PRAISE FOR JUDITH BOWEN

"Judith Bowen is a writer who knows how to warm the reader's heart. Her characters step off the page and make us care about them. Tender, poignant, cozy and beautifully written, Judith Bowen's books are a treat!"
—Deborah Smith, *New York Times* bestselling writer

"If you want to believe in the ability of love to transform ordinary lives and empower ordinary relationships, you cannot do better than to read Judith Bowen. She has the true romance writer's gift for taking ordinary people and ordinary circumstances and weaving about them an extraordinary love story."
—Mary Balogh, author of *Slightly Married* and *A Summer to Remember*

"Oh, how I love Judith Bowen's stories! Such gutsy heroines and such lovable men! You can't put the books down, and you remember them with a fond, tender feeling. Now, that's romance!"
—Anna Jacobs, author of *Our Eva*

"Judith Bowen's gift for creating strong, intelligent, savvy heroines sparkles in *The Man from Blue River*. An extraordinary read."
—Cindy Penn, *Wordweaving*

"As always, Judith Bowen has presented her fans with an entertaining and warm love story...."
—Elena Channing, *The Best Reviews.com* on *A Home of His Own*

"Judith Bowen delivers a unique, enchanting tale that stays with you long after you've read the last page."
—*Rendezvous*

Dear Reader,

Tamarack, Alberta, population 1900, is a Rocky Mountain town like no other—and like every other small town anywhere. It's a place where nothing ever happens and folks like it that way!

Only, of course, things *do* happen, even if the townsfolk would rather they didn't. The role of a newspaper, even a little weekly like *The Tamarack Times,* is to reflect the community, and Daisy Sutherland learns that hometown journalism can be just as satisfying as anything she's accomplished in the big city. Maybe even more satisfying.

I hope you enjoy your "visit" to Tamarack. Visit my Web site at www.judithbowen.com and send me a postcard to let me know, or write to me at P.O. Box 2333, Point Roberts, WA 98281-2333.

Judith Bowen

JUDITH BOWEN

WEST OF GLORY

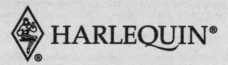

HARLEQUIN®

TORONTO • NEW YORK • LONDON
AMSTERDAM • PARIS • SYDNEY • HAMBURG
STOCKHOLM • ATHENS • TOKYO • MILAN • MADRID
PRAGUE • WARSAW • BUDAPEST • AUCKLAND

ISBN 0-373-83577-9

WEST OF GLORY

Visit us at www.eHarlequin.com

Printed in U.S.A.

Judith Bowen is an award-winning romance writer particularly known for her MEN OF GLORY series in Harlequin Superromance. She grew up in Alberta and knows its landscape intimately, as this book attests. Prior to becoming a novelist, she worked as a journalist. Judith lives in Vancouver, British Columbia, with her husband and three children.

CHAPTER ONE

DAISY SUTHERLAND could barely see where she was going, even with the wipers on full speed. She glanced in the mirror. Damn! Water trickled through the convertible's cracked vinyl rear window and dripped onto the seat. Uncle Leroy only drove the old Thunderbird on clear summer days with the top down, and he probably thought she'd do the same. Maybe she should have grabbed the keys to her father's Oldsmobile instead....

The 6:00 a.m. call from the paper's teenage reporter had woken her from a dead sleep and she'd jerked into action. Clothes, bathroom, shoes, keys, jump in the car, drive to the reserve. Now she was here, on the remote Rocky Mountain back road the boy had directed her to. But where exactly *was* she?

Rain yesterday and all night long had left the dirt track riddled with water-filled potholes of varying depths, some bonecracking, she'd discovered, thanks to the T-bird's aging suspension. She touched the brake lightly. If she didn't pay serious attention, she'd end up in a ditch herself instead of at the crime scene.

But now that she'd driven ten miles and her adrenaline had kicked back a little, she was wondering why she'd rushed. She wasn't in the big city anymore, fighting for a scoop with several other newspapers and a couple of TV stations. This was Tamarack, Alberta, pop. 1900, where nothing ever happened and folks liked it that way.

Only something *had* happened.

It turned out that John Spears, the high-school senior who wrote a video games column, developed photos and swept the premises at the *Times,* was also a devoted early morning eavesdropper on police scanner traffic. Interesting hobby. A talented kid, Daisy was beginning to realize. He'd heard the code for "cop down" and called her right away.

Crime scene—what was she thinking? More likely a traffic accident in this downpour.

Daisy frowned. She'd better focus on her driving. Okay, now turn right at the next crossroads and go about a mile or so and then look for some police activity.... She slowed to make a careful turn but even so, the convertible fish-tailed, giving her momentary heart failure.

Early June meant the sun rose around four in the morning, but in this weather, it didn't make much difference. Everything around her—the scrub grass, the sparsely forested hills climbing the mountain flanks, the treacherous narrow road that led who-knew-where in this part of the Pekisko Valley—had the gray, ghostly cast of predawn. She could hardly make out the Rockies looming massively to the west, a near impenetrable boundary between Alberta and the westernmost Canadian province, British Columbia.

Ah, police flashers just about where John said they'd be. There were three cruisers at the scene, and an ambulance pulled away just as Daisy arrived. No lights, no siren. That meant either no serious injuries or someone was dead. She was getting a horrible sinking feeling in the pit of her stomach. Excitement. Dread. That old, too familiar rush that went with big-city investigative journalism and all the crime, corruption and heartbreak—everything she'd vowed to leave behind when she returned to Tamarack to take over the family paper.

Nope. This is just another story, she told herself firmly. Simple, straightforward. You'll interview the cops, take a few photos, drive back to town, write it up for next week's paper. Even if someone was dead—well, someone was dead. Too bad. It was news. Accidents happened. She remembered the advice she got the day she started her first summer job at the *Sunshine Coast Record:* "Car crashes sell papers, kid, don't you forget it."

A policeman in rain gear appeared out of nowhere and waved her toward the left. She stopped where he indicated, facing north on the wrong side of the road, and rolled down the window.

"You live around here, miss?" The officer's moustache was heavily beaded with rain.

"No."

"Where you headed this morning?"

"Here."

He looked surprised. "Your name, please?"

"Daisy Sutherland, *Tamarack Times.*" Daisy held up her notepad and camera. "I'd like to ask a few questions, take a couple of pictures—"

"This is a crime scene," the Mountie snapped. "You shouldn't be here. Don't get out of your vehicle. I need to talk to the officer in charge."

"Okay." Daisy nodded. Normally she would've been more insistent. You didn't get anywhere in journalism by practicing meek and mild, but she'd been in town less than a month and there was no point in stepping on toes. Having a decent working relationship with the local police was vital to doing a good job running the *Tamarack Times.* Her father was putting a lot of faith in her by handing over the reins as he had. And, hey, the officer had a point—she could've used the extra sleep. There'd be details from the Mounties soon enough: who, what, where. The nuts-and-bolts facts of what had happened. They rarely went into why; that was her job. But maybe the *why* didn't matter so much here in small-town Alberta.

Crime scene. That meant it *wasn't* just a traffic accident. Daisy's heart was pounding. She watched the tall policeman retreat toward the cruisers, his image blurred by the rain, which still thumped on the roof of the convertible and vibrated puddles on the road.

Not great weather for a crime scene, was it? She tried to see through the annoying slap-slap, screech-screech of her wipers. Another car, a cruiser she hadn't noticed at first, was parked on the opposite side of the road, facing her, maybe thirty feet away. That made four. The driver's door hung open. No flashers. Brown, foamy water filled the ditch alongside the vehicle, just as it did on her side of the road.

She peered through the curtain of rain, watching for the policeman's return, and then realized there was *another* vehicle, a pickup truck parked on the edge of the ditch, slightly behind her and to her right. With all the police activity, not to mention the downpour, she hadn't noticed it immediately. Its driver's door was open as well.

There was a knock on her window and Daisy rolled it down. The officer had come back while she was gawking. "You're gonna have to move, miss," he said. "We're busy here. You can phone the Glory detachment later for anything you want to know."

"I won't even get out, I promise!" Daisy protested. Two cops were moving in their direction, stringing yellow tape. "I'll stay on this side of the road. I just need a photo—"

"Okay, okay," the officer grudgingly allowed, straightening. "One picture, and then you'd better be on your way," he warned, leaving to join the men putting up the tape.

Daisy scuttled over to the passenger side of the T-bird and rolled down that window, too. This angle wasn't bad; she could get the cop cars, a good length of the yellow tape—and what else was there? Rain, grass, mud. Nothing too exciting here, but she clicked off several exposures. She had to have *something* for the front page.

What was the crime? Stolen car? Truck? Whatever it was, Daisy hoped no one was seriously hurt. Actually, she was feeling a little silly now, jumping out of bed and high-tailing it out here barely awake. She hadn't even left a note for her parents, and Marian Sutherland was the worrying type.

How long would it take her to get back to town—half an hour? Mentally, Daisy reviewed the tortuous return trip, reversing John's directions. It was a wonder she hadn't gotten lost trying to find this place. Maybe she would on the way back, she thought grimly. Still, that'd make a nice light piece for the op-ed page. ''New editor lost ten miles from home.'' Give the town a laugh. Everyone liked to feel superior once in a while.

Another cruiser arrived and stopped between her and the other cars. Thanks, buddy! She started to squirm back into the driver's seat but something about the way the pickup was parked, door gaping, caught her attention.

She snapped a couple more pictures to finish the roll. It was an older truck, with rusted fenders and a battered Fiberglas canopy over the box. A red plastic streamer of some sort hung limply from the radio antenna, and she could see a pair of oversize dice hanging from the rearview mirror inside, the kind they sold in truck stops, along with deodorizers shaped like pine trees and cowboy hats. The upholstery on the driver's seat was torn in several places.

Whose truck? The bad guy's? *What* bad guy? Maybe it belonged to whoever had discovered the incident? Or just a helpful passerby. Or—

Then Daisy saw something that made her skin crawl. Beside the truck, rain had filled a large indentation in the muddy surface of the road.

The water was pink.

By the time Daisy got back to town, the downpour had started to ease a little. She put the convertible in the garage, mopped up the moisture that had collected below the rear window with a towel, and went up the back steps into the kitchen. Her mother was standing at the peninsula counter, slicing fresh strawberries to go with her father's morning pancakes.

"Hi, honey! I didn't know you were up already— *Daisy?*"

Daisy had taken one look at the plump soft berries, swimming in their own red juice in the glass bowl and raced for the powder room.

She stared unseeing at the swirl of water that flushed away the remains of her juice box and granola bar. *And bile.*

Oh, the terrible, bitter truth of this business.

Her eyes stung. She locked her elbows over the sink and tried to think about what she had to do. Wash her face with cold water, pat it dry, go back out to face Mother....

She gagged again, but there was nothing left. She shut her eyes but she couldn't shut out the image of the photograph the city editor had shown her before she'd left the *Sun.* Two emaciated babies had been discovered, clinging to life in a filthy basement suite in Vancouver's east end, victims of a baby-smuggling ring Daisy had uncovered and written about. Against the advice of the police, she'd gone public with the story before the arrests were made, with the result that the perpetrators had fled, leaving their tiny charges to fend for themselves.

It was her fault. If she hadn't been so stubborn about the public's right to know, so impatient to bring the criminals to justice, those babies would not have suffered....

"Daisy?" Her mother hammered on the bathroom door. "Are you all right in there? *Daisy, honey!*"

Daisy took a deep breath, rinsed her face and tried not to think about the pink puddle on the muddy road. *Death.* No matter how many times you saw it, you never got used to it.

RAIN FELL ON Florence Nolan's garden, so evenly and gently it was almost invisible. You could hear the rain, though, in the absolute stillness at the end of the valley where she had her shack, *pat-pat-pat*ting on the new leaves of the willows and the poplars and seeping silently into the June grass. Florence had planted her garden on the Victoria Day weekend, the third Monday in May, as was the custom in this part of Alberta, so not much showed yet, just radishes, beets and the Lincoln Homesteader peas she favored.

The fire was out and the door was closed but not locked. The five brown hens were shut up in their coop, for fear of coyotes.

Florence Nolan wasn't home; she was down at Pekisko at her grandson's funeral.

The Catholic church stood a space away from most of the houses on the reserve, which straggled along the riverbanks below, on both sides. Saint Jerome's had a small knoll all to itself, with the rectory and graveyard behind, parking in front. All the vehicles on the reserve were pulled up to the church. Drivers who couldn't find a spot in the gravel parking lot left their pickups in the neighboring field. There'd be ruts in the soft green of the sod when they drove away, like the black gash behind the church, the newly dug grave awaiting the mortal remains of Arlo Goodstriker, cop killer. No quantity of flowers, artificial or fresh-picked, could disguise a grave.

Water ran down the blistered white paint of the frame building and dripped from the corroded seams in the gutters. Rain fell on Morris Jack's dog until he finally gave up waiting for Morris on the steps and slunk beneath a pickup where another dog had already sought refuge. A short scrap ensued, the snarls of the dogfight rising above the congregation's rendering of "Amazing Grace," accompanied on the new electric organ badly played by Eunice Weaselfat, Morris's second cousin.

You'd think, Florence thought, sitting in the second row, that they could've got someone who could play a decent tune for Arlo's funeral. Just for once.

Florence's sister Ida sat on her left and Ben, one of her two remaining grandsons, the one who'd always been her favorite, sat on her right. She noticed Ben was holding the widow's hand in both of his. Poor Marie. Her eyes were red and swollen. And, Laverne, dear girl. So sad and wounded, so tender, so young. And Junior—Ben told her the boy hadn't said a word since the accident. Not one word. That was what Florence called it, an accident. What else could it have been?

Marie had been married to Arlo for thirteen years, because Laverne was just turned thirteen at the beginning of May, and she'd been well on the way at the wedding. Florence sighed. Her husband, Henry Nolan, mechanic, trapper, fiddle player, had been one in a hundred, and not a week had gone by these past twenty-five years that she didn't think of him. It was hard to lose a good man.

Not like Arlo, Mr. Happy-Go-Lucky who couldn't hold a job, no matter what. Florence had been fond of him— he was her grandson, wasn't he? He always brought her the first handful of wild raspberries in July and told her where the huckleberries were in August; he made her laugh with his stories. But anything serious he'd set his hand to, except rodeoing, had turned to dust. Maybe he'd been kicked by a bull one time too many. Who knew?

Arlo wasn't a bad man. He'd been good to Marie, good

to his kids. Just happened to be what Henry, God rest his soul, would've referred to as "lightweight." She'd known Henry to call a three-hundred-pound man "lightweight." It was nothing to do with size, more with attitude.

A man in years but not in deeds, that was Arlo Good-striker. A man who loved a joke, who was a little too easily influenced by others—maybe that was why Ben had looked out for him, more like a brother than a cousin. A man who meant well, who tried his best even if his best wasn't always very good. A man who'd flirted with the law—didn't they all, the young ones?—hunting out of season, driving drunk, burning purple gas siphoned from farmers' tanks at midnight, maybe even laying his hands on something he shouldn't now and then, if he was in need and the opportunity arose. He'd been in and out of trouble since he was nine years old.

But killing a cop? Florence had taken him on her trap line when he was a boy and remembered how he couldn't even skin out a beaver without retching. Arlo Goodstriker was no killer.

"Nan?" Ben, the best-looking of her grandsons, too, leaned toward her. He'd aged five years since Arlo had died but none of his sorrow showed today. Florence knew that was a front, for Marie and the kids. "I've got to go. You, uh—" He gave Marie a worried glance.

"You go," Florence said, patting his hand. *"Go!"*

She stood with the rest of the congregation and watched as Ben and five other strong young men lifted Arlo's coffin and began to carry it slowly down the aisle. She was an old woman. It wasn't right for the others to go before her. First Henry, then her oldest girl, Natasha, Ben's mother, and now poor foolish Arlo.

"Psst!" Florence prodded Marie and led her to the widow's rightful position behind the coffin. The church was only half-full, but it was a big church. An okay turnout for a youngster, never had time to make much of a mark on the world. Tina was there, Ben's sister, a big shot now in Calgary. All the council families were represented. The Weaselfats, the Georges, the Poundmakers. A few from town, Marie's boss—and who was that sitting at the end of the last pew by herself? Looked like she'd lost her best friend. Blond, pretty, town girl for sure, not too dressed up, either, in a rain slicker and rubber boots. Camera on her lap. Must be *somebody's* friend. Arlo's?

Marie stumbled and Florence grabbed her arm hard. *"You be strong!"*

Marie threw her a look. Florence wasn't sure if it was grateful or annoyed. She knew her grandson's wife had never had much affection for her, but Florence hadn't cared when Arlo was alive and she didn't care now. *"For the kids!"* she whispered fiercely, holding Marie's arm.

Clara, Arlo's mother, stepped up woodenly and took her place beside Marie. Poor little Clara. She lived in Edmonton now, with one of her daughters. Florence had always felt a special tenderness for her third-born, her only living daughter, such a gentle soul marrying such a fool of a man as Melvin Goodstriker.

They followed the coffin out into the rain. Many years ago, the Pekiskos, a small off-shoot of the Blackfoot Nation, would have lashed their departed one high in a tree for the magpies and crows to strip the flesh, for sun and wind to polish the bones and set free another spirit of The People to travel to the Sand Hills, land of the dead. The priests had changed everything. Florence Nolan was an old woman and she couldn't remember when the ancient ways had been followed.

The crowd milled on the church steps and beyond, some holding their funeral programs high to save their hairdos, others standing bare-headed and solemn, as the pallbearers continued down the rough path to the burying ground.

Morris Jack's dog howled as the coffin passed.

It was a bad sign.

CHAPTER TWO

HARD TO BELIEVE, Daisy thought as she did up the zipper on her skirt, that she hadn't worn this suit since she'd given her notice at that disastrous lunch meeting with the *Vancouver Sun*'s city editor two months ago. You're nuts, he'd shouted, no up-and-coming journalist with a big future leaves a city paper for a hick-town weekly!

Daisy'd had reason enough but she wasn't sure Oliver Crawford would've understood. Anything that didn't have to do with hard-nosed reporting, he didn't want to hear about. "Don't give me any of that 'quality of life' bullshit" was a missive he frequently fired at colleagues in the endless battle, as he saw it, between work, which was all that should matter to any reporter worthy of the name, and personal life, which was only a necessary evil, in his view. He tended to see home, family and friends as the boundary that separated one working day from another. He'd never married, he drank too much, he ate Christmas dinner by himself in the Sylvia Hotel, sitting at the same table every year. His proudest boast was that he hadn't missed a day of work in twenty-seven years.

Oliver Crawford was hardly a typical journalist—or "newspaperman" as he fondly referred to his ilk. But he *was* her boss and he'd taught her almost everything she knew and he would've been incredulous if she'd told him the *real* reasons she was leaving the *Sun*.

Daisy hadn't felt up to handling that incredulity, so she'd just said she was going home to take over the family weekly because her father was thinking of retiring. Which was true enough. Family loyalty? A newspaper dynasty? Well, a modest one but it was important to Owen Sutherland, whose father had started the paper back in the thirties in the heyday of the Tamarack Coal Company. Oliver Crawford would've scoffed and told her to get over it.

Get over it. That was just what she intended to do. Ironically, it was her very success as a young maverick journalist that had driven her back to the embrace of her hometown. She had an uncanny talent for digging out the ugliest stories, exposing the most horrific big-city crimes, shedding light on the nastiest coverups, and when she'd seen the pictures of the abandoned babies, she'd suddenly realized that she'd seen too much. Too much of the worst life had to offer. In Tamarack, she could concentrate on wholesome local issues, like the Friends of the Library strawberry social coming up soon, the new kiddie rodeo planned for the end of July and the annual slow-pitch tournament during the August long weekend.

Now she was wearing the gray suit to a funeral, which made a twisted kind of sense. She peered over her shoulder into the gilt-edged mirror above the dressing table in the second-floor guest room and eyed her bottom critically. Extra pound or two there? Since the prodigal daughter had returned, Marian Sutherland had been serving all of Daisy's favorite dishes. She glanced at her watch—the funeral was in half an hour—and resolved to cut back on the pasta, plus redouble her efforts to find more suitable accommodation. If this move to Tamarack was permanent, she'd need to find a place of her own.

Daisy took a deep breath and picked up a comb to engineer a last-minute fix on her hair. Who would've dreamed the events of that rain-soaked morning eight days ago would strike so close? Wayne Petrenko, constable in the Royal Canadian Mounted Police, the adopted only son of the Sutherlands' neighbors, Bill and Alice Petrenko, and the center of their lives, was dead at thirty-three, murdered in an ambush. She'd run the story, such as it was, in Thursday's paper—"Shoot-out at reserve leaves two dead"—with a front-page picture that didn't show much except a couple of blurry cop cars and a lot of mud.

Wayne had not only grown up next door, he was her parents' godson. The whole town was reeling. As a police officer and the son of a respected local lawyer, his funeral would be huge. Not like the service for Arlo Goodstriker a few days ago. The shooter. *The man who'd driven the pickup truck.*

Suddenly cold, Daisy put down the comb and reached for her jacket. Now, why had she gone to *that* funeral? No reason. She didn't know the deceased or his family. She'd felt compelled to go, responding to a need she recognized from her investigative reporting days in Vancouver. To dig deeper, to bring the people she wrote to life, more than a series of names and ages and addresses in a newspaper article. It was a quality, Oliver Crawford had grudgingly told her once, that elevated her work above the crowd and had won her a few awards. Maybe so, but it could be painful, too. When something went wrong, as so often happened, it was hard not to feel partly to blame, to feel that if she'd managed to do *more,* events might have worked out differently....

Going to the Goodstriker funeral, she told herself, was just getting a feel for her new community. She'd been late and had sneaked into the pew nearest the door, hoping no one would notice. The cavernous old church was nearly empty, and she'd left right after the coffin was carried out. She remembered the sight of those six tall dark men, two with braids, carrying one of their own, with a dog howling piteously and women crying. The dead man's children were weeping; she'd seen the small boy try manfully to hide the tears and it had broken her heart.

She squared her shoulders and checked for her handbag. Today would be different. Tamarack was very proud of Constable Petrenko, she'd discovered when she'd asked a few questions around town, looking for background. A small-town boy made good, the best kind.

"Dai-sy!"

Daisy shrugged on the jacket and grabbed her purse, glancing one last time in the mirror. The suit with its small peplum made her look more feminine than she usually felt. She liked it. *The new, improved Daisy Jean Sutherland, reporter.* Well, *editor,* now, of the hometown paper.

"Coming, Mother!"

"We'll be late. We'll never get a seat. Your father's having fits...."

Daisy slammed the door and clattered down the stairs in the shiny Italian pumps that had cost her half a paycheck and seemed so necessary six months ago. She hadn't worn them, either, since she'd left Vancouver. Tamarack, Alberta, was more inclined to cowboy boots and running shoes than patent leather.

In fact, she noticed as she accompanied her parents to the front of the church twenty minutes later, the mayor *was* wearing cowboy boots, albeit expensive, heavily tooled ones. Dress boots. Sid Brewster owned the feed store and probably hadn't worn anything else his entire adult life.

"Oh, Daisy," her mother whispered, "there's only two places—"

"Never mind, Mom. I'll sit at the back."

"Where?" Her mother seemed bewildered, much older than her fifty-nine years. The terrible news last week had devastated her parents. Daisy hadn't known Wayne well. He'd been eight years older, a chasm when you and your friends were ten and the most fun you could imagine was putting makeup on each other and pretending you were all top models on a Caribbean fashion shoot. The Sutherlands had adored their godson and had always found his hijinks hilarious—escapades that would have meant being grounded for life if Daisy or her older sister, Karen, had ever been caught at them.

"At the back." Daisy rested her hand on her mother's shoulder and bent down, adding in a whisper, "I may go outside." When they'd arrived, ten minutes early for the service, they saw that a loudspeaker had already been set up on the lawn for the overflow crowd. She'd also spotted a few city journalists she knew, as well as vans from Calgary and Edmonton television crews. This funeral was a big event.

The rustle of voices accompanied her as she walked to the back of the church. Even after a month, people still looked. Daisy knew there was plenty of speculation as to why she'd returned. Yes, Owen Sutherland wasn't getting any younger but he wasn't *that* old. And Daisy'd always been a bright girl with a headful of big dreams. Captain of the high-school volleyball team in her senior year—they'd even won the provincial championship. Turned down an athletic scholarship to go to journalism school back East, to everyone's dismay. Still single, too. Why, she'd hardly be happy here, would she, after working for a big paper out at the Coast, investigating crime and embarrassing people in high places? No, Tamarack wasn't a town with enough bad news to suit the likes of a fancy *journalist* like Daisy Sutherland.

"Psst." It was Ellin Brodie, her bookkeeper-receptionist-classified ad person at the *Tamarack Times* waving madly, inviting Daisy to join her in the last row. She spotted the paper's biker-turned-photographer, too, cameras dangling from his beefy neck. Sober, she hoped.

At least they'd have photos for the front page. No sign of Bunny McPhee, the *Times*'s part-time "society" reporter. Where did her father *get* these people?

As she'd expected, the church was filled, inside and out, with a sea of police representing law enforcement organizations from all over North America, as always happened when one of their own had been killed in the line of duty. To her left, eyes straight ahead, were several Royal Canadian Mounted Police officers, resplendent in their scarlet dress uniforms. Daisy recognized the tall, sandy-haired staff sergeant of the Glory RCMP detachment and was relieved he didn't catch her eye. Gordon Bass was in charge of the investigation into the shoot-out on the reserve. Shortly after it happened, she'd contacted him for details and he'd refused to give her more than a bare outline of the incident. Names, ages, addresses.

Was it because she was a pipsqueak local reporter now, from a pipsqueak local paper? She wondered if he'd be as tight-lipped with the big-city media here to cover the event. They'd want much more than she'd been told. After all, a cop was dead.

All anyone in town knew was that Wayne had been shot on an early-morning visit to the Pekisko Reserve. No reason given for his being there, no reason for Goodstriker to be involved. Those few official details weren't enough to write a decent story, even for the relaxed standards of the *Tamarack Times*. And the very fact that Daisy believed she was being stonewalled roused her reporter's instincts. All of which made her suspect, rightly or wrongly, that there was more to this story than the community was being told....

And there was another side to the tragedy, one no one in town seemed too concerned about. The shooter had died, which at least meant there'd be no drawn-out trial to torture the Petrenkos and their friends. But the shooter had a life. A family. Including a little boy out there on the Pekisko Reserve. Daisy couldn't get the image of the gunman's young son out of her mind. What was going on here? Was she being drawn back into exactly the kind of journalism she thoght she'd left behind in the city?

"I think that's Ben Goodstriker back there—isn't it?" Ellin whispered when Daisy reached the back row.

"I wouldn't know." Daisy squeezed into the space Ellin had saved for her, pleased to see that Ellin dispensed with her usual wad of chewing gum and toned down her makeup a little for the occasion. Maybe it was just the merciful light from the stained glass windows....

"Where?" She glanced around warily. She'd never met Ben Goodstriker, but she'd sure heard about him. The gunman was a cousin of his, double cousin, she'd been told, two sisters married to two brothers. Since the shootout, Ben Goodstriker's name had come up everywhere. Ask Ben Goodstriker, people said on the reserve and in town when she nosed around for background on the gunman. Call Ben, she'd been told when she inquired about the upcoming small-fry rodeo, a first for Tamarack.

Ask Ben, ask Ben. It wasn't as though she hadn't tried. He didn't return phone calls. She craned her neck slightly to get a better look at the crowd lining the back of the church. A group of natives stood in a knot by the open door, three women, one of them quite old, sitting in a folding chair. There was also a well-dressed heavyset man standing with several young men in beaded leather vests and long braids, and another man, standing a bit to one side, away from the rest, near the old woman.

He was tall, broad shouldered but slim in an easy, athletic way, with longish hair. Hands shoved in his pockets, he slouched against the wall, wearing black jeans, a leather jacket, reflective wraparound sunglasses. He stared straight ahead, appearing to ignore the chatter around him.

Ben Goodstriker?

Daisy raised her eyebrows. She was sure she'd seen some of these people at the funeral on the reserve and maybe when the service was over, she'd talk to them and finally get a chance to meet the elusive Ben Goodstriker. She found herself hoping he wasn't the pudgy one.

"Brothers and sisters, we are gathered today to celebrate the life of one among us, Wayne Alexander Dmitri Petrenko. Please rise to sing, er—" The preacher studied his notes, then called the hymn number.

Daisy reached for the book on the back of the pew in front of her and stood beside Ellin, sharing the hymnal. She frowned as the introductory music began, silencing the crowd.

Sunglasses? What was *that* all about?

BEN DIDN'T LIKE IT. He didn't like being here at all. If Florence hadn't insisted, and if he hadn't known that Casper Desjarlais planned to attend, he'd be home working Jilly Longquist's new gelding, trying to put together a haying crew or checking to see if he could do anything for Marie and the kids.

Look at it this way, he said to himself. *You've got a duty to be here. For Arlo's sake.* And why was Casper at Wayne Petrenko's funeral anyway? With his "warrior" hangers-on? Sure, they'd all been close once, even done a little business together—Ben and Casper and Wayne and Arlo—but that was when they were teenagers. Kids. Ben knew Casper and Arlo had been pretty tight in the last six months, ever since his cousin got fired from his last job, but it wasn't as though they were burying Arlo today.

"It's only right to pay last respects," his grandmother had insisted stubbornly. "I've lost a grandson and someone's lost a son in this terrible accident."

Accident. Ben didn't want to think about it. The reality

was that his cousin was dead. But what else could it have been? No, an accident involving a bullet usually meant one person was dead. Not two.

At least there was a crowd here for Wayne's funeral, including the Mounties in their full dress uniforms, he noted. Red serge and spit-polish. Not many from town had shown up last Wednesday, but that was no surprise. Marie's boss, Ed Sawchuk, who owned the gravel pit and the school bus fleet had been there. A few others, including the woman he'd seen muffled up in rain gear and a hood at the back of the church. Who the hell was that?

He looked around the interior of the wood-paneled church as the organ softly played in the background, just audible over the low buzz of the congregation—visiting, gossiping, speculating. Stained-glass windows, pictures of Jesus, a pulpit up front for the preacher, no candles, no saints, no altar, no crucifixes. Flowers everywhere, the closed coffin sitting there at the front, glossy mahogany, draped with a flag.

It gave him the creeps. Everything about funerals and death and too many cut flowers and the ridiculous notion of actually saying goodbye to someone you'd loved gave him the creeps.

That, and cops. The place was crawling. Ben never felt all that comfortable around officers of the law, just a little peculiarity of his since he'd first been picked up for mischief when he was eleven, caught turning over garbage cans with Arlo and Casper in the Glory municipal campground. They'd been looking for quick cash—beer bottles and pop cans. Yeah, they'd been rebels, all right. The ABC Gang, the folks on the reserve had called them.

He edged toward the door, closer to Florence, and noticed the blonde who'd come in with an older couple a few minutes earlier start back up the aisle alone. She paused once, glanced toward the RCMP contingent, then continued on to the last row, where someone was trying to catch her attention.

Something about her seemed familiar.

Young, pretty, short skirt. Honey-colored hair, all tucked up but it still looked good. He'd never seen her before. Undercover cop? He grimaced. No way. He was suspicious of everything and everybody these days, ever since he'd got the news about Arlo. And it wasn't as though he knew everyone in town anymore, far from it.

He watched her take a seat beside the woman who'd waved. Then, to his surprise, he saw her turn around, far enough to survey him and everyone else standing near the door, which made him think *cop* again. Ben noticed a fat guy taking photos—her partner?—and his suspicions went into overdrive. *Goodstriker,* he told himself, *you read too many crummy detective novels.*

He tried to stare straight ahead when the preacher came in and started talking, but his gaze kept wandering to the blonde dressed in gray. Luckily, in the sunglasses he'd worn because of the bright sunshine outside, no one could see him staring. He decided to leave them on.

By the time the service was over and the Mounties were standing at attention, along with all the other cops, on either side of the aisle as the coffin was carried out, Ben Goodstriker had memorized every detail, from the pale ringless hands holding the hymnbook right down to the tiny brown mole at the nape of her neck.

He'd also realized that he *had* seen her before. She'd been sitting in the last pew at Arlo's funeral.

CHAPTER THREE

BEN DROVE his grandmother back to the cabin at the head of the valley where she'd been living alone, running her husband's trapline, since his death twenty-five years ago.

He remembered Grandpa Henry, but just barely—a big guy with a moustache and wild gray hair. He'd been nine when Grandpa Henry died, Ben thought, musing on circumstances as he unloaded Florence's groceries from the back of his pickup. Arlo's son had turned nine the day before Arlo was killed. Would Junior remember his dad in twenty-five years?

"Nan?" he called, emerging from the small cabin. As many times as Ben suggested his grandmother move down to the ranch with him or to town, she refused. Setting traps and skinning out winter muskrats was a hard life for anyone, never mind an old woman, but she said she liked it.

Ben was already an orphan when his grandfather died. His parents had been killed in a New Year's Eve car crash near Lundbreck. Florence had taken him and Tina, his older sister, for a year, then Tina had left to live with a relative in Calgary and Ben had moved down to the reserve to stay with Auntie Clara and Uncle Mel. Arlo's family. Florence felt it was a better arrangement, closer to the school bus route and preferable to growing up alone with her on the trapline. She'd had so much grief in so little time: losing her husband to pneumonia and then a daughter and son-in-law just six months later.

Ben remembered living with different families on the

reserve for a while; he had no idea why. No one told a
ten- or eleven-year-old kid anything. Arlo was two years
younger, but they'd been inseparable right from the start.
Uncle Mel supposedly worked on a ranch north of Glory
but they rarely saw him, which suited the boys just fine.
They had the run of the reserve and no one ever chased
them down to tell them it was bedtime. Auntie Clara was
too busy sewing and cooking and cleaning house for the
priests in the rectory to worry about the whereabouts of
her third-born.

Ben had regarded his younger, smaller cousin as a
brother. When boys at Tamarack Elementary teased Arlo
because he was so small, Ben beat them up for him. When
Arlo got into trouble with Old Man Standish for stealing
his part-Staffordshire bitch and the litter of pups he intended to drown, Ben stuck up for him and told the old
man he'd get him back his dog *and* work off the theft
himself, splitting firewood, if Standish promised not to tell
the cops. Later, he realized Old Man Standish had got the
better of him. The old fool was glad to be rid of the pups
and wouldn't have told the cops even if he wasn't. No
wonder he'd laughed. He was a mountain man and mountain men didn't run to the police for *anything*.

It was a lesson Ben never forgot: don't make a deal if
there's nothing at stake.

Arlo had fixed up a nest with old clothes and straw in
an abandoned tool shed on the reserve and brought the
nursing bitch food his mother could ill afford. Then, when
the five puppies were weaned, Ben sneaked the mother
back to the Standish place in the middle of the night, tied
her to a fence rail and ran like blazes.

That was a hell of an adventure, Ben recalled, smiling.
They'd made money, too, twenty-five bucks apiece, selling
those pups on the rodeo grounds in Glory that summer.

"Ten dollars, sir, gen-u-ine huntin' dogs," Arlo told prospective buyers.

Ben had a notion he'd believed it, too. Hunting dogs? Little mutts were more like a cross between a pit bull and a coyote....

"Anything else I can do for you?" Ben spotted his grandmother finally coming back from the chicken house with her dogs following at a respectful distance—Bounder his usual cheerful self, Queenie beside him, her teats heavy and swollen from the litter she'd had a week ago. Florence wouldn't tolerate any harassment of her poultry, and the dogs knew it. She tossed out grain, watching the hens run every which way as the barley hit the ground.

"No, son," she said and looked up.

"I was just thinking about that time me 'n' Arlo sold those pups in Glory." Ben managed a dry laugh.

His grandmother regarded him keenly, her dark eyes sunken in her weathered face. Florence was half Sarcee and had been raised south of Bragg Creek, near Calgary; Grandpa Henry had been a white man, of Irish stock from New Brunswick.

"It's good to remember the dead," she said simply, touching his arm. "You want a cup of tea?"

"No." Ben shook his head. "I'd better go back. I got a green-broke colt I bought off Noah Winslow I want to work some this afternoon. And I'm training a new gelding for Jilly Longquist." *Why not the truth?* "I should check on how Marie and the kids are making out," he added, shrugging.

Florence stared, then looked away. "Lots of folks leanin' on you now, huh? Marie is a strong woman, son."

"I don't believe she is," Ben began. He hated what this had done to his cousin's wife, just when things had seemed to be leveling out for Arlo's family. His cousin appeared to have money lately, and Marie's job driving a school bus was secure. *Angry. That's what you are, you're angry at him for leaving you.* "She's pretty broken up. We all are." He paused. Cursing his voice for the hoarse note he heard, he said, "*I* am."

Florence patted his arm. "She's a strong woman," she repeated. "A Pekisko woman. Don't let her lean too hard. It's the kids I think about. Junior—" She stopped abruptly, her dark eyes searching his.

Ben knew what she meant. Arlo's youngest hadn't said a word since they'd received the news about his father.

Ben put his arm around Florence's shoulders and squeezed. He rested his forehead against hers. "Don't worry, old woman. You can always depend on me." He grinned as his grandmother batted at him and ducked from under his restraining arm. He headed toward his pickup. Florence appeared frail but she still split her own firewood if Ben forgot to send someone up to do it for her. He'd never heard her complain about anything.

"Pah! Too many depending on you. Better go home now. Change your clothes. Get to work. You done branding?"

"Couple weeks ago. I told Adam Garrick I'd give him a hand this year." Ben got in his truck and started the engine.

"When's that?"

"Week after next." He put his truck into reverse and drove backward for twenty feet or so, then turned in a loop worn into the long grass. He honked the horn as he entered the trees that surrounded her place and she waved, the two dogs beside her. She looked dignified and calm in her green print dress with her old checked black-and-red barn coat over it.

The funeral today and then Arlo's just three days ago— Ben didn't think he'd seen his grandmother wearing a dress before. Maybe he'd just never noticed.

But the woman in the pale-gray dress—or whatever it was she had on—he'd noticed her, all right. She was hard to ignore and he wasn't going to, now that he knew she'd shown up for his cousin's funeral. Not that he'd ever been particularly attracted to blondes, just that there was something about that quick little survey of the back of the church that flicked his senses onto high alert.

Caution.

Nosy. Smart. Something else he couldn't quite put his finger on…

Had she been a friend of Arlo's? Not likely. But Arlo didn't tell Ben everything, the way he used to. The past six months especially. Of course, Ben had been busy with his own affairs—pulling calves, riding range, fixing fences, and then, last month, moving the cattle down to the home ranch and branding. Now haying season was coming up fast.

Ben had a lot to think about without dwelling on sassy-looking blondes in city suits. He'd taken a graveled back road shortcut to his ranch so he could bypass the highway where he'd see people he knew, have to wave, never mind stop and talk as was the rural custom, considering all that had happened lately. As Arlo's cousin, like it or not, he was involved.

There was work to do tying up Arlo's affairs, not that he had any. No rush there, but the truck was in his name and he owned two roping horses—technically—which Ben had housed and fed for the past three years, plus Brownie, Laverne's barrel horse. Then there were some personal possessions, three rifles, two saddles, some sports equipment and fishing rods, not to mention, to everyone's surprise, an account in a Glory bank. Marie had found the passbook in a drawer, with the last entry, a fifty-buck deposit, two years ago. Probably nothing more in it than that lone fifty, if that, but as the one designated by the family to take care of these things, Ben would have to check it out.

Just like his cousin to have fantasies about saving up a bunch of money and then surprising Marie with it. Trouble was, Arlo's idea of a surprise tended along the lines of a high-powered snowmobile they didn't need and couldn't afford, or another horse.

For eight years, Ben and Arlo had ridden the rodeo circuit along with, from time to time, his friend Adam Garrick and another cousin, Lucas Yellowfly. Ben rode broncs, bareback and saddle, and Arlo rode the bulls. Neither one of them had ever made serious money, but it had been a living of sorts and exactly the kind of life they'd dreamed of as boys. They'd both quit when Ben ended up in hospital for the third time in two years; he didn't think Arlo had ever quite forgiven him for breaking his leg again. Old Moses, Ben recollected fondly, one of the rankest horses to come by in a long while. It was a privilege to be tossed by a horse like that.

Only crazy men like Adam and Arlo rode bulls. Not that Ben hadn't tried it himself, in the beginning. But he'd quickly realized there was only one winner in this game and it wasn't ever going to be the cowboy. Arlo didn't seem to care how many times he'd been stomped on or tossed, he always came up cussing that big old bull with a grin on his face and ready to try again. It was uncanny that in eight years he'd never been badly injured. The old-timers said he had an angel in the chute with him.

At least one of Arlo's dreams had come true.

Rodeo was in Ben's blood, too, but he had enough brains—and bruises—to understand that it was a young man's game. Lucas had gotten out with the money to study law, and Adam had left when his wife finally ran out on him, tired of being broke and living on promises.

Ben rounded the last curve before the turnoff to Meadow

Springs Ranch. This was where he'd put his rodeo money, plus every other cent he had. He had prospects with his bucking stock—which he hoped, one day, to turn into a business supplying roughstock for rodeos—and his cow-calf operation. In the meantime, his hayfields in the rich bottomland along the river paid the bills and made up for the price of his feeder steers in the bad years. With a little luck and a sympathetic banker, he'd make a go of it.

That was *his* dream.

He frowned as he neared the ranch house, approaching through the shade of the big cottonwoods and willows. There was a shiny late-model pickup he didn't recognize parked by Marie's trailer. Visitors?

Marie was a woman alone now. With Arlo gone, Ben needed to keep an eye on things even more than before. He pulled to a stop by the house in a cloud of dust and got out. Dodger, his heeler-terrier cross and a litter mate to Florence's dog, Bounder, rushed over to greet him and Ben hunkered down to fondle his chewed-up ears, grinning as the excited dog accidentally knocked his hat off. He generally took the dog everywhere with him, but he could hardly take him to a funeral. Dodger was a scrapper. He got into lots of trouble but Ben had never had a truer friend or a more loyal companion.

"Ben!"

Dodger barked and Ben stood slowly, slapping his hat against his thigh to knock the dust off. Casper Desjarlais was walking across the yard toward him.

CHAPTER FOUR

"HEY." Ben gave the hat a final thump against his thigh. "You been here a while? I took Florence home first."

The two men didn't shake hands; they'd known each other all their lives.

"Not long." Casper glanced over his shoulder. "Just wanted to see for myself how she was getting along, y'know. Marie and the kids."

Ben nodded. He'd suggested Arlo's family take over the trailer a year ago, when he moved into his new house. At the time, he'd thought about hiring his cousin to help his foreman, Harold Pappas, with the ranch chores but somehow that never quite happened. Arlo had never been crazy about regular work.

"Helluva note, ain't it?" Casper sighed and shook his head. He was still in the clothes he'd worn to the funeral—nice suit, pale-blue shirt, tasseled loafers. Loafers!

"She's okay," Ben said. "As well as can be expected, I guess. It's hard."

"Yeah." Casper glanced back at the trailer, then stepped a little closer. "I wanted to tell her she could count on me for anything she needed. I heard the boy's in bad shape." He looked at Ben, one eyebrow raised.

"Shock, Doc Pleasance told Marie. He'll get over it."

"Yeah?" Casper shook his head again. "Poor kid. It's not like I'm gonna just forget about Marie and the kids or nothing." He yanked at his tie, loosening it. "You and me and Arlo go way back."

"That's right. Haven't seen you out here for a while, though. Looks like you're doing well." Ben nodded toward the shiny new Dodge pickup.

Casper grinned. "Yeah. You know how it is. One scheme goes belly-up, and the next one takes off. Flea market's hot right now. Folks bring stuff and do all the work selling it, and I get my cut. Like taking candy from kids." He laughed.

"Arlo mentioned some kind of junk business you got involved in." Ben reached down and patted Dodger on the head to shut him up. He was alternately whining, yawning and growling. Probably hungry. "Lethbridge?"

Casper nodded.

"Didn't sound like anything too profitable to me, but then I'm no big shot businessman like you. You want to come in?"

"I got a few minutes." Casper checked his watch. "I'm driving straight to Calgary after this."

"I could crack you a beer. Dry work, that." Ben sent Casper a glance as they walked toward the house. It amused him how Casper let on that he was such a busy man. "Going to funerals, I mean."

"Yeah. I could use a beer, I guess. Sure, why not? Haven't had one all day."

Ben wanted to ask why he'd been at Wayne Petrenko's funeral, but maybe Casper was wondering the same thing about him. Ben hadn't thought about Wayne much in the years he'd been away and he wouldn't have gone to his funeral if Florence hadn't insisted. Wayne had been a happy-go-lucky, trigger-happy town kid, always ready to raise a ruckus and have a good time. His coming back a cop all these years later meant circumstances between them weren't quite the same....

"What's that?" Casper looked startled when Ben opened the door. A woman's voice came loud and clear from the kitchen. *"—and don't you ever answer your damn phone?"* Bang! Whoever it was slammed down her receiver.

"Answering machine," Ben said, grinning. "Great invention. Guess I ought to listen to it once in a while, eh?"

Casper seemed relieved. "Jeez, Ben. No wonder you're no businessman. You gotta answer your messages, could be important. Maybe something about that kiddie rodeo you and Arlo were trying to knock together. How's that going?"

"Not great. Not too many businesses beating each other up to sink money into a kiddie rodeo. Especially one put together by a couple of ex-rodeo guys with no management or organizational credentials. Not to mention being half-Indian," Ben said dryly. "Say, you want to toss in some cash? Sponsor an event?"

"Me? Hell, no!" Casper gave him a sheepish grin and draped his jacket on the counter beside the sink. "Not my kinda odds. I could make a donation, though."

"Talk to Lucas." Lucas Yellowfly was now a lawyer in Glory. "He and Adam are taking it over for me now that Arlo's—*shit!* I still can't believe it!"

"Arlo? Me, neither." Casper's homely face collapsed, and Ben thought for a second that he might actually start to cry.

He regretted his outburst. That was how it would happen. Every once in a while it'd hit him: Arlo was dead. *Dead!*

Ben inspected the contents of the fridge, while Casper perched on a stool at the island where Ben ate all his meals, at least the ones he didn't eat in front of the TV in the living room. Nothing there but a television set and a recliner that had seen better days. He hadn't quite got around to furnishing the place. Priorities. In fact, he hadn't even painted the living room yet. The walls were just bald white Gyproc with the seams taped and sanded. "Coors? Big Rock? What's your poison? Even a can of Old Stock kicking around in here somewhere…"

"Big Rock's fine." Casper had recovered from the emotion Ben's comment had apparently aroused. "Hey, you see that Sutherland girl there today? I didn't know she was back in town."

"What Sutherland girl? I don't know any Sutherland girl." Ben pulled two cans of Warthog out of the fridge and handed one to Casper.

"Daisy. The younger one. You remember Karen, her sister?" Casper popped the tab on his beer and took a deep pull. "She was about our age. Went off to private school in Calgary or somewhere halfway through high school."

"Rings a bell." It didn't really. Ben grabbed a loaf of bread, a bag of pepperoni, a jar of pickles and some sliced ham out of the refrigerator and set them on the counter. "Listen, you want a sandwich with that?"

Casper shook his head. "Nah. Anyway, Daisy, the one who was there today, was sitting beside Ellin Brodie. You know, that airhead lives over on South Willow, goes out with Ted Eberle who works at the Glory Co-op?"

"Big hair?" Ben went back to the fridge for the mayonnaise and mustard.

"That's her. You must've seen the two of them, they were in the last row."

"Gray outfit?" Ben was beginning to realize Casper was talking about the blonde.

"That's it. I hear she's taking over the paper from the old man." Casper stuffed several inches of pepperoni in his mouth and started chewing. "He's gonna ease off or retire or something," he mumbled. "Helluva fine-looking woman."

"Your point?"

"No point." Casper reached into the pickle jar with two

greasy fingers. "Just nice to see who's in town these days and who might be, uh, *available.*" He laughed and Ben had a sudden urge to punch him. He stood at the counter, putting together a ham-and-pickle sandwich. The way Casper talked about women had always bothered Ben. He was a big guy. Bulky, and not that good-looking, in Ben's opinion. The kind of guy who'd have freckles to go with his grin if he wasn't half-Indian. Who knew what women went for?

Dodger whined and Ben tossed him a stick of pepperoni. It was past suppertime for them both.

"Listen, forget that. Tell me more about this flea market of yours. You think you can sell some of Arlo's stuff? Marie wants me to take care of it."

"What kinda stuff?" Casper drained his beer and reached for another pickle, watching as Ben filled Dodger's dish with kibble and ran clean water into his bowl.

"Snowmobile, couple saddles, fishing rods…"

"Saddles, maybe. Fishing rods would be okay. I can find you a buyer for the snowmobile, no problem. Anything else?"

Ben shrugged. "Not much. Three rifles, some hockey gear—"

"Rifles?" Casper's eyes narrowed as he wiped his hands on a paper towel and picked up his suit jacket.

"Hunting rifles."

"He, uh, have those in the truck with him when—when it happened?"

"He always carried the .22 in the truck. You know Arlo—" Ben felt a pang shoot through him. Physical pain. The knowledge that his cousin was gone, that his crazy, devil-may-care cousin would never walk through that door again, struck him hard. Arlo would never come over to watch a hockey game anymore, or shoot some pool or try to talk him into going fishing in the middle of branding or haying or some other sixteen-hour-a-day job on a working ranch....

"Yeah. Ready to pop a partridge for the supper table if it happened to run across the road. Necessities of life. Oh, well." Casper sighed and squeezed into his jacket. "Hockey gear'll go, for sure. Rifles? You can't just sell guns. They're registered these days. You need a license."

"I know that. I wasn't going to get rid of his rifles." Ben had thought he'd keep them for Junior some day, when he grew up. Dumb sentiment? Maybe. Arlo was no hunter, except, as Casper had said, for necessities, but he loved fishing and being in the bush. Junior took after his dad.

"What about the truck?" Casper was buttoning his jacket, adjusting the sleeves. "Piece of junk but I could take it off your hands, I guess. Maybe bring another two hundred bucks for Marie."

"The cops took it."

"They did?" Casper looked surprised.

"Evidence." Ben raised his eyebrows. "Whatever. When they let it go, you can have the damn thing. You off?"

"Yeah." Casper shoved his tie in a pocket. "Big date." He winked. "Gotta love those Calgary girls, eh?"

What an idiot. Casper could be so exasperating—Ben had almost forgotten *how* exasperating until this little visit, but his heart was in the right place. "So, where's your warriors? Not often I see you traveling alone these days."

"Warriors?" Casper laughed. "Oh, you mean the boys from Pekisko? Gave 'em the day off." He winked again. "Hey, don't say nothin' bad about those boys, they'd do anything for me...."

"You're a bad influence on them. They should be working. There's lots of oil patch jobs out there. Listen, tell me the truth, Casper.'' Ben stood at the door, facing his boy-hood friend. They'd met when Casper had moved in with a foster family on the reserve, when he was twelve and Ben was ten. Their paths rarely crossed anymore, but Ben valued his opinion, if only because Casper had a wily kind of smarts. He'd also traveled in the same circles Arlo had. ''You think he did it? You think Arlo shot Wayne?''

''You don't?'' Casper frowned. ''Jeez, Ben. The cops say that's what happened, so that's what happened, okay? Since when do you care how the cops do their jobs?''

''But you know Arlo. He wouldn't hurt a fly.'' Ben held his breath, searching Casper's expression.

''Yeah, I know. Weird stuff happens, though. It *might* have been like the cops say. Freak accident, maybe.''

Ben nodded. He'd thought of that.

''All I'm saying is, don't go stirrin' things up,'' Casper continued. ''Don't go puttin' Marie through more hell than she's already had. Arlo's gone. She needs to put this be-hind her.''

''Behind her! For God's sake, he was her *husband,* Cas-per. She loved the guy!'' Casper could be such a pain in the ass sometimes. ''It's not like she's going to just *for-get.*''

Casper reached for the doorknob. ''Stay out of it, that's all I'm saying.'' Ben held his gaze for a long moment.

The phone rang. Damn, he'd better pick it up this time. ''Okay. I hear you. See you around, pal.''

Casper left, slamming the door behind him. The phone stopped ringing, then started again a few seconds later. Ben picked up before the answering machine came on, noting that the red light was blinking madly, showing seven new messages.

''Ben?'' Marie. She sounded scared. ''I didn't know if you were home— Ben, Junior's run off again! I can't find him anywhere.''

BEN WAS AT the trailer in under three minutes.

"Settle down, Marie. You know he's around here somewhere." He put his hands on her shoulders and gently eased her down onto the banquette that ran two-thirds of the way around the kitchen table. "Laverne home?"

"She's sleeping. I didn't want to call her. She's exhausted, Ben." Marie's tear-stained face looked awful. When she was happy and dressed up, she was a beautiful woman. Pale, smooth, coffee-colored skin, glossy black hair, big dark eyes. A gorgeous smile. There was a time when Ben hadn't been immune to her charms....

"Let her rest." Ben ran water into the teakettle and set it on the stove. He'd lived in this trailer himself for four years, since he'd bought the ranch and before he'd started to build his house, and knew where everything was. "Make yourself a cup of tea while I take a look around. He's just scared. Wants to be off on his own, think things through."

"You're right." Marie sighed. "I *know* you're right. But since—since what happened last week, I just can't bear to have Junior out of my sight." She pressed a used tissue against her mouth. She was shaking. "I'm sorry," she whispered.

It was all Ben could do to stand there, steel himself against the raw pain in her voice, stop himself from taking her in his arms. But he couldn't make the hurt go away; no one could.

"When did you last see him? Was he here when Casper arrived?"

"What? Oh, yes. He was in his bedroom. I thought he was playing video games. Then, when I checked, he was gone. He must've slipped out the back door." Marie clenched her trembling hands together. "Ben?"

"Yeah?"

"Casper gave me some money—"

"Money!" Ben swung around from the counter, where he'd arranged the empty teapot, a mug and the tea canister, ready for Marie to brew her tea when the kettle boiled.

"A check. Said I should spend it on whatever I needed." Marie met his surprised gaze. "Should I cash it? What do you think?"

"How much?"

"Five hundred dollars. He said Arlo was his pal and he never wanted to see his kids go hungry...."

"Cash it. Not that Laverne and Junior would *ever* go hungry, you understand, not while I'm around. See that suit he had on? He didn't pick that up at the Army and Navy. Go ahead. If the check doesn't bounce, buy yourself a new dress."

That brought a smile, no matter how teary.

Ben stepped outside the trailer and whistled, closing the door behind him. Both Dodger and Junior's dog, Ringo, came running.

"Hey, Ringo! Go find Junior. Hey, fella—where's Junior?" Seeing Junior's dog gave Ben a sinking feeling. The two were usually inseparable.

To his relief, Ringo, a collie cross named for the white marking on his neck, trotted toward the barn, looking back and whining. Ben followed. Ringo led him straight to the stairs that went to the loft.

"Junior?" Ben climbed the steps, both dogs crowding behind him. The hayloft was dim, with only the light from the cracks in the siding and the cobwebby windows high in the gable ends. The missing boy was lying on his back in a nest of hay, his hands behind his head. He sat up when Ben appeared. "Your mom's worried. You shouldn't have run off, not without telling her."

It was so easy to forget that Junior wasn't telling anyone anything these days; he never answered a question, never spoke a word. Ben reached out a hand and pulled him to his feet. He'd been crying.

"You been here long?"

Junior just stared at him, his dark eyes huge.

Junior nodded. Ringo had probably been with the boy but had finally gotten bored and gone home looking for his supper.

They walked toward the trailer. Ben stopped, his hand on the child's shoulder. "Now, I want you to go in there and give your mom a great big hug—you got that? You're the man of the family now, right?"

Junior nodded, his lower lip trembling.

Poor kid. "You got any problems in the future, anything at all, I want you to come and see me. We can figure it out. You understand? No more taking off like that."

Junior shook his head. Ben ruffled his hair, as he'd seen Arlo do so many times and watched the boy race toward the trailer, Ringo behind him. When Ben heard Marie's happy cry, he continued toward his own place, Dodger at his heels.

Poor kid, he thought. Man of the family and he's only just turned nine.

CHAPTER FIVE

"CHARITY SQUARE *DANCE*?" Daisy waved the piece of paper that had appeared on her desk. She'd been gone for two minutes while she grabbed a mug of the ghastly brew Ellin referred to as coffee, stopped to check the photos pegged up outside the darkroom and then returned to the newsroom. Newsroom? Well, it was a large open space with big windows fronting Frank Street. There were several scarred oak desks, including hers, and a reception area where Ellin took classifieds and answered the phone. "And who is Lucas Yellowfly?"

Ellin spun around in the new swivel chair that had been delivered the day before from McPherson's Furniture. "Glory lawyer. Ben Goodstriker's cousin or something."

Ah. Ben Goodstriker. The man who didn't return phone calls. "And?"

"It's to do with that kiddie rodeo. Bunny's not here so I gave it to you." Ellin whirled again, reaching for the phone. She loved that chair. "Good morning, *Tamarack Times*. How may I help you?"

Daisy stared at the scrawled message in her hand. This was Bunny McPhee's assignment. She'd reluctantly taken on the kiddie rodeo while Daisy had been busy with the Pekisko shoot-out.

"Did Gordon Bass call back?" she asked when Ellin hung up.

"Not yet."

Not that Daisy expected he would. The staff sergeant

had told her point-blank that she had all the details the Mounties intended to release at this time. And now that they'd gotten that piece of business out of the way, was she free to go out with him this weekend?

Daisy had considered the offer for about two seconds—he was one of those handsome, competent men, arrogant but charming when he wanted to be—then turned him down, saying she didn't like to mix business with pleasure and she was sure the RCMP had the same policy. She said she'd call later. And she would. Damn it, she needed an update to go with the terrific pictures Duncan had taken at the funeral. It was embarrassing having to monitor the big-city competition, as she'd done surreptitiously over the weekend, for details on a story that had happened in her own backyard. The *Herald* and *The Journal* and the CTV network should be coming to *her* for details....

Daisy wasn't giving up quite that easily.

"Anyone call from the *Sun?*"

"In Vancouver?" Ellin looked up from the message she was writing. "No. Are you expecting one?"

"No. Just my old boss," Daisy said. She'd left a message on Oliver Crawford's voice mail, but she had no idea when she'd hear from him.

Her friend Emily Parrish had managed to get the two of them invited to a spring branding, and Daisy wanted to sound out Oliver on whether the *Sun* might be interested in a color piece for their weekend edition. While she was at it, she was going to run this Pekisko thing by him. He could tell her if she was trying to read something into the situation that very likely wasn't there.

She knew she should just rewrite what she'd had in the *Times* last week and hope that with all the funeral pictures no one would notice that she had nothing new. Then move on to other riveting small-town stories, like this kiddie rodeo—what exactly, she wondered, was a kiddie rodeo?—

the track and field day at the high school, the grand opening of a new restaurant in the old station building on Saturday. The kinds of stories she'd come home to write. Safe. Sensible. Nothing brutal or grim.

Nothing that could have life-and-death consequences…

What really bothered her—and this was tough to admit—was how closemouthed people were. Everyone suggested she ask someone else. It was almost like no one in the town or on the reserve *wanted* to know what had really happened or why. What had Wayne been doing out on the reserve so early, for instance? The cops wouldn't say. Did they know? Why had he been gunned down? Who was the bad guy? Well, she knew who he was, or at least who he seemed to be. Arlo Goodstriker, an out-of-work ex-rodeo cowboy who'd left behind a wife and two children and whose high point in life had probably been the three seconds he'd spent on a bull at the Calgary Stampede seven years ago. That was a little item she'd found going through back issues of the *Times*.

But…why? Sure, he had a criminal record with a list of petty misdemeanors a mile long, going back to practically the day he turned sixteen. If he also had a juvenile record, which he probably did, it was sealed. But stealing gas and speeding didn't add up to a dawn shoot-out that left two people dead.

One last try. "Chief George call back?" Chief Winston George was head of the Pekisko band. Daisy hoped that if he talked to her, gave her his seal of approval, so to speak, others would, too.

"No. Daisy, you *know* if you get any calls, I pass them on." Ellin looked hurt.

"Of course I do. Just antsy, I guess. I wish people would return calls, answer my questions.…"

"It's just because you're new. People aren't used to being asked questions in this town. That isn't how it's—

well, your dad likes to do things his way," Ellin finished loyally. Daisy knew what she meant. Owen Sutherland had a network of cronies who fed him information, usually of the don't-rock-the-boat variety. He knew what was on a press release before it arrived in the mail.

So maybe it was just habit that kept her picking away at the edges of a story, like a loose thread on a sleeve, until the whole thing unraveled. That was what she wanted to run by Oliver. She wasn't proud of everything she'd done as a journalist but, right or wrong, she hadn't gotten as far as she had at the *Sun* by sitting on her hands and relying on press releases for information.

The scene that rainy morning still haunted her. She kept replaying the tape in her brain. The officer shouting at her to back up and turn around when she began to drive forward. The pickup and cruiser, both empty, both with drivers' doors hanging open. All that rain dumping down, a lot of it right through the crack in the back window of Uncle Leroy's car. Owen Sutherland's brother was in the Middle East on a two-year drilling project, and Daisy knew he loved that car, the way only a bachelor of fiftysomething could.

Maybe the setup made sense to the cops, who obviously had a lot more information than she did, but it didn't to her. How did two guys manage to shoot each other so conveniently? *Bang, bang—you're both dead.* And why?

Daisy made up her mind. She grabbed her cell from her desk drawer and stuffed it into her bag, along with a camera and an apple. Bunny didn't want this rodeo story, anyway. And it gave Daisy an excuse to speak to the man who was supposed to know everything and always ignored her calls. "Ellin? I'm going out for an hour or so. If Bunny shows up, tell her she can have the town council meeting tonight. I should be back by noon."

"If not, where should I send the ambulance?"

Ellin's idea of a joke. "Ben Goodstriker's place."

IF NOTHING ELSE, it was great just getting out of town. Only half-past ten, but already the pavement was hot. Tamarack was an odd town, stuck between a past it was very proud of and a future that was less certain. Its fortunes had been built on coal mined back in the fifties and sixties in the Rocky Mountains that loomed at the end of Main Street, history shared with other Crowsnest towns like Blairmore, Coleman and Bellevue. During its heyday, the town's population had been twice what it was now. Since then, ranching and hardscrabble farming—a few cows, a kitchen garden, perhaps some hay to sell—had been the mainstay for most people. Fortunately, a number of merchants had clung on through the lean years. The province's current burst of oil and gas exploration was supposed to be the ticket to Tamarack's future, and new stores had begun to sprout up. And there was even talk of Fording looking into the viability of the old coal properties.

Which was good for business if you were the newly hatched editor of the family weekly newspaper.

The Tamarack road snaked around Miller's Hill, then continued two or three miles northeast before meeting Highway 22A, where Daisy turned north.

The pavement stretched before her, the magnificent foothills rising to her left, with the snowcapped Rockies behind, and the Porcupine Hills, a sixty-mile-long geological anomaly running from Nanton to Pincher Creek, to her right. The sky was the blue of a...well, an Alberta summer sky. There was just nothing in the world like it. Daisy had the convertible's top down, the wind deafening her and making a mess of her hair. She intended to buy a vehicle of her own soon, something small and secondhand, but in the meantime, it was fun driving Uncle Leroy's car. People noticed it.

Actually, Daisy was excited about making some changes at the *Times*, the paper started by her grandfather in the thirties. He'd been from Ontario, a rabble-rouser who'd come out west to dig coal but been fired when he tried to organize the miners. He'd had his revenge on the company when he'd started a town newspaper. Then he'd met Daisy's grandmother, a local rancher's daughter, and had put down roots in the community. Daisy sometimes wondered if a little of that rabble-rouser blood ran in her veins.

All of which made being part of the hometown paper an exciting prospect. If she was going to put the *Times* on the map, she needed more than a part-time society reporter, a ditzy office manager and a high-school kid who ran the darkroom, swept out the place, wrote the odd column and eavesdropped on the police radio. A-student, too. Come to think of it, John Spears was quite a busy boy. Then there was Duncan Fairlie, the part-time photographer, who did okay work when he wasn't drunk or hadn't booked time off to search for the legendary Lost Lemon Gold Mine in the Crowsnest Mountains—his passion. Fairlie wrote the occasional story, too, which was a help, since Bunny had been threatening to quit ever since Daisy arrived. Daisy suspected the Tamarack matron had a crush on her father and found it wasn't quite the same coming in two days a week to work for his daughter. She needed to bump Bunny McPhee up to full-time reporting or replace her.

Then there was the redundantly named Bob Roberts, who sold advertising and was still more or less under her father's jurisdiction. Owen Sutherland remained on the masthead as publisher, which was fine by her. The business of running a weekly paper wasn't nearly as interesting as the editorial side. Like this little expedition to see Ben Goodstriker, the man everyone said she should talk to.

She was ashamed to recall how she'd lost her temper when she'd phoned the evening after Wayne's funeral.

That would have been the fifth or sixth message she'd left. Not that it mattered; Ben Goodstriker didn't seem to check his messages anyway. Yelling at him on his answering machine wouldn't improve the situation, though, would it? Well, with luck, he wouldn't have bothered to check *that* message, either.

Daisy slowed for the turnoff onto the Mosquito Creek Trail, which led to Goodstriker's ranch. She could actually hear birds singing in the ditches, western meadowlarks and warblers. There, above the power lines as she turned, she saw a kingbird launching himself, the show-off, from the high wire to perform some crazy aerial acrobatics for whatever female happened to be in the vicinity.

Men! Weren't they the same everywhere?

THE RANCH YARD looked deserted. There was a dusty pickup parked near the house, but no sign of anyone. A dog barked somewhere in the distance.

Daisy got out and smoothed her hair, wishing she'd worn a scarf or at least had the sense to stop at the turnoff to find a comb. The house was a modest-looking white-painted rancher that appeared to be brand-new, right down to the unfinished sidewalk and handful of wires poking out of the hole where the doorbell should be. Daisy rapped on the door and waited.

She rapped again, then turned to survey the yard. A huge cottonwood grew off to one side near the river. In the middle distance behind it were several buildings, granaries, sheds, corrals, a big red barn. The grass near the house was neatly clipped, but the flower beds were empty. A few elderly lawn chairs formed a ragtag grouping on the grass under the cottonwood.

No answer. Clearly she couldn't beard the lion in his den because he wasn't *in* his den. At least he wasn't answering his door.

Daisy spotted the outlines of another structure through the copse of poplars and willows across the yard, maybe fifty yards away. It turned out to be a house trailer next to a large open shed containing a parked school bus and an old station wagon. A dog yawned and came toward her as she approached, slowly waving its plume of a tail.

"Good boy!" Daisy risked a pat on the broad head and was rewarded with an adoring look. "Some watchdog you are," she muttered and knocked on the trailer door.

It was going to be a scorcher. She could smell the heat already, rising from the dust on the battered stoop, from the faded Fiberglas awning above the window....

Daisy noticed a movement, glimpsed a boy's face before it disappeared behind checked curtains.

"Yes?" A frightened-looking woman opened the door a few inches, then opened it wider, her features relaxing. "Can I help you?"

"Hi, I'm Daisy Sutherland," Daisy said, extending her hand. After a few seconds' hesitation, the other woman took it. She wore jeans and a sleeveless blouse and was very pretty, obviously of Native Indian ancestry, with large eyes and clear skin. She seemed very tired, though, as if she hadn't slept well for days. "And you're—?"

A frown. "Listen, are you selling something, ma'am, because—"

"Oh, no! I'm here to see Ben Goodstriker. This is his ranch, right?" The woman nodded. "I knocked at his door. At least I guess that's where he lives." She felt rather silly. Maybe he lived *here* and this was his wife. "Over there in that house." She pointed.

"Yes, that's his." The woman nodded again. "Built it himself."

"Oh?" Maybe that was why the doorbell hadn't been installed. On the other hand, why encourage visitors? From all the evidence so far, Ben Goodstriker was not exactly social. "Anyway, do you know where I might find him?"

"He's probably working a horse. Maybe in the corral behind the barn. Would you like me to take you there? Or I could send my boy."

"Oh, no. Thanks, anyway. I'll find it. I'll just—" Daisy waggled her fingers, feeling a bit embarrassed "—wander over there myself. Thanks!"

"Maybe I could help you with something?" The woman's eyes were only faintly curious.

"I work for the paper in town. I'm doing a story on the junior rodeo. And—well, I'd like to ask him a few questions about his cousin, too, while I'm here."

"His cousin?" she repeated sharply.

"The one who was killed on the reserve two weeks ago."

The woman's eyes clouded and she hunched forward and wrapped her arms tightly around her waist, as though she felt cold. "That was my husband," she whispered.

Daisy was appalled. "I'm sorry." She touched the woman's forearm lightly. "Please. Forgive me—"

"Never mind," Marie Goodstriker interrupted, stepping back. "Ben'll be out at the barn. If he isn't there, I don't know where he'd be."

She shut the door and Daisy began to walk, hot-faced, in the direction of the barn she could see a few hundred yards away, downstream from the house and set well back from the river.

Oh-my-Lord-in-heaven! How could she have shoved her foot in it like that? That poor, poor woman—Arlo Goodstriker's widow!

CHAPTER SIX

BEHIND THE BARN were various corrals. In one, she saw a man with a black horse that shook its head constantly and ran around the enclosure. The man kept facing the horse, moving in toward the animal, almost, it seemed, forcing the horse to run. Then he turned and took a few steps away and Daisy could see the horse's ears prick with interest, eyes following every movement the man made. After a minute or so, the horse bobbed its head low to the ground, up and down, then shook its head vigorously and approached the man. The man turned away again, and this time the horse turned with him. Then the man reached out and started to rub the horse's face, its ears, its neck.

Daisy caught her breath. She realized she'd actually seen Ben Goodstriker twice before. He been one of his cousin's pall bearers and he'd been with the old woman at Wayne Petrenko's funeral.

She stood at the fence awkwardly, not quite sure what else to do, hoping he'd notice her. His dog did. The mutt had been lying in the shade of a nearby shed but when she walked up, it stood and stared at her, ears pricked. Then it sauntered over, stiff-legged, and began to inspect her shoes, her knees, even her bag, in which she kept everything from her steno pad to her eyeliner and which she'd dropped on the ground. She hoped he wouldn't pee on it.

"Good doggie," she muttered. She liked dogs and they generally liked her, but this grizzled little mutt didn't look as though it could be trusted somehow....

Goodstriker turned toward her but continued working with the horse, touching it continually, running his other hand along its back. He gave no indication that he'd noticed her but Daisy knew he had. He wasn't the kind of man who missed things.

She felt awkward waiting there but she didn't want to disturb him, either. Even though the horse was standing with him now, it looked skittish, as though it really would rather be running in the opposite direction. But the pole corral was circular and there was nowhere to go. So, for some reason probably known only to horses, it stayed close to the man, moving forward a step or two when he moved, turning when he turned.

Finally, after what seemed like an eternity but was probably no more than five or six minutes, Goodstriker began to walk toward her. He was taller than she'd remembered and wore a dark hat, jeans, blue chambray shirt and scuffed riding boots. Standard cowboy gear.

Daisy waved awkwardly. "Hi! I'm sorry to disturb you...."

He nodded. "What can I do for you?" It was the usual western business-conversation opener. He was a lot handsomer, close up, than he'd seemed in church the day of Wayne's funeral. Tanned, dark hair, dark eyes, a tiny scar to one side of his mouth. Of course, then he'd been wearing sunglasses, which had given him a faintly menacing air. Not that he looked particularly friendly now, but he did look polite.

"I'm Daisy Sutherland," she said, thrusting out her hand.

He ignored her gesture. So much for polite. She quickly buried her hand back in the pocket of her capris.

"Ben Goodstriker. Maybe you already know that."

"I do. In fact—" Daisy laughed weakly "—you're who I came to see today."

"About what?"

"Well." The direct gaze was disconcerting. He hadn't glanced back at the horse, which had moved to the other side of the enclosure and was regarding them with alert ears. "A couple of things. I'm with the *Tamarack Times*—"

"I know who you are," he said flatly. He had greenish-brown eyes, she decided, and right now they were as cold as the river that ran by his ranch.

"You do?" Daisy was surprised.

"Word spreads. You're taking over the paper. You're single. You're looking for a place to rent in town. You've been asking a lot of nosy questions about my cousin."

"For a man who doesn't answer his phone or return calls, you sure know a lot!" Daisy's face was flushed.

Goodstriker leaned over, plucked a long blade of grass growing near a fence post and stuck the end of it in his mouth. He adjusted his hat, so the brim shadowed his face, and glanced up at the sky. "I get around."

He ignored her outburst. "So," he continued, his eyes following the blade of grass as he removed it from his mouth and tossed it over the fence, "what can I do for you, ma'am?"

Daisy made a heroic attempt to rein in her temper, although her first impulse was to storm off, get in Uncle Leroy's convertible and burn rubber all the way back to Tamarack.

"I guess it's more about what I can do for *you*," she returned. "The boys' and girls' rodeo?"

That caught his attention. "What about it?" He put one foot up on the second pole and swung his leg over the top to join her on the outside of the corral. His little dog barked, ran in a tight circle, then sat down at his feet, looking up at them both. One ear dangled comically.

"I thought you might want to see an article in the *Times* on it."

He nodded. "Sounds like a good idea."

"Well, I'll need to know a bit more about it. And now there's this charity dance coming up in a couple of weeks and—"

"Dance?"

"Fund-raiser." She was pleased that she seemed to know something he didn't. "I got a message from Lucas Yellowfly. He wants to get together and talk about some kind of charity dance he's planned to raise money for your rodeo."

Goodstriker sighed and leaned against the fence. "Is that what you're here for—to find out about the dance? Because if you are, this is the first I've heard of it."

Daisy rummaged in her bag for the message from Yellowfly. "No. I've got his number. I'll talk to him myself."

"Fine." He studied her for a few seconds. "Let me turn that horse out, then we can talk."

Daisy watched him vault the fence again and stride toward the black horse, each step sending up a tiny puff of dust. The dog went with him. Daisy watched the horse wheel and run away from the man, then turn as Goodstriker opened the gate at the far end of the corral. He whistled and his dog took a run at the horse. The horse dashed through the open gate, snorted, bucked a few times and galloped off to join a knot of horses Daisy could see under some trees at the far end of the pasture.

She'd slung her bag onto her shoulder when he returned and was determined to make a fresh start. Bass was close-mouthed. Chief George didn't return her calls. Now him. Why were all the men in this town so difficult? "What's your dog's name?"

"Dodger."

"What kind is he?"

"You interested in dogs?" He started toward the house. She walked quickly to keep pace.

"I like dogs," she admitted, "but I've never seen one quite like him."

"That's because he's one of a kind," Goodstriker answered with a sideways glance, and Daisy realized that was about as close to a joke as he was going to make. This was a lot harder than she'd thought it would be. He didn't like her; that was clear enough. Because she was a reporter? Because she'd been asking questions about his cousin? Lots of people were suspicious of the press—not that the *Tamarack Times* was *the press,* exactly!

When they reached the house, he waved her toward the grouping of lawn chairs under the cottonwood.

"Ma'am?"

"Please, call me Daisy."

"You want a beer?" He looked perplexed, as though surprised to hear his own offer. "Or something?"

"Water would be very welcome," she said stiffly. "Thank you."

He disappeared into the house and Daisy tried a chair, then another, pulling it onto more level ground as it wobbled dangerously. She sat down and rummaged in her bag for the steno pad, which contained a list of questions about the kiddie rodeo, plus a few notes she'd jotted down regarding the slayings at the reserve. Just in case Ben Goodstriker actually did know anything about that, as so many people seemed to think. She wished she could let this go: *no one* wanted to talk about it. Her own better judgement said, *give it a rest.* What had she come to Tamarack for, if it wasn't to leave this kind of journalism behind? She wished Oliver would call.

Her host approached with a glass of water in one hand and a can of something in the other. She sipped the water and set the glass down on the grass. He popped the tab—

it looked like a soft drink—and stood in front of her. "Fire away."

"Okay." She glanced at her notes. "I gather this is new for Tamarack?"

"The kids' rodeo?"

"Yes."

"It's new. I don't know why there's never been one before." He shrugged. "Maybe because Tamarack doesn't have the real rodeo, Glory does."

"Real?"

"Pro rodeo."

"I see. Why a kids' rodeo? If you don't mind me asking." She could think of all kinds of activities this man might be involved in, none of them having to do with good works in the community.

"Why not?" He hunkered down on the grass in front of her, which put them at eye level, and began to scratch his dog's ears. The mutt groaned and collapsed into a heap of grizzled fur between them. "Kids growing up on ranches like to test their cowboy skills. It's a western tradition."

"Oh? You're a rodeo cowboy?"

"Used to be. This is cowboy country." His gesture took in the mountains, the hills, the wide-open grassland to the east. "Kids here grow up riding and roping, skills they need for their own ranches and, sure, a few of them do end up in professional rodeo. What we're putting on is for little kids, six to, oh, say, twelve or thirteen. Older than that, they usually ride in what's called a high school rodeo."

"No bucking broncs, I assume?"

He rested his forearms on his knees and looked directly at her. "No broncs. More like roping straw bales and riding sheep. It's fun for the kids."

"How about you? What kind of rodeo stuff did you do?"

"Broncs, bareback and saddle." He raised one eyebrow, apparently wondering what that had to do with anything. She was just curious. He'd struck her as an athlete the first time she'd seen him, leaning against the wall of the church with the deceptive ease of a mountain lion before the big pounce. "I finally got busted up one time too many and called it quits."

"I guess it's a dangerous sport," Daisy acknowledged.

He took another quick draught of his cola. "You could say that," he agreed coolly, then added, "This isn't about me, though, is it?"

His gaze held hers until Daisy managed to wrench her attention back to her notes. "No," she said hurriedly. "It isn't."

"This small-fry rodeo was actually my cousin's idea," he went on smoothly. "His daughter's a fine little barrel racer and—well, we were working on it together before—" He paused and stared up at her. "Before my cousin was killed. I guess you know all about that."

"Yes," Daisy said, too quickly. She bit her lip. "I talked to his wife—"

"Marie?" He frowned.

"I knocked on the trailer door and she told me where I could find you. She was very helpful. Actually, I was hoping we could talk a bit about that, too, you know—what happened to your cousin. Background, stuff like that."

He scratched Dodger's belly again. After a few long seconds, he went on as though she hadn't spoken. "Boys' and girls' rodeos are a tradition in Alberta. Most rodeo towns have what they call Little Britches rodeos. There's a big one each year at High River. Maybe this one will turn into an annual event."

"Do *you* think your cousin killed Wayne Petrenko?"

He stood suddenly, and the sun was so high Daisy had to shade her eyes when she looked up at him. "Why do you ask?"

"I just wondered if it made any sense to you. If you thought your cousin was that kind of man. I'm curious."

"A killer, you mean." His face was unreadable.

"Well, yeah. I heard he knew Wayne. Is that true?"

Goodstriker nodded. He took his hat off and ran his hand through his hair. "Sure he did. He knew Wayne well. So did I, years ago."

This was news. Daisy had wondered if there was a personal connection, since Ben had been at the funeral. Of course, there'd been a lot of people at Wayne's funeral who would've had only a passing acquaintance with him or the family or none at all.

"Why are you asking me this stuff?" he demanded. "Don't you believe the cops' story?"

"Do you?" Daisy picked up her water and took a sip.

"To tell you the truth, I don't know what to think."

"It seems strange to me. Two guys happen to kill each other, and no one knows why," Daisy continued. "I'd like to write a decent story for the newspaper, but no one seems to want to talk about it. Your name keeps coming up and—"

"Mine?" Goodstriker laughed, but she could tell it wasn't because he was amused. "What the hell do I know about what happened? All I know is what the cops say."

"Seriously, have you ever heard of two people shooting each other dead like that?" she burst out. "Except on television? Not that it couldn't happen, I guess. Just seems unlikely to me. But let's say it *did* happen like that. What was Wayne doing out there on the reserve so early? On a back road in the middle of nowhere. I understand he was a traffic cop, mostly. Was he trying to arrest your cousin? For what? The Mounties give me the brush-off. Half of what I've got on this story came from the CTV national news on the weekend. Nobody in town wants to talk.''

"Well, why would they?'' Goodstriker hunched his shoulders and jammed his hands in his jeans pockets. "Think about it. There's a tidy little story here. Cop gets shot by a bad guy and, son of a gun, the bad guy turns out to be a shiftless, unemployed Indian who happens to have a long list of relatively small crimes and misdemeanors going back to when he was a kid. Add 'drunk' to that and you've got your stereotype all wrapped up and tied with a bow.''

"I never heard he was drunk.''

"Me, neither. He probably wasn't. That early in the morning? Hung over, if anything. Who knows? Who cares? But the Indian's dead, too, so—'' he shrugged "—end of story.''

"Why aren't the Indians talking then?'' Daisy felt a thrill. Did that mean he'd help her sort this out? "You'd think they'd want to stick up for him.''

"Stick up for him? You're forgetting something. A cop was shot. My cousin was there and he's dead, too. Both parties are *dead,* so why bother worrying about the kind of job the cops are doing?''

Daisy stared at him. Bitter disappointment washed through her. For a few minutes, she'd thought he actually believed the same thing she did. "So you don't care about the truth, either?''

"What truth?'' he asked angrily. "As far as we know, it happened exactly the way the cops say it did.''

"I get the feeling you don't think your cousin would shoot a boyhood pal. But if you don't think your cousin would do something like that, well, maybe he didn't....''

"What? You're saying Wayne shot Arlo and then he shot himself? Get real!''

"Nobody actually saw what happened, right?'' Daisy

reached down for her empty glass, then searched his expression for some softness, some curiosity. There was none. She wished she'd just shut up. "There's a lot of supposition here," she began.

"Yeah—by you."

"I was hoping you'd help me get to the bottom of this."

"How? Do the cops' work for them?"

"No. Just find out a bit more. Like, what crime was your cousin being arrested for, if he was being arrested? And why he might try and resist that arrest and—"

"Listen, lady, who *cares* who did it? They're both dead! What don't you get about that? Nothing's going to bring my cousin back!"

He made an abrupt gesture of dismissal and started walking toward the house. Daisy caught up with him and glanced into his face. "I care. I'm sorry this is disturbing you."

"*Disturbing* me?" He wheeled. "Goddammit, woman! You're asking questions about me around town, you're pestering people on the reserve about my cousin, you're in my face on my own damn ranch...." He growled something else, something indistinguishable, which was maybe just as well, and began to stride toward the house again.

Daisy hurried along beside him, not sure what tack to take. This wasn't going well. When they'd gone another fifteen yards, he whirled again, so suddenly she ran into him. His hands went out to steady her, then he abruptly let her go and stepped back.

"That's why you're here, isn't it?" he charged. "It's got nothing to do with this kids' rodeo. You just want to poke around about my cousin, ask questions, talk to the widow, pry into my family's business—"

"I *am* interested in the kiddie rodeo. It's a big story for Tamarack. But so is the business out on the reserve."

"There is no *business* out on the reserve!"

He began moving, quickly, and when they got to the house she walked toward the convertible. The dog trotted up the steps and sat down beside the door. Goodstriker stayed several paces back, on the unfinished sidewalk.

She paused, one hand on the door handle. *One last shot…* "Will you help me?"

He swore again. "No, I will not."

"Not even if you don't think your cousin would ever do something like that?"

"Nope."

Daisy held out the empty glass. He hesitated, then stepped toward her and took it from her hand. She tossed her bag onto the passenger seat and pulled her sunglasses from the visor, where she'd left them hanging. Then she opened the door, sliding into the driver's seat. "Not even to clear his reputation?"

He shook his head.

"What about his good name?"

"He didn't have a good name."

"What about his wife? His kids?" She put on her sunglasses.

"What about them?" Goodstriker came closer and leaned on the passenger door as she turned the key in the ignition. "Anything I pass on to you going to bring a father back? A husband?"

"No." That wasn't the point.

"And there's something else you maybe haven't thought through, Ms. Sutherland."

She knew he was being sarcastic. "Yeah? What's that?"

"If my cousin didn't kill Wayne Petrenko, then who did?"

She revved the engine, then, with her foot on the brake, pushed the gearshift into Drive. "I don't know."

"No, *you* don't know. And *I* don't know. And it's not my job to find out. Or yours." He stood back as she took her foot off the brake and the car eased forward. "Stick to making sure the summer pool schedule gets into the paper and the mayor's daughter gets her picture on the front page."

"Thanks for the water," Daisy said.

"Don't mention it. And something else—"

"What's that?" Daisy forced herself to meet his angry gaze.

"Leave Marie alone. She's got enough to deal with. She doesn't need a nosy reporter playing investigator. If you're going to keep poking around, talk to me in the future, not her."

"I tried to talk to you," Daisy retorted, stung at the implication that she was harassing a grieving relative. "Didn't do me much good, did it? If you don't want to see me out here again, try answering your damn phone!" She resisted the childish urge to stomp on the gas; instead, she drove extra slowly down the graveled drive that wound along the river. She glanced in her mirror several times, each time seeing him standing there looking at her until a bend in the drive hid him from view.

So he wasn't going to help. Well, he had something to think about, at least.

An unwelcome thought niggled at the back of her mind as she turned south onto the highway toward Tamarack. Ben Goodstriker had given her something to think about, too.

This really *was* work for the police.

CHAPTER SEVEN

WELL, SONUVABITCH.

If he was the type to abuse animals—which he wasn't—he'd kick Dodger into next Tuesday. Or take out that flighty buckskin he'd bought from Noah Winslow, run him hard and put him away wet.

The red convertible disappeared around the bend, flashing chrome. Where did that kind of woman, didn't look a day over twenty-two, get a car like that? The girl-next-door type, all pretty blond hair and innocent blue eyes. Running the *Tamarack Times* these days, according to Casper!

Casper was right about one thing—she was a babe. He definitely didn't recall her—or her sister—from school but why would he? He had to have at least ten years on her. She was just a kid!

A kid with a big problem. Sticking her nose where it was liable to get bumped real hard.

He turned toward the house, crumpling the empty cola can in his hand, satisfying some of the urge he had to wreak havoc, and tossed it in the trash can by the corner of the house.

Now, where would *she* get such a notion about his cousin? Not that the idea hadn't crossed Ben's mind, but it was based on nothing more than instinct. Loyalty. The Arlo he knew was incapable of forming the thought, never mind the action. Ben had decided to accept the double shoot-out story because...well, who could know for sure? Arlo *might* have done it. Some bizarre accident, maybe.

The small-fry rodeo was one thing. What had happened out at Pekisko was another.

He was more than happy to talk to any reporter, including her, about the rodeo, which, now that Lucas and Adam were involved, looked like it might actually take place. He'd help out a friend in a flash, no questions asked. But don't make him draw up some kind of business plan, the kind the town wanted to see before they'd commit the playing fields. When Arlo first came up with the idea, he and Ben had thought they'd stage the rodeo out at the reserve. Now, with Adam and Lucas on board, the plan had grown and there was talk of having the one-day event at the municipal ball park in Tamarack. That meant insurance, liability, concessions, guarantees, all that crap. Lucas was good at the fine print; he was a lawyer, after all.

Now a dance, too! Whose idea was that, for God's sake? Probably Virginia's, Lucas's wife. In a way, Ben was glad Lucas and Adam had stepped in.

He walked in the direction of Marie's trailer. There was a quick tug at the kitchen curtains when he knocked, something he hadn't always bothered with when his cousin was around, and then Junior opened the door.

"How come you're not in school?" Ben asked, stepping inside. Marie was on the phone. She gestured to him to sit down but Ben shook his head. He didn't plan to stay, just find out if Daisy Sutherland had poked around a little more than she'd let on. Then he'd drive across the river to check on his hayfield. With the hot weather the past ten days, the hay was maturing faster than usual.

Junior went back to the stove and stirred something in a pot. Ben saw an empty cream of mushroom soup can on the counter and glanced at the wall clock over the table. Twenty minutes to twelve.

"Sorry, Ben." Marie looked flushed. Tired, but she had color in her cheeks again, which was a good sign. "I'm taking Junior to the doctor in Glory, Laverne's in school." She threw an anguished look at the back of her son's head. "I know he should be, too, but he didn't want to go," she stated softly. "He'll be there tomorrow for sports day."

Marie had driven the bus in the morning, and Ben knew she'd be taking it out again at half-past two to pick up kids from school in Tamarack. "You want me to bring him to the doctor's? Save you a trip?" He wouldn't mind the opportunity to ask Doc Pleasance a few questions about the boy's condition.

"No, that's all right," she said hurriedly. "Ed offered to drive me. That was him on the phone—"

"Ed Sawchuk?" Ben was surprised. He knew Ed was a good guy—he'd been one of the few white men who'd shown up for Arlo's funeral—but he also knew he was a busy man with half a dozen other business interests in the area. Hardly a man with the time to run a kid to the doctor in the middle of the day.

"Yes." She moved closer to the boy. "Honey, you watch that soup now. Keep stirring, don't let it scorch." Ben had the distinct impression Marie was avoiding eye contact.

"Daisy Sutherland bother you?"

"Who?" Marie gave him a puzzled look. "That reporter? Oh, no. She just stopped by to ask where you were."

Ben felt a little silly. Ben wondered if he was making a mountain out of a molehill, just because Daisy had caught him off guard with her questions about Arlo. Ben hoped she hadn't floated her dumb theory by Marie but he wasn't going to ask. Old habits died hard. Every time Arlo climbed on a bull when they were rodeoing, Ben contemplated what might happen if he got hooked. Or trampled.

Marie hadn't had many breaks in life, and now that her husband was gone, she needed someone to look after her more than ever—not that Arlo had done such a helluva good job while he was alive.

"You want some lunch?" Marie was slapping butter on a couple of slices of bread at the counter.

Ben shook his head. "Thanks but no thanks, Marie. I might go over to the other side of the river, check on the timothy. You need anything, you just call my cell."

"Sure, Ben," she replied. Sometimes she didn't look a day older than Laverne. Sometimes she reminded him painfully of the girl she'd been at eighteen, the year she graduated. She'd gone out with him a few times that endless summer. She'd gone out with Wayne before he left for Regina, too, and then she'd up and married Arlo that October, when he got back from bull-riding school. Surprised them all.

Ben walked toward his pickup, whistling for Dodger. He needed to think about putting together a haying crew. Harold usually managed to round up a few hands, but Ben couldn't leave all the responsibility to his foreman. Finding seasonal labor, whether it was branding or haying, was difficult these days with so much oil and gas work in the district paying big wages.

Maybe before he checked the timothy, he'd go into town and scout out some of the bars, grab a sandwich. Most years he had good luck hiring hands in the Tamarack drinking establishments. It seemed able-bodied men sitting around swilling draft and playing shuffleboard on a fine June afternoon were often in need of short-term employment. Not every layabout was cut out for the tough, dirty, round-the-clock shifts on the oil rigs.

Ben opened the door of his truck and Dodger settled on the passenger seat. Yeah, town was a good idea. Might even drive down the alley behind Frank Street, make sure that shiny red Thunderbird was parked behind the *Times* where it belonged.

Ben climbed in and turned the key in the ignition. Besides, he might hear some news. Bars were places where you heard things.

"NOTHING FROM THE Glory detachment yet," Ellin sang out the instant Daisy walked into the office, "but you got a call from someone at the *Vancouver Sun*. I put it on your desk."

"Thanks, Ellin!" Daisy dumped her bag, picked up the phone and dialed the familiar number. Finally...

"Oliver? It's Daisy. Yes, everything's just fine. Thank you for asking," she said gaily. It wasn't Oliver Crawford's style to comment on either the weather or the well-being of his staff, present or former. His question pleased her; maybe the crusty old editor even missed her a little. His familiar, slow-talking voice was remarkably welcome, and Daisy felt a twinge of what she could only describe as homesickness, the first she'd had since she left Vancouver. They'd had plenty of differences but she realized now how very fond she was of the man who'd shepherded her through the past few years. Distance made the heart grow fonder? She'd been a maverick right from the start, a thorn in the side of many at the *Sun,* who'd felt the stories she'd jumped on were above and beyond her years and experience. With Crawford's guidance, she'd managed to pull most of them off....

Not all.

"Thought you might be in trouble or you wouldn't have called."

"No trouble, Oliver. Just wanted to hear your voice."

He didn't laugh.

"Actually," she went on, feeling a bit silly that she'd even attempted a joke with him, "I wanted to tell you about a piece I'm doing on spring branding. I thought you might want it for the Saturday edition.''

There was complete silence for several seconds. "You're going to be branding *cattle?*" He sounded more than skeptical.

"Helping. I'm going to be *helping.* My best friend from high school, Emily Parrish, set this up for me. Kind of a 'city girl goes country' thing. What do you think?"

"It could be amusing," he said dismissively. Daisy knew him well enough to interpret that as genuine interest. "You didn't call from—where the hell is it again?"

"Tamarack."

"—Tamarack, Alberta, to offer me freelance bumpf, now, did you, Daisy?" Typical Oliver Crawford, blunt and to the point.

So Daisy told him about the shoot-out at the Pekisko reserve, including her misgivings about pursuing the story at all. "Maybe I'm just imagining half of this, Oliver," Daisy concluded. "I wanted to run it by you."

One of Oliver's lengthy silences told Daisy he was thinking it over. "Any idea why the cop might've been arresting the Indian?"

"None."

"What kind of bullet from what kind of gun killed the cop?"

"I don't know." Daisy bit her lip. That was an obvious question, all right.

"You should find out, Daisy," Oliver said dryly.

"That's part of the problem, Oliver—no one will talk. The police have been tight-lipped, and no one at the reserve will return my calls."

"Have you seen a police report?"

"Not yet. It's supposed to be coming soon. I think they're sitting on it."

"What does your father say? Have you talked to him about this?"

"Not yet." Daisy bit her lip. "I—I'm hoping to find out what I can on my own, Oliver—"

"It's his town, Daisy!" her former boss broke in. "You should be talking to him."

"I think he'd rather I didn't pursue it," she said in a small voice.

Another of Oliver's silences ensued. "What do your instincts tell you, Daisy?"

"I don't know what to think, Oliver. I came out here to leave all that behind me." Daisy paused. She'd never really told Oliver why she'd left the *Sun*.

"The adoption story?"

"Yes," Daisy whispered, shutting her eyes and gripping the receiver tightly. *The baby story*. Her knuckles were white. Of course he'd know…

"You did damn fine work on that piece, Daisy." Oliver's voice was gruff.

"But those pictures!" Daisy couldn't open her eyes. "Those babies were—"

"One of those babies died, but the story is that he would've died anyway. He was scheduled for heart surgery when he was kidnapped. The other one lived. She recovered and has been reunited with her family in Guatemala.

"You have nothing to be ashamed of," Oliver growled. "There's news in small towns just like there's news in the city. Trust yourself, Daisy. I've rarely worked with a reporter who had better instincts. You'll be all right."

He hung up. Daisy stared at the receiver, which buzzed angrily. That was a compliment, she supposed. Bastard! He'd hung up.

TAMARACK MIGHT NOT be big enough to have its own Legion but there was plenty of choice for the drinking crowd. The Blue Room in the Croft Hotel was a traditional watering hole with smoke-stained ceilings and moth-eaten trophy heads, mostly antelope and five-point mule deer, on the pine-paneled walls. With its grease-spattered sign by the kitchen pass-through—Our Chili's Like Sex. When It's Good, It's Great. When It's Bad, It's Still Pretty Good— the place clearly didn't cater to women.

Wiley's Bar and Grill did a brisk business, mainly with the boys from the feed store and the hockey arena, situated right across the street, and with truckers ducking through Tamarack on a shortcut to the Crowsnest Pass. The Rose and Crown Pub was the only licensed establishment the cowboys and Indians stayed away from—it wasn't their kind of place, with a huge nonsmoking area, plenty of greenery, hardwood floors, upholstered bar stools and no dartboard or pool table. Plus, the Rose and Crown's lunch ran more to quiche with funny cheese and shrimp salad on a croissant, a long way from a working man's fare.

Ben didn't bother with the Rose and Crown. He stopped at Wiley's but there were only a few truckers arguing over long-haul rates and ogling the waitress, Lonny Harris, a flashy blonde who'd graduated from high school with Ben and was raising her three kids alone since her husband had walked out on her five years before. And who was also, Ben suspected, seeing a fair amount of Sid Brewster, Tamarack's mayor and owner of the feed store, mainly when his wife, Amy, was out of town....

All of which, Ben figured, was none of his business. This was a small town and things happened.

The Blue Room, most likely named for the eternal haze of cigarette smoke hanging over the pool tables, was fairly busy for a Tuesday afternoon. He spotted Morris Jack and a couple of pals near the jukebox.

"Lookin' for somebody, Ben?"

Ben could tell Morris was responsible for most of the

empties standing on the table. "Haying. Week or two away still. Can I count you in, Mo?" Ben grinned. He knew very well that Morris Jack had no interest in work that was hot, sweaty or hard, and haying was all of that.

"I'll let you know." Morris frowned as though determined to actually give the offer some thought. He waved one hand toward an empty chair. "Take a load off."

Ben scanned the room for other prospects, spotted a table of cowboys near the window and decided to join Morris and his pals for now.

"A glass of draft and a roast beef sandwich, Jeannie," he said as the waitress approached with a platterful of used glasses and ashtrays.

"Comin' right up, hon." She switched the overfilled foil ashtray on the table for a new one, picked up the empties and continued on to the back of the bar.

Ben deposited his hat on the seat next to him. "Anything new, boys?"

Morris gave him a bleary look. "Pat here is startin' tomorrow with the gas company. Driving delivery. Tha's why we're celebratin'."

Ben nodded. There was always *something* to celebrate for Morris Jack and his cronies. "Southwest Propane? Good for you, Pat."

The boy blushed under his peach fuzz. Pat Lawrence was just a kid, maybe twenty years old, and a job would do him more good than hanging out with Morris Jack and company.

Morris caught Ben's eye and, in an exaggerated gesture, hunched his bony shoulder meaningfully toward the side door. Three of Casper's "warriors" had entered the room and were standing at the bar. The only one Ben thought he recognized was Alan Poundmaker, a youth Harold had hired to help with spring branding the year before last.

Ben pulled his chair closer. "What's with those guys,

anyway? I didn't know they were legal.'' The drinking age in Alberta was eighteen.

"Oh, they're old enough. Toughs from out at the reserve,'' Morris said, with a nervous glance toward the bar. "Do little jobs for Casper Desjarlais. I hear stuff,'' he finished in a low voice.

Ben thanked the waitress, who'd brought his beer and sandwich. "What do you hear?''

"No good, the lot of 'em,'' Morris whispered hoarsely. His eyes were bloodshot. "Fencin', poachin', running smokes. Hey—'' he pawed the air ''—I know what I'm talkin' about.''

"That's ridiculous. They're just kids.'' Ben drank off half his beer. Some Indian bands down east, he knew, made big money running tax-free American cigarettes across the border and selling them illegally to retailers and middlemen. A setup like that took organization, which this bunch didn't have.

"Casper might fence small stuff here and there, bootleg to high school kids, buy and sell junk in that flea market of his. He's a two-bit player, always has been. You know that, Mo.''

Even drunk, Morris Jack was able to convey his dismay at Ben's ignorance. "Flea market?'' He began to laugh, then coughed loudly. "What rock you been hidin' under, Goodstriker? You ask what them boys bring across from Montana every week. It ain't old TVs and secondhand Barbie dolls, I can tell you that.''

"Montana?'' Ben had never heard anything like this before. "Where?''

"Browning, for one.'' Morris mentioned the biggest town on the Piegan reservation across the border. The Piegans, spelled differently on the U.S. side, were the same aboriginal group as the Peigans of Alberta, now called the Piikani, all related to the Blackfoot and Blood tribes and all speaking the same Algonquin language. "Why, your own cousin—"

Morris broke off abruptly and raised his bottle of Molson Ex to his mouth.

Ben's eyes narrowed. "What's that, Mo?"

"Arlo musta told you," the old man muttered, wiping his upper lip with a torn sleeve. "Have another beer, Ben." He gestured suddenly, his eyes wild. "He knew. Poor stupid bastard—Arlo *knew!*"

"Knew what?"

"Nothin'." Morris Jack buried his face in his beer again. "I ain't sayin' *nothin'.*"

Ben hesitated. He wanted to grill the old cowpoke, but why drag his cousin's name into this conversation any more than necessary? He glanced at Pat Lawrence, who was studying his glass as if it was the first time he'd ever seen a brew. His ears were red. The other fool at the table, a grader operator by the name of Tiny Lapointe, was dozing, tobacco-colored spittle dribbling from the corner of his mouth.

Ben got up in disgust. This wasn't about Arlo. Arlo was dead. This was about a bunch of young bucks who didn't have enough to occupy their time…. He wondered if Chief George had any information on their activities with Casper Desjarlais, which Ben was convinced didn't amount to much more than penny-ante stuff, one step up from vandalizing park benches and joyriding. Casper had never been the brightest light on the Christmas tree.

"No more for me. And you've had enough, Mo," Ben advised, tossing down a five-dollar bill. "Go home and sleep it off." He picked up his sandwich and walked toward a table of cowboys, some of whom he knew. Could be they were looking for work.

He felt seriously annoyed, even if he *had* come to town thinking he might hear something. First Daisy Sutherland, now Morris Jack… What the hell was Arlo, his poor dead, bumbling cousin, supposed to have known?

CHAPTER EIGHT

AT SIX, Daisy went home for dinner sorely disappointed. Chief George hadn't called, and neither had Gordon Bass. She would've gone out to the reserve to track down the chief if she hadn't suddenly realized there were no Pet of the Week photos and she had to zip over to the pound, a couple of kennels kept at the Archie Deverall farm just outside town, to take some. She'd sent Duncan Fairlie out with Bunny McPhee earlier to get a story and some photos on a runaway grass fire behind the swimming pool, and neither had returned by the time the office closed.

The Sutherland family home was one of the oldest in town, a two-and-a-half-story brick house built for the original mine owner and his family in 1942. There were four big bedrooms upstairs, one for Karen, one for Daisy, one for their parents, one for guests. The Petrenkos, next door, had a large white-painted frame house with a screened veranda running across two sides, dating from the fifties. Although the Petrenkos had lived beside the Sutherlands as long as she could remember, Daisy hadn't known Wayne well. He'd been a typical boy, from what she'd gathered, full of high spirits and dumb schemes. Maybe more than ordinary high spirits. He'd stolen a car when he was fifteen, and the Petrenkos had had to turn themselves inside out to keep the incident quiet. There'd been other stories, rumors about the succession of girls he dated and why he'd been let go from Mr. Valentine's hardware store when he'd only worked there for a month in his senior year. Then he'd graduated from high school with a surprisingly decent average and, after a summer spent working for the Diamond Seven, one of the big ranches near Glory, he'd announced his intention to join the RCMP. That fall he'd gone off to basic training in Regina, and everyone in Tamarack had breathed a huge sigh of relief.

There followed, apparently, the usual itinerant Royal Canadian Mounted Police career. He'd been stationed here and there at various places in Ontario and the prairie provinces and ten months ago, he'd been posted back to Glory, which was close enough that he could live in his home town. All she knew about his personal life since he'd come back was that he'd rented an older house behind the hardware store, a place once owned by an elderly spinster, now deceased, who'd lived a solitary life and been considered a witch by most children in town. Desdemona Birch. Daisy recalled that she and Emily Parrish had been so frightened of the old woman they'd crossed the street when they saw her coming. Poor old thing.

It occurred to Daisy that she was looking for a place to rent and the Birch house was now empty. She shuddered. What she wanted was a nice bright apartment, not a run-down rental with a ghost....

The fact that Bass hadn't called didn't surprise her. She intended to drive to Glory tomorrow to see if she could catch the staff sergeant at his office.

She still wasn't sure what she thought about his asking her out. Maybe there was a shortage of single women in the area. Since she'd returned home, she'd been flattered by the number of men who'd made a point of chatting her up. In the post office, the drugstore, even the library when she'd gone in to look through old issues of the *Herald*. Two former classmates had asked her out already, and now Gordon Bass.

Daisy signaled to enter the alley behind her parents'

house. Hmm. What if she encouraged him a little? Would that be consorting with the enemy? Bass wasn't the enemy by a long shot, but he wasn't on her side, either.

And what was she going to do about Ben Goodstriker? She could have sworn he'd had exactly the same idea she had—that something about the Pekisko shoot-out didn't add up. Despite the hundred-and-one details she'd had to deal with that afternoon, she hadn't been able to put the ex-rodeo-cowboy-turned-horse-trainer out of her mind. Why? It was maddening!

So, okay, her knees had wobbled a bit when she finally met him. There'd been a lot of hype and buildup—mostly from Ellin, who seemed quite smitten, even though she had a steady boyfriend who worked at the Glory Co-op. And, yes, Goodstriker *had* turned out to be a good-looking man in a rough, outdoorsy way. But was he friendly? Helpful? Forget it! He'd practically run her off his ranch.

She yanked on the emergency brake and got out of the Thunderbird. At least Bass was attracted to her. Or appeared to be, if flirting meant anything. She shook her head—dating a guy to squeeze a story out of him. She hadn't stooped to *that* tactic in her journalistic career....

Yet.

When she went in the kitchen door, her mother was pulling one of her famous casseroles out of the oven. She asked Daisy to bring it to the dining room while she tossed the salad, and also, could Daisy please call her father?

"Dad?" Daisy poked her head into the den, a room that might once have been a bedroom, although the Sutherlands had never used it as such. "Game over? Dinner's ready."

"Okay, okay," her father muttered, getting up from the sofa. Toby, the family spaniel, looked up from his spot on the carpet, yawned, then closed his eyes again. "The Bruins are down two and this is the sixth game of the Stanley Cup. I'd hoped—"

"Here, Dad." Daisy shoved a tape in the VCR, then took the remote from him and hit what she hoped were the right buttons. "You can see it later without the commercials."

"It's not the same," he grumbled as they went to the dining room. Daisy knew her father was finding so-called retirement hard. Owen Sutherland was sixty-eight and had spent every working day of his life at the newspaper his father had founded. Since Daisy had come home, he was taking a rare summer holiday, ostensibly overseeing only the advertising side of the paper until Daisy was ready to manage that as well.

"How was your golf game today?" Daisy asked, taking her usual place at the dining room table.

"Golf, schmolf!" Owen Sutherland sat down at the head of the table and spread his napkin on his lap. "You know something, Daisy? Golfing was a lot more fun when I had to sneak out for the afternoon."

"Oh, Owen—"

"It's true, Marian." Daisy's parents exchanged defiant glances. Daisy knew how much her mother had looked forward to having her father at home more. "So, how are things at the *Times?*"

"Maybe you should consider coming in one morning a week," she suggested tentatively. "Write the editorials. I hate those and you're good at it."

"Don't even mention it, Daisy!" Her mother gave her a severe look. "Your father's promised me we're going to have a real holiday for a change, and we are. I feel poor Alice and Bill need our support just now, or we'd be gone already. Please pass the salad, dear."

"There might be something to that idea," her father went on, as though he hadn't noticed his wife's firmly pressed lips and clear disapproval. "It wouldn't be like *really* working, would it? One morning a week's nothing."

"You know how involved you get, Owen. Next thing you'll be at the office every day and there goes our vacation. My sister's planned a family reunion for years and we're going!"

"Yes, we are," Daisy's father soothed. "Writing the occasional editorial does not mean I'm back in the harness, honey. I could do those in my sleep. Use the typewriter in the den. Say," he continued brightly, "how's Bunny doing?"

"She says she's quitting."

"No!"

"She doesn't like working for me." Daisy shrugged. "I sent her out on an oil field story last week, and she came back fuming. They'd made her wear some man's rubber boots on the platform. No wonder—who wears high heels to a drill site?"

"That's Bunny, all right." Her father smiled. "Good for you. I've never been able to get her to do anything but Women's League meetings and that gossip column. She doesn't cost much, but sometimes I wonder why I keep her on the payroll at all. How's Ellin?"

"Oh, the usual. She's working on John, trying to get him to change the spelling of his name. Says J-O-N-N is better numerically, I have no idea why. More *auspicious*."

The *Times*'s receptionist-bookkeeper had many fervent beliefs, Daisy had discovered, astrology and numerology among them.

Owen Sutherland beamed at his wife. "That's why she spells her name with an *i*. Even her last name, it used to be Brody with a *y*. Now it's *i-e*. You see the kind of stuff I had to put up with, Marian?"

Daisy knew he loved every minute of it. "John's mother wants him to get another summer job," she went on. "She thinks Ellin's a bad influence on him."

"Only son, that's why," Daisy's mother broke in, picking up Daisy's empty plate. "Alice used to be like that with Wayne, I remember."

Daisy stood, hoping to change the direction of the conversation. "I'll take care of these dishes. You sit down, Mom. Is there dessert?"

But it was too late. Owen Sutherland's face fell. "Not that Wayne ever listened to Alice, did he, Marian? You know, I still can't believe it...." His voice trailed off miserably.

Marian Sutherland took his hand. "It's a parent's worst nightmare, Daisy," she said, in a low, strained voice. "You never *ever* think you'll outlive your own children."

"Can I bring out that angel food cake in the kitchen?"

Food always diverted her mother, and while she fussed with the cake and sauce, Daisy carried the casserole and salad bowl into the kitchen.

The phone rang, and Owen Sutherland had picked up the living room extension when they returned. "Yes? Oh, hello, Winston."

Daisy frowned. Chief George?

"Listen, before you say anything, don't tell me the score on the hockey game, y'hear? I'm taping it to watch later. Daisy?"

Her father fixed her with his hard blue gaze. "Yes, she's here. What? You don't want to speak to her? Ah, I see." Her father nodded. "Uh-huh. Did she? Uh-huh. I see. Well, never mind, Winston. I'm sure it's all a misunderstanding. She's a city girl, you know! I'll take care of it right away. How's Doris? That's good. Thanks for calling." He put down the receiver and returned to the table.

"Problems, Owen?"

Daisy was glad her mother had asked. Why hadn't the chief called *her* at the *Times* this afternoon? And why hadn't he wanted to talk to her now?

"Oh, I don't think so." Her father took his chair again

and reached for his dessert fork. "Something about Daisy calling folks on the reserve, asking a lot of questions. Digging into that business with Wayne and Arlo Goodstriker."

"I left him a message," Daisy said tautly. "Several messages, I don't know why he didn't call me at the office."

"Because he knows I'm still responsible for the paper, that's why. He knows I wouldn't want my daughter bothering folks when it's not—"

"Dad! I just need a little background. What's wrong with that?" Daisy glanced from her father to her mother and back again. She knew her face was red; she didn't care. "Why doesn't anybody want to talk about this? It's as if the whole thing never happened! The cops won't talk. Chief George and the rest of them out at Pekisko won't talk. They—"

"Daisy, Daisy," her father said, taking a soothing tone. "It's not that they don't *want* to talk, honey, it's that there's nothing to say. What happened happened, and what's best for the town is to put it behind us and look to the future."

"It's a strange story, you've got to admit that, Dad. Why would those two shoot each other? They were boyhood friends! I'm not sure I—"

"Daisy!" Her mother sounded shocked.

"If they did do it, why? Over what? Drugs, murder—a speeding ticket?"

"But, Daisy, what's the difference to us?" Her father was truly baffled. "The police have checked everything out, you can be sure of that. They've done their jobs. You've run a couple of stories, and now all you have to do is put in another short item, maybe on one of the inside pages, when the police report comes out."

"Maybe you can tell me, Dad, what kind of crime goes on around here that's bad enough for this level of violence? Crack houses? Biker gangs? I'm serious!'' Daisy put down her napkin.

"Well, sure, honey, we have a little crime here in Tamarack, just like they do in the city.'' Her father's brow wrinkled. ''Wiley's was broken into last winter and the safe was stolen, and of course there's always a snowmobile or bicycle going missing. We had something in the paper a while back about a few B and Es in Cardston and Pincher Creek. The police thought they might be connected. But drugs? Oh, I don't think so—''

"I believe there's a real story here,'' Daisy repeated stubbornly, ''and I want the *Times* to get it.''

"You mean put *more* stuff in the paper about Wayne and that Goodstriker fellow?'' Marian Sutherland was standing, collecting the dessert dishes, and she sat down again with a thump. "What you call 'background'? For heaven's sake, Daisy! What about his family? His wife and children? What about poor Bill and Alice?''

"I hate having to consider stuff like that, Mom! That's not journalism. Isn't it the truth that matters? If I'm going to be the editor, I want to turn the *Times* into a paper I can be proud of!''

Her father was obviously bewildered, and Daisy realized she'd gone too far. "Of course, I'm proud of the *Times* and this family's role in Tamarack, Dad,'' she added hastily. "Your role. I couldn't be prouder. But—well, you know, maybe we could change things a little bit. Move with the times,'' she finished lamely, knowing she was at the mercy of her own hotly spoken words. What she'd wanted to say was "move into the next century.''

To her amazement, her father seemed suddenly amused. "Oh, Daisy. You're quite the girl! This isn't the *Globe and Mail*, honey. This isn't the *Calgary Herald*. We're just a little weekly and we depend on the merchants in town, our friends, for advertising dollars. Where would this family be if everyone pulled their advertising because of some big ruckus in the paper? Then what?''

Daisy realized she wasn't getting anywhere. Neither of them seemed to see her point. ''Well, we'll just see how things work out, Dad. I've spoken to Oliver Crawford at the *Sun*—''

''Your—your old boss?'' Her father paid close attention to his cake.

Too late Daisy realized her gaffe. ''Yes. He advised me to speak to you. This is great cake, Mom!'' She turned to her mother for help, but Marian said nothing, just worried the crumbs on her plate with the tines of her fork.

Her father cleared his throat. ''I, ah, I told Chief George I'd speak to you,'' he said quietly. His ears were red, a sure sign that he was upset. ''He'd like you to quit calling folks out at the reserve, asking about Goodstriker, and I said I'd pass the message on. Okay, honey?''

''I still have a few ends to tie up,'' Daisy replied, avoiding the implication of her father's words: no more investigating, whether on the reserve or anywhere else. ''And the police report hasn't come out yet.''

''Well, yes. I suppose if the police have more details when they release their report, fine and dandy. No one could object to that,'' he said with a smile. ''Public record. I'm sure you'll handle it the right way. We're proud of you, your mother and I.'' He patted her shoulder awkwardly and smiled at his wife. ''Very proud. Say, any more of that lemon sauce, Marian?''

AFTER DINNER, Daisy put Toby on his leash and took the arthritic old spaniel for a walk, ostensibly to relieve her parents of the duty, but really to get a breather and think things through. Now what? Never mind investigating anything—forget that—all she wanted was a decent wrap-up on the shooting. But at what cost? Her parents obviously didn't want her to produce anything beyond a small-town-boy-made-good article.

And, worse, her dad's feelings had been hurt that she'd gone to Oliver Crawford for advice.

No matter what Oliver had said, maybe she was looking for something that just wasn't there. Why? Because she was a stubborn person who just couldn't take no for an answer? Was she going to put her parents in an unpleasant situation in the town where they'd lived all their lives?

She kicked at a stick on the sidewalk sending it bouncing onto the street and numbing her toe in the process. Toby paused, leg suspended against a hydrant, and gave her an incredulous look, as if to say *surely* she didn't expect him to retrieve that!

The little mutt out at the ranch today would've been all over it in a second, tearing it to sawdust, no doubt.

Not like his owner. Mr. Laid-Back Horse Guy. Mr. Mind-Your-Own-Business. Mr. Let-The-Cops-Do-Their-Jobs.

Just like her dad.

Damn! Okay, she wouldn't visit the reserve tomorrow, as she'd planned; out of respect for Chief George's request. Maybe the next day. But she'd still go see Gordon Bass. Demand some answers. What kind of bullet had killed Wayne? Why had Wayne been arresting Arlo Goodstriker, *if* he'd been arresting him?

She'd give it a darn good last shot and then, when she felt she'd made her best effort under the circumstances, she'd be happy to run a press release story.

Well, maybe not happy. But she'd move on to the next item of business. Do a bang-up piece on the kids' rodeo, maybe. Or the Friends of the Hospital strawberry social. Or the spring branding. Or a story on the new vet in town.

She wasn't complaining. After all, wasn't that what she'd come back to Tamarack for—nice, straightforward, *heartwarming* journalism?

CHAPTER NINE

THE SOFT KNOCK at her bedroom door caught Daisy by surprise. She put down her book and jumped up, grabbing her terry cloth bathrobe and pulling it on as she went to the door. "Yes?"

It was her mother, looking strangely discomfited. "Can I come in for a minute, darling—oh, were you in bed?"

"Just reading."

"I won't disturb you for long."

Daisy stepped back and her mother slipped inside, closing the door behind her after a quick glance down the darkened hallway. Daisy's father was an up-with-the-birds man and generally went to bed early. Daisy checked her bedside clock: nearly eleven.

"Sit down, Mom." Daisy sat down on the bed and indicated the one comfortable chair in the room, an upholstered armchair that stood in the corner by the window.

"Oh, dear," her mother said, plucking at a loose thread on the arm of the chair. "I don't know where to begin."

"Is it about Dad?" Daisy felt a sort of dread gather in the bottom of her stomach. *Cancer, alcoholism, an affair...*

"Oh, no! Dad's just fine. No, it's about—about Wayne."

"*Wayne?*"

"Listen, honey, I know you were upset by what Dad had to say at dinner. I understand how important it is for you to do a good job. You're a fine journalist and, as Dad said, we're very proud of you. We know it's been a sacrifice for you, winning those awards and everything, giving it all up to come back here...."

"Oh, Mom." Daisy felt a little embarrassed. "You know I wanted to come back. It was my idea." If they knew, *really* knew, everything about her journalistic career so far...

"Of course, you're the editor now but you need to understand why we don't want you putting all kinds of things in the paper about Wayne."

"Just him?"

"And Arlo Goodstriker. I know he killed Wayne and I don't feel sorry for him, not a bit, but he's got a wife and two children, and I can't help thinking of them. His wife—widow, I guess—drives one of the school buses for Ed Sawchuk. You know, the Sawchuk who owns the gravel pit south of town."

"Mom," Daisy interrupted gently. "You didn't come in here to tell me who owns the gravel pit."

Her mother stared at her for a few seconds. "No, I didn't," she said quickly. "It's just that I thought you ought to know there's a reason, a *good* reason to drop all this nonsense about trying to do some extra-big story, which is what it sounds like you want to do. We don't think you should put things in the paper that maybe shouldn't be there." Marian paused to take a breath.

"What's the reason, Mom?" Daisy asked patiently.

"Well, it's nothing definite. Just some hints Alice and Bill have dropped from time to time, and I believe it has to do with why Wayne came back to Tamarack—not that we weren't all thrilled when we heard he was coming back. Actually, Dad put two and two together from things the Petrenkos said. Your father's not the worst newspaperman in the world, you know." Her mother looked directly at Daisy, her eyes bright, a spot of hot color in each cheek.

"Oh, Mom. I'm sorry about what I said at dinner. I was

just so surprised that Chief George wanted to talk to Dad and not me....'' Daisy felt miserable. She'd hurt her parents, both of them, with her quick words. "No one's been cooperating with me. I guess I just overreacted."

"Don't worry about that. Your father figures something must've happened back East, something that wasn't good at all, and Wayne may've been sent back here by way of punishment—oh, not *punishment,* that's too strong a word. More like *discipline.*"

Her mother peered at her, as if she assumed Daisy could now see why she shouldn't dig any further.

"And?"

"*And?* Why, I don't think it would be appropriate to risk information like that coming out in the paper with Wayne dead and all. Dragging up stuff from the past. You can see that it would upset Bill and Alice terribly."

"*What* would upset Bill and Alice?" Daisy persisted. "What could Wayne possibly have done that would get him sent—sent back here?" She'd almost said "to this backwater" but managed to stop herself in time. Well, from an RCMP career standpoint, it probably *was* a backwater. "Not that I'd put it in the paper anyway."

"We don't know for sure what he did, but—" her mother bit her lip and looked worriedly at the door "—I believe it had to do with what they call substance abuse these days."

"Drugs?"

"Oh, no! Drugs sounds so *awful,* doesn't it? Liquor, maybe. Maybe drinking a little too much. I'm sure he was never an alcoholic, but they probably have strict rules about that in the Mounties."

"Did Alice tell you this?"

"She mentioned that word, you know—*substance* abuse. It's not something she'd want the town to hear. Nor would your father or I. No one would." She pressed her lips tightly together. "What's done is done. So, you see, Daisy? You really must forget this idea of digging things up. And besides, what could any of that possibly have to do with him getting killed? He was just doing his duty trying to make an arrest. He was a hero! *That's* what should be in the paper." Her mother got up, then turned to remove the loose thread from the arm of the chair, dropping it into the wastebasket beside the dresser. "So there you go, darling." She smiled. "That's how it is. I feel a lot better telling you."

Daisy gave her a hug. "Thanks, Mom. I appreciate your filling me in. Now a few other things are starting to make sense to me." She decided not to say any more. She wasn't going to tell her mother that she'd been wondering why Wayne Petrenko, boy wonder, had never made it past constable in his ten-year career.

Her mother went to the door, then paused, her hand on the knob.

"Is there something else, Mother?"

"Well, yes, there is, darling." Marian Sutherland came back and sat on the edge of the bed. She reached for Daisy's hand.

"You know how much your father and I love you, don't you, Daisy?"

"Of course I do." Daisy was mystified. "And I love the two of you just as much."

Marian flushed. "I hope you know you could come to us if you have any problems, my dear, any problems at all."

Daisy wasn't so sure about that, but she didn't intend to upset her mother's view of the world at this stage. Daisy was nearly twenty-six years old and had been keeping her own counsel since before she'd left high school. Marian Sutherland was a kind, well-meaning soul with rather exacting ideas of right and wrong—

"Daisy, are you going to have a baby?"

"A *baby!*" Nothing could have prepared Daisy for her mother's words. If possible, Marian's cheeks grew even redder, her eyes brighter.

"Darling, I know the world isn't the way it was when I grew up, but you need to know that your father and I will stand by you, no matter what happens and—"

"B-but, Mom, I'm not going to have a baby. What in heaven's name gave you that idea?"

"Two weeks ago. You rushed into the kitchen when I was fixing your father's breakfast and you threw up in the powder room. I know you did. I could hear you through the door." Marian's eyes were watering dangerously.

"Oh, Mom!" Daisy threw her arms around her mother's shoulders. "Yes, I threw up, but, no, it wasn't because I'm pregnant."

"Now I feel rather foolish," her mother said, groping in the pocket of her robe for a tissue.

"No, I'm so glad you said something. I—I just felt a little sick that morning. I had no idea you and Dad were thinking I'd come home to have a baby!"

Marian stood and tucked the tissue back into her pocket. She patted Daisy's knee. "Well, I must say I'm relieved. No harm done. I mean, I'd love to have another grandchild, no matter what the circumstances, but I'm just not sure it's the right thing for you at this time in your life."

"Because I'm not married?"

"Call me old-fashioned, Daisy, but I do think it's important to have an upright, honest, reliable man to share your life with if you're going to bring a baby into this world. Someone you can depend on. I never hear you talk about a man who's important to you. Maybe this Oliver—" Her mother darted an inquiring look Daisy's way.

"Good grief! Oliver's about a hundred years old and everyone in the news room calls him Grumpy. No, there's no particular man in my life, Mother. But I'm hoping one day there will be...." Daisy's throat felt tight.

Daisy accompanied her mother back to the door. A baby! Who would've guessed?

"So, now. About that other business, dear. You won't put anything in the paper?"

"Not about that specifically, Mom. Of course not. I mean, not by itself," she qualified. "It would need to tie in to other things."

"This is all by-the-by." Her mother made a face. "For Bill and Alice, you understand. And don't forget that everything I've told you is secondhand. Third-hand, really. What's done is done. Good night, darling."

Daisy kissed her mother and closed the door after she'd left.

What's done is done.

Wouldn't it be nice if that was true?

CHAPTER TEN

"MISS! MISS!"

Daisy turned to see a small girl in glasses running across the grass, all knobby knees and blond hair flying. "What is it, honey?"

"Did you get a picture of *me?*" The child was almost too excited to talk. She couldn't have been more than eight. "Did you? I came second in the long jump. See?" She tugged at the green ribbon pinned to her red T-shirt. "Amy won and she's my best friend! She's over there!"

Daisy quickly snapped a photo of the girl jumping up and down and gesticulating wildly for her friend, Amy, to join them. Then, when Amy arrived, she snapped two more and left the girls smiling.

The day wasn't turning out quite as she'd planned. Ellin had called in sick that morning, and John couldn't come in until noon, so that meant the end of Daisy's trip to the RCMP detachment in Glory, at least for today. To her amazement, she'd felt relieved.

The last couple of weeks hadn't been easy. On the one hand, she'd come to Tamarack to get away from investigative-style journalism, always probing, always looking beyond the surface. On the other hand, she couldn't help feeling that she ought to be asking hard questions about what had happened at the reserve. What she really preferred, she kept telling herself, was fun stuff, like today's event at Tamarack Elementary.

Daisy had already sent Bunny and Duncan to get pic-

tures and details on a forest fire that had broken out in the
Porcupine Hills, ten miles east of town, when a ten-thirty
call from the elementary school principal reminded her of
sports day. She'd immediately locked the office and
headed over to Second Avenue. Sports days were big news
in small towns.

Closing down the *Times* office just because someone
had called in sick didn't make any sense, though. Which
underlined the need for more staff if she was ever going
to run the paper properly. At least one full-time reporter,
in addition to her and Bunny, whether Bunny stayed or
not, and another person to help out in the office, maybe
relieve Ellin of the classifieds so she could take over as
office manager. Plus someone to work with the computers
on the technical side, doing layout and production.

It was all very well for her father to have run the *Times*
largely from the comfort of his pine-paneled office, relying
on press releases, the rumor mill and telephone calls to
cronies for most of the paper's news, plus the odd bit of
fluff thrown in by Bunny and Duncan. But that wasn't
Daisy's style. It was important, she felt, to be out in the
community, active and visible. Then, if she did happen to
run a piece that raised a few hackles, she'd have some
goodwill to draw upon with advertisers. If that meant mentioning Bill's Plumbing or the Tamarack Co-op or Henderson's Hardware as sponsors in a Little League story, it
was a sacrifice she could make.

"Thanks!" Daisy accepted a Popsicle from another
child who'd run up, blushing, to report that "Teacher said
to give this to you." Daisy waved across the field at the
male teacher supervising the refreshment stand—another
suitor?—and got a wave back.

Small towns. Sometimes you really felt like you belonged.... She peeled the paper off the blue Popsicle and
licked it. Blueberry? Whatever it was, it tasted surprisingly

good. Now where? The relay race, the hundred-meter dash, the kindergarten three-legged sack race…

An hour later, after taking notes at the high jump event, Daisy decided she might as well shoot off one more roll of film before heading back to the office. *Pictures, Daisy!* she could hear her father saying. *Folks like to see themselves in the paper! And if it's their kid or grandkid? All the better!* She knelt down by a big poplar tree that marked one corner of the playground and rifled through her canvas bag for a fresh roll, looking up when she felt someone touch her shoulder.

"Miss?" It was the little girl who'd wanted her picture taken earlier, Belinda somebody-or-other. She seemed frightened, her eyes enormous behind her glasses.

"Yes?" Daisy gave her a friendly smile, locating a canister of film at the same time.

"Miss, I think you should come," the girl whispered. "Somebody's getting beat up!"

"Beaten up?" Daisy was on her feet instantly, shoving the new roll of film into her camera and dropping it in her bag. "Where?"

"Over there behind the school." Belinda pointed. "The big boys are picking on the boy that can't say anything anymore."

Can't say anything anymore? What was she talking about? With the girl trotting beside her, Daisy set off in the direction of the school, a wing that extended toward the nearby baseball diamond. "Have you told a teacher?" She frowned. This was hardly her problem.

"Everybody's too busy," the girl answered, still trying to whisper although she was half running beside Daisy. "You're so nice, I thought I should tell you."

Daisy could tell that Belinda was wondering if she'd made the right decision. She reached for the child's hand and smiled, giving her hand a quick squeeze. "I'm glad you did. I'll take care of this. Why don't you run and see if you can find a teacher anyway?''

''Okay.'' The girl brightened considerably and veered off toward the crowd standing near the long-jump pit.

Daisy hurried around the wing of the school that blocked the playing field, where the track meet was taking place, from the asphalt area where there were basketball hoops and bike racks. Off to one side, she saw an unused batting cage that belonged to the municipal baseball diamond adjacent to the school.

''Cop killer! Cop killer!'' Four boys had cornered a fifth, who was on his knees and nearly obscured by the bullies.

''Hey!'' Daisy hurried forward. ''What's going on here?''

The bullies turned as one, obviously surprised to see her. The boy they'd trapped against the concrete building hid his face with one arm. He was covered in dirt and there were chunks of dirt and grass all around him, as if he'd been pelted with clods of dried turf. The boys started to run, but Daisy dashed forward and grabbed one of them by the shirt.

''What's your name?''

''Byron, miss.'' He looked like he was about to cry. His eyes darted desperately after the disappearing shadows of his buddies.

''Byron who?''

''Byron Mendez.''

''What grade?''

''Five,'' he whined. ''Let go of me, miss!''

''Not until I'm done.'' She shook his shirt a little for effect. ''What's your teacher's name, Byron?''

''Mr. Chesterfield.''

''What do you boys think you're doing?'' She glanced at the victim, who was standing now, his clothes filthy, his face turned away from her. "Picking on someone half your size! You should be ashamed of yourself."

"Aw, we were just teasing him. He started it! He tried to fight us! We didn't mean anything—"

Daisy let go of the boy's shirt and he nearly fell. "We'll see about that. Mr. Chesterfield and the principal might have something to say, as well."

She went to the boy who'd been bullied. "Are you all right?" He just stared at her, his face blotchy with tears and mud. There was a trickle of blood down his chin that he'd smeared with his sleeve, as well as dirt ground into his nose and ears. The bullies had done a job on him, all right. "Huh? You okay?"

He nodded slightly and Daisy dug into her bag for a tissue. She came up with a Wet Wipe, even better. She held it out to him, not sure he'd appreciate a stranger wiping his face. Then, when he made no move to take it, she stepped forward and began to dab gently at his bloodied nose. Fresh tears kept running down his face but he hadn't said a word—what had Belinda said?

The boy that can't say anything anymore.

"What's this all about? Oh, my goodness! Junior, what happened?" A teacher scurried around the corner, accompanied by the wide-eyed Belinda and her equally wide-eyed friend, Amy. "Are you all right, dear?"

"Thank heavens you were here," the teacher said to Daisy. "I'm Margaret Peabody. You must be the lady from the newspaper—Daisy, isn't it? Owen Sutherland's daughter?"

Daisy nodded.

"Amy, dear, you run and find Mr. Sangster. That's a girl. Are you okay, Junior?" the teacher asked, whipping a handkerchief out of her sleeve. She started wiping the child's face where Daisy had left off.

Daisy studied him. A handsome boy, dark hair, dark

eyes, long dark lashes, clearly of native ancestry. Somehow, he looked familiar. Had he been one of the athletes she'd captured on film earlier? He couldn't be much more than eight or nine.

"Daisy, can you stay here a few minutes?" Margaret Peabody straightened. "I'm going to call his mother to come and get him. Mr. Sangster—that's our principal—will try to catch whoever did this. Did you happen to see it?"

"Yes. A boy called Byron Mendez was one of them."

"Byron! Well, I guess we know who the others were. They're quite the little gang. And this poor child—" She leaned toward Daisy and whispered. "Just lost his father, too."

This was the Goodstriker boy! Daisy produced another Wet Wipe from her bag. "You go and take care of calling his mother, Ms. Peabody. I'll stay right here with—sorry, I didn't catch your name," she said, smiling at the boy. He just stared at her with huge brown eyes. The tears had begun to dry on his cheeks, forming white rivulets against the tan of his skin.

"This is Junior. Well, his name is really Arlo—" Daisy wondered if the teacher saw the wave of pain cross the boy's face "—after his dad, but everyone calls him Junior. Don't they, dear?" She hurried off. Daisy watched, alarmed, as Junior sank to the ground again and buried his face against his knees. His small shoulders quivered.

Daisy felt her own gut wrench in sympathy. Those bullies! Brutes! Teasing a boy whose father had just been killed, calling him names, calling his *father* names... Cop killer.

The two girls reappeared with another teacher, who immediately sent them for wet paper towels from the rest room. Daisy was relieved that someone seemed to be in charge, but she felt strangely reluctant to leave. *This boy needed her.*

Just then Margaret Peabody hurried back to report that there was no answer at the Goodstriker house.

"I'll call his uncle to come and get him," Daisy announced, pulling her cell out of her bag and quickly punching in the numbers. Well, he was *like* an uncle.... She'd called Ben Goodstriker often enough to know his number. She should put him on speed dial.

"Ben?" He'd actually answered! Daisy turned away briefly and plugged her free ear with her finger so she could hear better. She missed the look exchanged between the two teachers, including the very definite pursing of Margaret Peabody's freshly lipsticked mouth.

BEN WHEELED into a parking spot on the street in front of the school and strode toward the main entrance. They'd be in the principal's office, she'd said.

Damn kids. Every school had its share of bullies. Time Junior learned to fight back. Bullies were cowards; when you fought, they ran. Ben and Junior's dad had learned that lesson twenty-five years ago, at the same damn school. Back then, Casper and Wayne had picked on them. Eventually, when the four boys had sorted things out with a few fistfights, they'd become the best of friends.

And Daisy Sutherland—imagine *her* being mixed up in this. Man, that woman was everywhere!

When he saw Junior, he was glad she was. The boy looked pretty desperate, his face dirty, his shirt ripped. He'd been crying. Daisy was sitting beside him, her arm along the back of the bench seat, hovering near his shoulders. *As though to protect him from the world's cruelty...*

"Ready to go?" He had his hat in his hand. No sense in a bunch of messy explanations here. He needed to get the kid out of town. Marie could phone the school tomorrow and find out what happened.

She jumped up, bag in her hand. "Yes, we're ready." *She was coming, too?* He threw her a disapproving frown but she ignored it. "Come on, Junior. Ben's here now and we can go home with him."

"Don't you, uh, have your car?" he asked carefully. He refrained from inspecting the damage to the boy. He knew Junior would be embarrassed by this wretched ending to what should have been a wonderful day. Nobody could beat him in the hundred-meter dash for his age group. He was a good swimmer, too, a real little athlete, and Arlo, who'd been picked on in school, only realizing when he began to ride bulls that his slight stature gave him an advantage, had always been proud of his son.

"No, I walked. I told Junior I'd go home with him, make sure he got there all right." She raised one eyebrow, then both eyebrows, apparently trying to telegraph something over the kid's head. He had no idea what message she was trying to get across.

He sighed. "Okay. Get in the truck, both of you." They walked out into the sunshine. Daisy waved at two women by the chain-link fence. Looked like teachers. They both waved back and stared at him as he went by. He winked at the older one and she quickly averted her head. Ben grinned.

Old biddies.

CHAPTER ELEVEN

DODGER WAS BANISHED to the box of the truck and Junior sat in the cab between Daisy and Ben. Ben found himself inexplicably conscious of the condition of his truck, something he rarely noticed. There was a length of chain on the floor on the passenger side, and a broken halter he'd been meaning to drop off at the harness shop in Glory. Two Red Robin coffee cups rolled around near Daisy's feet, as well as an empty Doritos bag, a handful of unopened bills and one of Dodger's chew toys. The mail had been on the passenger seat but he'd dumped it on the floor before going into the school to get Junior. The whole mess, not to mention the dog slobber on the passenger window, didn't make a very positive impression.

But then, why did he care what kind of impression he made? Daisy Sutherland had invited herself along for the ride. He shot a quick glance her way as he set off down Second Avenue. Green T-shirt, bare arms, that canvas bag she'd brought out to his place the other day, those form-fitting sawed-off pants women wore in the summer, the kind that went just past the knees. Blue. Sandals with orange-painted toenails showing. That fabulous hair tied back with a polka-dot scarf…

Ben came to the stop sign at Frank Street. "You're sure you don't want me to drop you at the office?"

Her cheeks were red but she met his gaze full on. "No, thanks. I've taken care of everything. The high school student who works there—do you know John Spears?"

He shook his head. "Nope."

"Well, he had an exam this morning and was able to come in at noon. Hard to believe school's almost over, isn't it?"

He gave her a hard look and ignored her question, which was just designed to fill air, anyway, he figured. Chitchat. She sure was nervous. About what?

"I'd like to talk to you a little later, so this is really quite convenient. I have, uh—" here she looked down at Junior and made a small grimace "—a few things to discuss."

Something about the boy, obviously. Hell. Ben let out the clutch and turned in the other direction, the road that led out of town. "Fine. Junior, I'm taking you to Granny's, okay? Your mom took Laverne to dance class, and then she's got to drive the bus after school."

The boy nodded. The news seemed to cheer him up a little.

"Granny's?" Daisy asked with interest.

"*My* grandmother, actually," Ben replied, glancing at Daisy. "Florence Nolan. Lives out in the bush north of Pekisko. I was going to run Junior over to Granny's when he came home from school, anyway."

They drove for several miles in silence. Ben sensed that she was itching to ask more questions. She must have decided not to, considering the presence of the boy.

"Well," she finally burst out, "at least you answered your phone."

"Yeah." He was taking the back way and paid careful attention to the road in front of him, which had been freshly graveled. "I happened to be inside changing my shirt."

He knew it was driving her nuts not to ask why he'd been changing his shirt, so after a full five minutes, he put her out of her misery. "One of the four-year-olds threw me and I landed in a fresh pile of you-know-what."

Her laughter was refreshing. Ben didn't know when he'd heard someone laugh with such merriment. Not for a long, long time. He noticed that Junior was trying hard to keep a straight face, too.

"Nugget," he said, by way of explanation to the boy. "He's going to be a great horse someday."

"Great horse! He bucked you off! I don't call that *great*." She shared a grin with Junior. It was a relief to clear the air after their less than amicable parting the day before, and it did his heart good to see the boy smiling.

"When you raise bucking stock," he said, narrowing his eyes against the sun as they topped the last ridge before descending into the valley, "believe me, a horse that throws you is the best news you can get. He's your meal ticket."

Florence was in her garden when they drove up. Bounder raced toward the truck and barked once, just for effect. Dodger leaped out of the truck and there was a brief stiff-legged sniff fest among the three dogs, ending in tails wagging all round.

"Queenie's got some new pups, Junior."

The boy raised his head briefly, then gazed out the window, his face soft. Sentimental. Dreamy. For a minute, he looked so much like the old Arlo, the childhood pal Ben remembered from long ago, that it hurt.

Ben opened the door and got out, and Junior slid under the steering wheel and clambered down beside him. "You go see Granny first, okay?"

Florence stood watching them, but as the boy approached, she made her way to the side of the garden, where the rhubarb and dill grew riotously among the moonflowers nodding their foolish faces. His grandmother had a well-deserved reputation as a gardener in this part of the world.

He glanced at Daisy. "We won't be long. You want to get out?"

"I—I think I'll just stay here." She seemed shy, which surprised him. She hadn't struck him as the shy type.

He walked toward the rickety fence Arlo had built one summer, an attempt to keep the deer out. Like so many of his cousin's projects, this one hadn't worked out particularly well. Florence was always cursing the deer or shooing them away or, sometimes, bagging one for her smokehouse.

Junior tossed a stick for Bounder and then ambled after the dog as he raced to get it.

"Company?" Florence nodded at the pickup.

"The newspaper lady. She was with Junior at the school."

"She the one doing all the poking aound? Eunice told me she was out at the store last week."

"Yeah. Listen, can I leave Junior with you? Marie will come by for him at suppertime."

"Sure. He can help me pull weeds." The boy came back with the stick, Bounder and Dodger behind him. "You want to go see the pups first, Junior? They're under the steps. You be careful now, don't be squeezin' them. They're just young."

Junior streaked off toward the back of Florence's cabin. Ben watched him go. He was glad Florence hadn't said anything about the kind of questions Daisy was asking. At least, not in front of Junior. Anyway, since he'd been in town talking to Morris Jack the other day, Ben had been asking a few himself.

"What happened to him?"

"Fight at school." He gestured toward the truck. "She helped him out."

"Oh." Florence reached in the pocket of the baggy work pants she wore and pulled out a tissue. She wiped her nose. "He talkin' yet, son?"

Ben shook his head. "Not yet. Doctor says he's had a shock. He'll be okay. Just takes time. Marie thinks now it may have started earlier, the weekend before Arlo got killed when we had that wreck after branding." Florence looked past him, over his shoulder.

"Wreck?"

He wheeled. He thought he'd heard the truck door open....

Daisy approached, her bag over her shoulder. "Hi!" Her face was flushed; she seemed self-conscious. "I wanted to come over and say hello. What's this about a wreck?"

"Why? You figure it's news?" Ben snapped. "Something should go in the paper?"

"Maybe." Daisy stuck out her hand and after a split second's hesitation, Florence took it, with a wondering glance his way. "I'm Daisy Sutherland!"

"I'm Ben's granny. People call me Flo. Would you like some tea?"

"Oh, no thanks. I think Ben's in a hurry."

Ben was a little taken aback at his grandmother's offer. She wasn't the friendliest of souls—certainly not to a stranger asking questions about her dead grandson.

"Glass of water? It's a hot day."

Daisy looked at him uncertainly and he bent down and pulled up a stem of grass. "We should get going, Nan," he said, ignoring Daisy. "I have to take Ms. Sutherland back to Tamarack before I head home."

"Maybe she wants to see the pups," Florence persisted, and Ben tossed down the blade of grass. What the devil was the old woman up to?

"I'd love to! Do we have a few extra minutes?" Daisy's eyes held his. "No need to rush on my account. Really."

Well, hell. How could he refuse? He led her to the back steps where Junior was perched, two of the little sausage-like creatures in his lap. The pups didn't quite have their eyes open. Queenie sat alertly on the grass near him with a worried expression.

Daisy knelt down and gently stroked one of the puppies. Junior's dark eyes regarded her solemnly. Wonderingly. *Like a boy in love.* Queenie appeared to have a little more sense—she growled.

"Are there any more?" Daisy asked.

Junior pointed to the steps, then bent sideways and pointed to the space underneath, where Queenie had dug down into the soft earth to make a den.

Crawling closer, Daisy peered into the darkness. Queenie growled menacingly, glancing nervously at him, as though asking for help in getting this stranger away from her puppies. Ben immediately hunkered down and stroked Queenie's head, ready to grab hard if necessary. That was all he needed—Dog Bites Reporter. More headlines involving the Goodstriker family, this time for setting a vicious animal on the press.

"Okay, Mama!" Daisy rocked back on her heels and smiled at him. It was hard not to respond. Whenever he made up his mind he didn't like her, she'd do something like that, flash him one of those sunny, sweet smiles that made him think—for a second or two—that she was just what she appeared to be, a pretty fresh-faced city woman visiting her country cousins.

"I'll leave you alone with your little family," she said to the dog. "Bye for now, Junior." She waggled her fingers at the boy.

Junior smiled shyly. Ben hoped Florence would give

him a good wash before his mother showed up. He was a mess. They began to walk toward the truck.

"What kind of dogs are those?"

"Hilton hounds. Like Dodger. Named for Henry J. Hilton. What, you never heard of them?"

"No." She sent him a tentative grin. "Are they an actual breed?"

Ben laughed. "Only if you're from this part of Alberta. Henry's the foreman on Cal Blake's ranch, northeast of here. He's been mixing and matching dogs for as long as anyone can remember. Hobby of his. Some coon hound, some blue heeler, a little border collie, a handful of terrier thrown in. This and that. Most folks with cattle have owned a Hilton hound at one time or other."

"Cal Blake. I think he owns the ranch where my friend Emily arranged for us to help with spring branding next week," she mused.

Ben stared at her. *Branding? She must be joking.*

She seemed preoccupied. "Ben, what's this about a wreck? What you were telling your grandmother—"

"Rodeo talk for a bust-up." He sighed. "Freak accident. A horse broke his neck and front legs and had to be put down."

"That's horrible!"

"It was," Ben said grimly. Shooting that horse was one of the toughest things he'd ever had to do.

"What happened?" She sounded so sympathetic. Eager to understand. He couldn't figure this woman out—how much was genuine emotion and how much was calculated to drag a story out of him, maybe a story he didn't want to tell.

"One of the hands we'd hired for branding was trying to show off and got on a young horse that hadn't been ridden much. Horse started to act up, nothing serious. Then something spooked him big. Maybe a piece of paper blowing into the corral, who knows? Some noise, maybe? He started bucking blind and piled straight into the corral fence, head first.''

"And you think Junior saw it?''

"He did. Turned out he was in the hayloft and saw the whole thing. He cried all night, Marie said.''

"Poor kid,'' she said softly.

Florence was bent over, staking a row of peas when they got back to the truck. Daisy waved. "Nice meeting you, Florence!''

Ben's grandmother straightened and waved back.

He held the door for Daisy and she got in.

Quite the gentleman. Just like your pal Casper Desjarlais. Next thing you'll be wearing tasseled loafers.

Not likely.

He went around to the driver's side, wondering what the hell had gotten into him all the same.

FLORENCE WATCHED the pickup drive out of sight, then turned her attention to her beets. The young leaves were bright green, a foot tall, with roots nearly an inch across. A boiled egg and steamed beet thinnings with a little butter and vinegar made a fine spring meal. She filled her basket and walked slowly to the edge of the garden, pausing to run her hands over the leathery rhubarb fronds, stooping to peer under the leaves to see if she could spot Jupiter, the toad that lived down in the dampness, there in the shade. Toads brought luck. Good for the garden, too.

What about a pot of rhubarb sauce this afternoon? Junior's favorite. She'd stoke the stove and the boy could pick some rhubarb while she washed the beets. Give him something to do.

He was a good boy.

In the cabin, Florence went to the woodstove and put her hand on the fat metal belly of the teakettle. She'd let the fire burn down after breakfast, but the kettle was still warm. Better wash the boy's face before his mother saw him. No sense Marie getting hysterical about her son being in a fight. Boys were boys. She should know; she'd raised two girls and three boys herself, plus her grandson, Ben, for a while. She got a cloth, a tin basin and a bar of soap, then grabbed the kettle and carried the works to the back door, which was propped open to catch the breeze. Junior sat on the top step, his back to her. She could see the dark crown of his head through the screen door.

"Nice puppy. Nice little puppy, aren't you?"

Florence stayed where she was. The boy was hunched over one of the new pups in his lap, with Queenie lying in the grass in front of them, eyes sharp, ears alert.

"You could be *my* puppy if I didn't already have Ringo. Would you like that?" the boy murmured. "Ringo's a big dog. He might not like you. No, you better stay with Granny, little guy, it's safer here...."

Florence remained where she was for a few seconds, then stepped back and put the basin down on the unpainted table in the middle of her kitchen. The shack was really only two rooms—one small one at the side for her bed and dresser and the larger combination kitchen-sitting area. She poked crumpled paper and a few sticks of kindling into the stove and lit it. Then she went to the sink, dipped water from the five-gallon pail that stood by the counter and started to scrub the beets.

CHAPTER TWELVE

"IT WAS NICE to meet your grandmother," Daisy began. She had the window open and the breeze was welcome, even though it was making a mess of what was left of her ponytail. Ben was driving a little too fast, she thought. "Too bad it was in such an unfortunate circumstance."

"You mean Junior getting beaten up?"

"Well, yes." She decided to pull the scarf off altogether and shook out her hair. "Bullied. I'm going to speak to the principal since I saw the incident myself."

Ben's expression was grim. "That kid needs a few boxing lessons."

"Ben!"

"What? Is he going to let kids pick on him all his life? He needs someone to teach him how to fight back."

"That's a *terrible* thing to say. Violence begets violence."

"You're damn right it does. Kids need to know that hitting someone hurts."

"Kids should be taught to talk about their differences, not fight about them!"

"You think so?"

"Don't you?"

"Talk's cheap."

One-two-three… She began to count to herself.

The sun shone through the trees as they drove over the narrow grassy lane that led to his grandmother's place, lighting the cab of the truck in alternating strips of shade and sun. It was cool and green, pleasant in the woods. Daisy tried her best to keep her emotions in check. This man had an uncanny ability to get under her skin....

...*eight-nine-ten*. "So you're saying the answer to Junior's problem at school is to teach him to fight."

"Stand up for himself. It has to be done. School, life, whatever, a man has to act like a man."

"Act like a man! By beating someone up!"

"Correction—*defending* himself. And the people he cares about."

"Those boys were bigger than him! There were four of them! That's bullying, pure and simple."

"Okay, okay." He didn't look too happy about conceding a point to her. "If they were bigger than he was, that's different. But there's nothing wrong with two kids the same size squaring off against each other, one on one. Fair fighting, no dirty stuff."

"Just fists," she said sarcastically. She couldn't believe what she was hearing.

He nodded. "If kids were allowed to wrestle and fight more when they were younger, before they could really hurt each other, there'd be less of it when they got older. It's when they get older that they turn mean. Start ganging up. Use knives or worse. Couple of seven- or eight-year-olds dukin' it out? Hell, that's no problem." He cast her an impatient glance. "All they get is dirty and maybe a nosebleed. It's a helluva useful lesson, in my opinion. Keeps them in touch with reality."

"Reality!"

"Being physical is part of life," he said matter-of-factly. "Too many folks think life is something that happens in your head and in books, but it's—"

"You're advocating violence!" Daisy broke in, unable to contain herself for a second longer. "That's just about the craziest thing I ever heard!"

"Yeah?" He glanced at her. "And what you said about talking out their differences at that age is just about the most naive thing *I* ever heard."

Daisy stared blindly out the window. Was there anything they could discuss without getting into an argument? At the end of the lane, Ben turned left. A change of subject, Daisy decided, might be good idea.

"So. Does your grandmother drive?" They were on the gravel road now, the shortcut that led over the spine of the hill from the paved highway several miles to the east. They'd passed only one car coming and none, so far, going back.

"No. Well," he added, with a sly grin. "Maybe I should say she's never gotten a license. She can drive when she has to."

"How does she get groceries? Go to town?"

"Someone takes her. Me or—or Arlo when he was alive. Or she walks to the road and hitchhikes."

"Hitchhikes!"

"Everyone knows her. She never has trouble getting a ride."

"But—but isn't that *dangerous?*"

Ben shook his head several times. "My, my, Ms. Daisy Suth-er-land," he said mockingly. "Don't you sometimes feel you're *way* in over your head these days? Out here in the wild West?" Ben gave her a level look from knees to nose that sent her pulse ricocheting wildly, for one illogical second. "Driving around the backcountry alone with an Indian you just met, someone who advocates *violence…*"

"Your point?"

"My point?" He seemed startled by her question. "*Any*thing could happen, couldn't it?"

As if to illustrate, he put his foot on the brake and turned off the gravel road onto a grassy track that led through lodgepole pines dotting the open, grassy hillside. The truck banged over a few ruts and hummocks and then rolled into a clearing near the summit. Daisy's heart lurched into her throat. "Where are we going?"

"You mean, where am I *taking* you?" Ben's slow smile didn't do much to quiet her nerves. She clutched her bag, which contained her cell phone. *She'd jump out, she'd run, she'd dial 911.* He stopped the vehicle and reached forward to turn off the ignition. All at once, it was achingly quiet.

"You wanted to talk. This is as good a place as any. Don't worry, I won't harm a hair on your lovely head." He placed his right hand on his chest. "Scout's honor."

Your lovely head. Hardly. It made her wonder what her hair looked like.

"Of course, that would be a lie," he continued, removing his hand from his chest. "I never made it to Boy Scouts. We were happy sticking to that old standby, Cowboys and Indians. Little white guys always got to be the cowboys, and Arlo and Casper and me were always the Indians. Was that fair?" He grinned suddenly, as though delighted with the memory. "Then I grew up to be a cowboy, after all."

"*And* an Indian."

"Right." He was smiling.

"How much? You keep mentioning it," she replied. She was in a temper. He could have *asked* her if she wanted to pull off the road for their conversation!

"My father was Pekisko. My mother had a little Sarcee blood." Dodger had jumped out and stood in front of the truck barking, one ear cocked, the other hanging down. He was definitely a funny-looking dog. "You want to get out? Enjoy the view?"

"Sure." She could use the air, too. It seemed awfully close quarters in the pickup, even with the windows open.

She got out and walked to the crest of the hill. They were quite high, and she could see well up the valley in the direction of Florence's cabin, plus a good way down the valley. The Livingstone Range stood against the clear blue sky in the background, piercingly white with snow, hard-edged, commanding. *Magnificent.*

Ben came up beside her. "That's the reserve over there," he offered, waving his left arm to the south. "I guess you know where it is."

Was that a reference to the inquiries she'd been making? "As a matter of fact, I've made a lot of phone calls but I've never been to the settled part of the reserve, except the church and the corner store. And I was there, of course, the morning your cousin and Constable Petrenko died."

"You were?" He seemed surprised. Surely he'd known. "Taking pictures, I suppose, bugging the cops?"

"Pictures." Daisy dropped her bag at her feet and bent down to pick up a stick, which she lobbed for Dodger. As she'd expected, he was on it like a terrier on a three-legged rat, shaking it this way and that. He didn't seem inclined to return it, but then maybe the legendary Henry J. Hilton hadn't included any retrievers in his mix. "No one would talk to me. In fact, I was pretty much ordered off."

"You saw my cousin's truck there?" He looked interested, which Daisy took as a good sign. It might help her, after all.

"Yes." She lobbed another stick. "I didn't know it was his, of course, at the time. I didn't know anything about what had happened. It was pouring rain. I don't know how the cops found any clues at all, but they were stringing up yellow tape when I left."

"You got a picture of Arlo's truck?"

She nodded. "Why?"

"Just wondered." He kicked at a small stone and sent

it rolling down the hill. "I picked it up yesterday from the RCMP compound in Glory."

"The cops had it?"

"Evidence. Part of their investigation, I guess."

"Oh."

He sighed and shoved his hands in the pockets of his jeans. "Happens maybe there *was* a reason my cousin took a shot at Wayne. Apparently there was contraband in the truck."

"Drugs?"

"No. Illegal animal parts."

"Animal *parts?*"

"Gallbladders from black bears, an item that's apparently in high demand in the Far East."

"Gallbladders!" Daisy thought about that for a while. "Let me guess. They have something to do with fertility—*male* fertility—"

"Nothing to do with fertility. Or sex," he observed dryly, gazing out over the valley. "Black bear bile is an ingredient in traditional Chinese medicine. For all kinds of things."

Daisy felt a little light-headed and it wasn't the elevation. "Do you think your cousin was *poaching* then?"

"Arlo had a hard time cleaning a duck or gutting a fish when he caught one. Poaching for profit?" He shook his head. "You wouldn't think a guy who tried to make a living riding bulls would be squeamish, but he was. Arlo didn't mind pain but he hated blood."

Ben scuffed his boot on the ground again, sending up a small puff of dust from the tinder-dry mountain soil. The air was clean and soft with the intoxicating scent of alpine flowers in bloom. Tiny clusters of milk vetch covered the ground in a bluish-purple haze, interspersed here and there with mountain lupines and harebells.

"Don't get me wrong," Ben continued. "My cousin

was no saint. He didn't have any more respect for the law than the rest of us, but his idea of breaking it ran along the lines of speeding or driving drunk from time to time or not filing an income tax return. Hell, he never *had* any income!'' He turned to her, his expression serious. "You're right. I've never believed my cousin was a cold-blooded killer. And the gallbladders make no sense, either. I hate to say it, but even if he could stand the blood, he was just too damn lazy.''

He looked at her. "I didn't want to listen to you yesterday. Maybe because what you said had already occurred to me and I'd made my mind up not to pursue it.''

"Why not?''

"No point.'' He shrugged. "Arlo's dead. Period. That's the reality. That's what I keep coming back to.''

"And now?'' Maybe she wouldn't have to do any arm twisting after all....

"You could be onto something," he said slowly, grudgingly.

"There's serious money in this stuff?'' Daisy still felt skeptical. Money laundering, drugs...but animal *parts?*

"Big money. That's what doesn't make sense to me. Arlo's needs were minimal and short-term. He wasn't a gambler. He didn't drink that much. He never ran around on Marie—''

"What does that have to do with anything—whether or not he cheated on his wife?''

He gave her a surprised look. "Money. Women cost money.''

"*Some* women,'' she said stubbornly, adding, "I suppose.''

He ignored her comment. "The poaching, the big money angle, the connections necessary, none of it sounds like Arlo. But maybe you're right. Maybe I do have an obligation to check this out.''

"Even if the truth is worse than you think?" she asked softly. "He *could* have been a poacher, you know. There could've been a whole lot you didn't know about your cousin."

"Maybe."

Daisy felt sorry for him. Ben had obviously been very close to this happy-go-lucky relative. They'd been boy-hood friends.

"Until I heard about the gallbladders, I was prepared to accept the cops' version," he said. "A mix-up, maybe an accident, and somehow they both ended up dead. But now the poaching—" He shook his head. "I just don't buy it."

"Those cops really infuriate me!" Daisy muttered. "I've been trying to get a few simple facts out of them since it happened. Nothing! Now one of them tells you there was contraband in your cousin's truck. No one told me *anything* like that."

"I didn't get that from the cops."

She stared at him. "Who told you then?"

"Someone in town—"

"Someone in town," she repeated. "See? People tell you things. Why don't they tell me? And that staff ser-geant! Gordon Bass! It's like dealing with a stone wall, a stone wall that tries to *date* you! What? Is this town *that* short of single women?"

He shot her a puzzled look but seemed prepared to let the comment slide. She wasn't sure why she'd blurted out that little detail.

A sudden thought struck her. "You don't think the cops might have planted that box of stuff?"

"Hell, no. Why? This is the Royal Canadian Mounted Police we're talking about. Canada's finest. They may be incompetent occasionally, but even *I* don't think they'd plant evidence and I'm no fan of cops."

"It gets stranger," Daisy said slowly. "Maybe Wayne

wasn't what he seemed, either. My mother told me—in confidence—that he might've been sent back from Ontario because he'd been abusing drugs or alcohol or both.'' Now she was telling Ben. But damn it, she trusted him! She couldn't help feeling they were in this together....

"Come on! How would your mother know that?"

"She and Dad are close to the Petrenkos. They've heard hints. My folks worshipped Wayne and now that he's dead, well—'' Daisy paused, reaching down pick up her bag "—they still worship him. He was their godson, the son they never had and all that. Believe me, they do *not* want me stirring things up and writing an article for the paper, unless it's favorable.''

He regarded her curiously. "So why *are* you stirring things up?"

CHAPTER THIRTEEN

"I DON'T KNOW," she said miserably. "Maybe it's because so many people don't want me to."

He looked incredulous. "You're doing this because you're *stubborn?*"

"I know that sounds awful, but sometimes I almost think it's true." Daisy drew a shaky breath, held it for a few seconds, then let it out. "I thought I'd put that behind me when I left my last job. All that digging around. Apparently not." She threw her hands in the air and took a few steps forward, then wheeled to face him again. "No matter how much I tell myself I'm through turning over rocks and inspecting the lowlife beneath, I can't just walk away when something like this happens."

"You had problems in the city?" His eyes were guarded but curious.

She nodded. The wound was still so raw. She'd been warned that she might be jeopardizing an investigation but she'd just plowed ahead. Then that photograph—she'd never forget the photograph that convinced her she should've listened to the police. Her front-page story had sent the baby kidnappers fleeing before the police could locate their hiding place and put an end to the illegal adoption ring. They'd been arrested two days after abandoning their tiny charges.

"I was a reporter," she whispered. "A damn good one. But things happen in that business, things you don't always want to see happen—" She bit her lip, proud that her voice remained steady. She'd already bared more of her heart and soul than she'd intended.

Ben strolled downhill a dozen yards or so. He bent to pick up the stick she'd thrown earlier and tossed it again for Dodger. Daisy snapped off several pictures of the view, including him and Dodger in a couple of them.

She stowed the camera in her bag, glad of the few minutes alone to regain her composure.

"But you *are* stubborn," he said, with a gleam in his eye when he returned. "Right?"

It was an icebreaker.

She smiled tremulously. "I guess I am. Sorry." She felt a sudden rush of feeling—gratitude—toward this taciturn man who seemed so rough and yet so tender and caring at the same time—toward his loser cousin and Junior, Arlo's widow, his old granny....

"Damn!" He sighed and looked out over the valley. "I hate to stir up anything that might hurt Marie or the kids."

"You mean like real evidence that Arlo was poaching?"

"Among other things, yes."

"Maybe they're already hurt. Those bullies called Junior's dad a cop killer," Daisy said in low tones. "They said Junior started the fight."

"He *started* it?"

"Maybe he was trying to stick up for his father. Ever think of that? Kids do. That child's got a lot to live with these days. And why doesn't he talk?"

"Who told you that?" Ben asked angrily.

"A little girl at school. She told me Junior was 'the boy that didn't say anything anymore.' And he didn't say a word at the school—or all the way out here—did he?"

"He's been having some problems lately. Emotional stuff. Is that what you wanted to talk to me about—earlier?" Ben frowned.

Daisy nodded.

He glanced at the sun. "Time to head back," he said abruptly. "I've got work to do this afternoon. I'm sure you do, too."

Daisy remained quiet the rest of the way. She felt drained. It had been a busy day and she still had a meeting to attend that evening.

When Ben stopped in front of the *Times,* her mother was on the sidewalk, about to go into the building. She paused when Daisy jumped out of the pickup and slammed the door.

"Daisy?" Ben's voice was low through the open window.

"Yes?" She peered back inside the cab. Had she forgotten something? No, she had her bag and her scarf.

"I'll call you."

He drove off, leaving Daisy staring after him, only vaguely aware that her mother was holding the door, waiting for her.

"STAFF SERGEANT Bass, please."

"Is he expecting you, Ms.—?"

"Sutherland. Daisy Sutherland. And, no, he is not expecting me." *But he is darn well going to see me.* Daisy turned and surveyed the five scarred wooden chairs in the small waiting area of the Glory RCMP detachment. Two chairs were filled, one with a woman dozing in the corner, her handbag gaping open beside her, exposing a half bottle of a popular brand of rye whisky. The other held a teenager with fingernails bitten to the quick. He kept getting up and looking out the window, then sitting down again and gnawing at his thumbnail, which made Daisy nervous. She stood near the door for a few minutes, then decided she might as well sit down. She could be here for a while.

She'd just taken a seat and reached for a tattered copy

of *Alberta Report* to leaf through when the receptionist peered over the high counter. "Ms. Sutherland?"

Daisy followed her down the hall to the office at the end. Staff Sergeant Gordon Bass had a corner office, both windows overlooking a dusty parking lot and an alley filled with trash cans, old cars and sagging wooden garages. It was a run-down area, between Painter's Flats and the lower side, the Horsethief River side, of downtown Glory.

Bass was behind his gray metal desk but he stood when she entered and stepped forward with a smile. "This is a pleasant surprise?"

"It can hardly be a surprise, sir," Daisy returned, giving his hand a quick shake. "I've called you half a dozen times since the funeral. I've left messages. You must have realized I wanted to see you," she finished with more than a hint of sarcasm.

"See *me?*" He grinned. Gordon Bass was tall and fit, the kind of man for whom uniforms were made. He had thick blond hair, clipped short, a terrific tan and a small moustache, the style favored by the young Robert Redford in *Butch Cassidy and the Sundance Kid.* A good-looking guy—and well aware of it. "I'm flattered."

"*Talk* to you," Daisy corrected.

"Sit down." He indicated the plum-coloured Naugahyde chair in one corner and moved back to his desk. A fake philodendron trained up a bamboo pole in a Mexican-style pot climbed ceilingward between two visitor's chairs and a small square glass-and-brass coffee table. "Something to drink? Coffee? Tea?" He paused, one hand on the telephone receiver.

"Not for me," Daisy said. She perched on the edge of the seat and plopped her bag on the coffee table. "I don't want to take up too much of your valuable time."

Bass flashed her a smile. "I've always got time for you,

or—should I say?—the press. What's on your mind today?''

"The shoot-out at Pekisko," Daisy returned promptly. No sense beating around the bush. The smile tightened; the blue eyes cooled ever so slightly.

"What about it? You know we've almost wound up our investigation. Not much to it. Details are in the press release we'll be sending out later this week." He shook his head in an expression of sympathy. "Bad luck on both sides, I guess. Terrible thing to lose an officer like that."

"And Goodstriker had a family, you know. Wife and two kids."

"Of course. Tragedy all round." Bass shrugged. "But what can I say? You don't go around shooting cops."

"Why was there a shoot-out at all, sir?"

Bass glanced at her sharply; she preferred to remain on relatively formal terms with him. "Why?"

"Yes. I presume Wayne was arresting Goodstriker for something, or in the process of arresting him. For what crime?"

Bass chose his words carefully. "We have reason to believe, yes, that Constable Petrenko may have been executing an arrest when he was killed." He gave Daisy a level look. "We have various investigations going on at all times, I'm sure you know that. I can't really give you any more information at the moment."

"What strikes me as a pretty incredible coincidence is two guys, two boyhood pals, hauling out guns and firing on each other at the *exact* same time. How do you explain that?"

Bass shrugged again. "What can I say? It's unusual but it can happen."

"You're an experienced officer. How often have you seen two people shoot each other dead like that?"

"We don't know that they were both killed instantly,"

Bass said. "One of them could have lived a few minutes, maybe more. There were indications that Constable Petrenko died immediately, but it appeared Goodstriker moved around some before succumbing to his injuries."

The pool of pink water in the mud.

"How did Wayne die?"

"Gunshot wounds. He was hit in the neck."

"What kind of weapon?"

"I can't give you that information."

"Arlo Goodstriker had a couple of legally registered rifles, his cousin says, hunting rifles, but that's all." A hazy image of Goodstriker's truck at the scene of the crime swam into Daisy's mind. *The door hanging open, the torn upholstery, the cracked back window...*

"You don't need a legally registered gun to kill someone. Any gun will do." She realized that was Bass's idea of a joke. "Not many people own legally registered *handguns,* but most rural guys around here own rifles."

What was that supposed to mean? What kind of gun killed Wayne? Handgun or rifle? Daisy felt frustrated. "Goodstriker's cousin said Arlo wasn't a killer, that he could hardly kill a fish when he caught it."

"He would, wouldn't he?" Bass scoffed. "Please don't be naive, Daisy. You're too good a journalist for that, if half of what I hear about you is true. If the RCMP relied on the opinions of surviving relatives in order to lay charges, we'd hardly be one of the premier law enforcement organizations in the world, would we?"

She was a little surprised he'd gone to the trouble of checking her out. "What have you heard about me?"

"That you're a pain in the butt to the police," he said pleasantly, his smile mitigating—barely—the blunt words. "Or you *have* been in the past. You jeopardized an investigation we were doing into insurance fraud in Winnipeg. You interviewed witnesses in a potential drug trial, which set us back quite a few months and blew cover on one of our operatives.''

"I did?" Daisy hadn't known about that one. The police didn't make a practice of informing journalists of everything they were investigating.

"Plus a few other incidents that are best forgotten."

"The baby kidnapping case?" she offered weakly.

He shrugged. "Actually, you did a good job on that one, Daisy. I think even the Vancouver police might admit that now."

"Those two babies suffered because of me," Daisy said in a low voice. "If I hadn't run that story—"

"What are you talking about? You flushed out the kidnappers. If you hadn't run that story, the police might still be looking for them. As it was, they were arrested trying to cross the border in the States. They're in jail awaiting trial as we speak."

"One of the babies lived," Daisy whispered. "Thank heavens for that."

"Yes." Bass picked up his pen and played with it for a few seconds, avoiding her eyes. "One lived and one died. However, the fact remains that you have a reputation for getting in the way of police work, and in this particular case, under my jurisdiction, I have no intention of letting you jeopardize anything by running with any half-cocked ideas."

"I can understand your reservations, sir," Daisy said stiffly. She could see that—from a police point of view—she might be a liability. But... *Jeopardize anything?* That meant they must *have* something....

"I really must insist that you call me Gordon." He smiled and dropped the pen in his desk drawer and shut it firmly. "Listen, I hear there's a fund-raiser dance for the kids' rodeo coming up next week. Want to go with me?"

Daisy stared at him. "Don't you have some kind of—of conflict of interest guidelines about this?"

Bass laughed. "Nothing in the procedures manual says an unmarried officer can't date a good-looking eligible woman he—"

"Eligible?"

"Unmarried." His eyes narrowed slightly at her response. "No boyfriends, are there?"

"Would I tell you? No comment, sir." She ignored his laughter and flipped her steno pad to the page where she'd jotted notes. "Let's see. Sorry to trouble you further, but I have one or two more questions, if I may. What's this about Arlo Goodstriker having illegal animal parts in his truck?"

"Who told you that?" Suddenly Bass looked very serious.

"Why? Is that the mysterious crime?"

"Who *told* you?" he repeated.

Daisy's instinct was to protect her source. Besides, Ben hadn't exactly said where he'd gotten the information. "It's a story that's going around town."

"At any given time, we are investigating many potential crimes, Daisy." He spoke carefully, repeating what he'd said before. "Small towns have their share of break-and-enters, stolen goods, fencing, drugs, gang activity, money laundering—"

"Money laundering!"

"I'm not saying we're investigating that particular problem, just that these matters come to the attention of the police from time to time, even in small towns. Poaching, for instance. Usually it's a provincial matter for the Fish and Game wardens. Sometimes it's bigger and we get called in. Now, I'm not saying Goodstriker had animal parts in his truck, you understand, but if he *did*, trade in illegal animal parts is a very lucrative international busi-

ness. A major crime, second only to drug traffic. Not many
people know that."

"Is it?" Daisy quickly scribbled down his comments.

"When that Air Canada flight bound for India went
down over Ireland a few years ago—you remember that?"
Daisy nodded. "A suitcase of dried bear gallbladders
worth over a million dollars was aboard."

Daisy let out a breath. *That* kind of money? She'd had
no idea....

"It's our belief that Arlo Goodstriker may have gunned
Officer Petrenko down to prevent him making an arrest.
Whether for contraband, as you've heard rumored or for
other reasons I can't tell you about. Luckily, our man got
off a shot and the perp is dead. End of story." He smiled
grimly. "Saves the taxpayer a lot of money, going to trial
and then locking him up for twenty-five years." Killing a
police officer in Canada warranted an automatic twenty-
five-year jail sentence, no parole.

Daisy stood and shoved her steno pad back in her bag.
"Call me crazy, but I get the distinct impression there's
something to this animal-parts-found-in-truck scenario.
Am I right?"

"No comment." His blue eyes practically twinkled.
"Suffice it to say, I'm going to shut you down if you tell
another soul about our conversation. Understand?"

"Perfectly."

Bass held out his hand. "You mind if I have a look in
that bag of yours?"

Daisy was stunned. "Why?" She wouldn't dignify the
request by telling him he'd need a warrant to search her
bag. "You think I'm hiding something in here?"

Bass laughed. "No, let's just say I'm playing a hunch.
Cops have hunches, too, you know."

Indignant, Daisy handed over her canvas carry-all and
watched as Bass went through it. Camera, film canisters,

Lifesavers, purse-size Kleenex package, eyeliner, wallet, three Luna bars, a half-liter bottle of water, lip gloss, a tube of hand cream, a spare maxipad in its pink plastic sleeve, her notebook, three pens and a highlighter, cell phone, a book of wedding matches, her Timex with the broken strap—

Daisy made an attempt to grab the bag before he got to the lint, the loose change and the cookie crumbs at the bottom, but Bass jerked it away, holding up the book of matches. "'Hannah and Jack, March 14.'"

Daisy snatched the matchbook from him. "Friends of mine." She held out her hand and he gave her the bag. "What, no tape recorder in there?" she asked sweetly.

"Just checking," Bass said with a grin. "You're a damned fine reporter, and I wouldn't put it past you. Now, about that dance, I'm available until Wednesday noon next week. After that, if you haven't accepted my offer, I'm going to have to ask someone else. It's only fair to give my second choice some notice."

"I'll try to remember that," Daisy said, with an attempt at sarcasm. It was hard not to like Gordon Bass. He was doing his job, as he saw it, just as she was trying to do hers. In this situation, he held all the cards. Her impulse to reject his invitation was tempered with a feeling that she needed to think the situation through before limiting her options.

Maybe she *would* date a guy just to see what kind of info she could squeeze out of him…. There was always a first time. Even if she never used anything he said, she'd feel better just knowing she'd gotten the upper hand with Gordon Bass—for once!

When she went back into the reception area, the woman was gone but the jumpy teenager was still there. Daisy slung her bag onto her shoulder and stood for a moment on the cement steps outside, staring at the parched lawn, neatly ringed with a painted black chain looped on short steel posts and dotted with gum wrappers and cigarette packages that had blown in with the prairie wind. A Canadian flag flapped loudly on the flagpole in the center of the lawn, the only sound except for the distant yells of kids in a playground somewhere.

What should she do next? Her first thought was to rush to Meadow Springs Ranch and tell Ben everything. But she needed to think that one over, too. He'd said, "I'll call you." Despite Daisy's lingering at the office the night before and staying up long past the time she usually turned out her light, there'd been no call.

Maybe she should drop in at Lucas Yellowfly's office while she was in Glory to see if there were any more details on the dance. She needed an update for next week's paper.

She had a village council meeting in Tamarack to cover that night, the Rocking Bar S spring branding on Saturday and then she'd promised her mother they'd go to Lethbridge to shop after church on Sunday while her father golfed. With the paper coming out Thursday, the office was generally closed on Sunday and Monday.

Next week was the rodeo dance and after that the big summer sidewalk sale and then the kiddie rodeo and then the Glory hearing into health hazards of accidental sour gas flares, big news in a rural community overwhelmed with oil and gas exploration. There was a big baseball tournament the first week in August and...

Daisy had never been so busy. She'd been in Tamarack six weeks already and still hadn't gotten around to looking for a place of her own.

CHAPTER FOURTEEN

"RASSLIN'?" The old cowboy pushed his battered straw hat higher on his grizzled pate and scratched his sunburned right ear. "Why, that's when you hold them little calves down for the fella with the branding iron and the fella that does them, uh, *other* things that has to be done...."

"Stop!" She'd done her research. She knew what he meant: the vaccinating and "cutting" or castration. "What do you think, Em?"

"*Rasslin'* sounds just fine with me," Emily said with a big grin and a tug on the broad-brimmed hat she was wearing. When Daisy had picked her up at her parents' house at eight that morning, Emily had appeared with hats for them both. "I mean, are the two of us likely to be *ropin'*?" She laughed. Emily Parrish, Daisy's best friend from high school days, ran her own small catering business in Calgary and was always up for an adventure....

The old cowman looked relieved. "I wouldn't presume to tell you ladies what to do, no sir, but I'm kinda glad you picked rasslin'. There ain't never no shortage of ropers on this job. It's the glamour factor, y'see," he said, surveying the melee of cows, calves, dogs, horses and helpers. "*Everybody* wants to rope."

This, Daisy had discovered, was the famous Henry J. Hilton, breeder of the renowned Hilton hounds and foreman at the Rocking Bar S, the ranch owned by the Cal Blake family. Emily, who knew Cal's wife, Nina, had made arrangements for them to participate in spring branding. Daisy was looking forward to getting the kind of city-gal-meets-country story that would appeal to big-city readers. It was a start to what she hoped would become a lucrative freelance sideline to her new career editing the *Tamarack Times*.

"We look okay for this?" Emily held her hands wide and glanced down at the fancy-tooled boots and designer jeans she had on. Both wore jeans—although Daisy's were plain old Wranglers—and T-shirts in addition to the cowboy hats. Daisy felt a little foolish, but had agreed to go along with the "cowgirl" fashion just for the day.

"The calves don't care, Em."

"You ladies look just fine to me," Henry drawled. "Maybe even finer than fine," he added with a twinkle in his blue eyes. "Now, let me show you what you need to do."

"Give me a few minutes," Daisy said, looping her camera strap around her neck. "You two get started. I'd like to take some pictures first." Duncan Fairlie was off on another of his endless searches for the fabled lost gold mine and, besides, Daisy wanted to get her own pictures for this story.

"You go right ahead, miss," Henry said magnanimously, and Daisy took her first two shots of him alone, then another one with his arm around Emily. Daisy left them grinning at each other and walked toward the area with the most activity.

On one side of the lane, cows—what looked to be hundreds of them—were bunched along the fence, bellowing. In other corrals, on the opposite side of the lane, she saw bawling white-faced Hereford calves. Cowboys on horses moved here and there in both enclosures, a lot more slowly than she would've thought, but then most of her ideas of ranch life came from watching rodeo on television.

She shot half a dozen pictures by the fence. The cows

seemed surprised to see her and many of them regarded her curiously—and quietly—for a few moments. Then, as if giving up on the idea that she might be an ally, they started bellowing again. What a racket!

A small boy who couldn't have been more than ten stood near one of the gates. A girl, about the same age or maybe a bit younger, perched on the top rail nearby. The boy grinned at her as she walked toward him, his grin getting even wider as she snapped his picture. He practically swaggered as he took a step toward her and pulled his hat down to shade his eyes, the way she'd seen cowboys do.

"What's your name?"

"Ryan, miss. Ryan Webster," he said proudly. "I'm the chute boy."

"I'm Rosie!" called the girl on the fence. "Rosie Garrick! I'm eight-almost-nine!" She was a sweet-looking child, with curly black hair and blue eyes. Both children were dressed in jeans, boots and long-sleeved shirts, miniature cowboys.

"Mind if I take your picture?" Daisy called back.

"No way!" The girl covered her face with her arms but when she peeked out after a few seconds, Daisy snapped the picture and Rosie giggled.

"So, you open the gate for these cows, do you?" Daisy asked, looking around doubtfully. One pint-size boy could hardly hold back this tide of hooves and horns if it decided to surge through an open gate.

"Nope. I just let in the calves when Adam and Ben bring 'em over." He pointed. "They bring 'em in that pen and I open that chute over there and then they put 'em through to the cows to mother up."

"Ben?"

"Ben Longquist. He goes to college. He works for Adam in the summer."

"Oh."

Daisy's face must have betrayed some disappointment, because the boy quickly added, "If you're looking for the other Ben, he's ropin'."

The other Ben. Did he mean Ben Goodstriker, as she half hoped and half feared?

"Adam's my dad," the girl said helpfully, kicking her heels against the smooth weathered pole of the fence. "I've got a little brother who's three and another little brother who's just a baby."

"I see." She took her microcassette out of her shirt pocket and recorded the children's names and ages. How was she going to keep any of this straight? If she truly planned to become part of life here, she'd need to learn who all these people were and where they fit into the Glory and Tamarack communities. "I think I'll just walk around a bit and take some more pictures. What are they doing over there, Ryan?"

Daisy pointed to the corral that seemed to contain the most activity—saddled horses tied to posts, heads down, tails lazily swatting flies in the morning sun, riders on other horses, people on foot, smoke, dust, plenty of yelling back and forth, the occasional burst of laughter.

"That's the branding pen, miss," the boy said, with a look of polite disbelief that anyone wouldn't know something *that* elementary. "Say, are you the new reporter?"

"I guess I am," Daisy said, smiling and taking another quick shot of the boy, with the cows behind him.

"Am I going to be in the paper?" Daisy could tell he was pleased at the prospect.

"Maybe."

"Her, too?" He pointed fenceward.

"Maybe. See you two later." Daisy walked along the fence line, back the way she'd come. There was a grassy knoll about a hundred or so yards away, well situated to let her get a terrific wide-angle shot of the entire operation, but unfortunately in the same field as the cows. She stopped to study the cows briefly. They appeared to be quite preoccupied with what was going on in the branding pen.

And who'd ever heard of cows bothering anyone, anyway?

BEN COULDN'T believe his eyes. He'd seen the Thunderbird drive into the ranch yard—who could miss it?—and he'd noticed Daisy and her friend talking to Henry. Then he'd gotten distracted with a couple of calves that had ducked out of Laverne's loop, and by the time he'd put that right, Daisy was over by the fence talking to one of the Webster twins.

Maybe five minutes had gone by. He'd roped another calf and brought it to the branding area for his partner, Trevor Longquist, to heel, then glanced back—and there she was on the other side of the fence walking toward the hill!

Ben muttered a profanity and began to ease his horse through the calves, all bewildered, all darting this way and that. Laverne, who had recently turned thirteen, was roping with him and Trevor, taking one calf to Trevor's two or three. Laverne's dream was to enter an all-girl rodeo like the one at Claresholm. She was a decent roper already and dynamite on the barrels, although she'd never make the big-time with her old pony. Besides, no one knew better than Ben that only one or two percent of rodeo contestants ever won real money in rodeo; all the rest "donated," as the old-timers said. Donated blood, sweat and tears. Cash prospects were even slimmer in all-girl events, which were few and far between.

He brought his horse up next to Trevor's. "Can you

take the next couple with Laverne? There's something I need to check out."

"Sure." Trevor, an intense boy of eighteen, had his loop built and his eyes fixed on his next calf. "No problem."

Ben urged the big rawboned gelding he was riding, one of Cal's horses, toward the mothering-up pen. Daisy was nearly halfway to the hill. Adam Garrick and Ben Longquist—known in the branding pen as Young Ben today—were minding the calves that would soon be going back to the cow pasture. He approached Adam and nodded in Daisy's direction.

"Sonuvabitch!" Adam was an experienced cowman; his first reaction, Ben knew, had matched his exactly. Normally cows were mild-mannered and no danger to anyone. But these cows, with their calves taken away, were overwrought and unpredictable. "Who's that?"

"The newspaper lady. I'm going in there to get her out. If you'll keep an eye on these cows—"

"Hell, I'm coming in with you. If they decide to follow her, you'll need help turning them."

"Let's hope it doesn't come to that." But Ben appreciated Adam's offer.

"Ryan, you tell Young Ben to bring in some of the branded calves," Adam said as they rode through the chute. "That'll keep the cows busy."

Good idea, Ben thought. It was early enough in the day that there weren't a whole lot of calves ready to be reunited with their mothers. Those that were could be turned in, a process that always occupied the attention of all the cows—until they found that their own calves were still missing and the bellowing began again.

Ben picked his way carefully through the cattle, skirting the press nearest the fence and trying to work slowly toward the hill. He didn't want to upset the herd by making any quick movements, nor did he want to yell to get

Daisy's attention, for fear of starting something. To his dismay, she still had her back to the whole operation and was wandering merrily toward the knoll, snapping photos of the countryside as she went.

Several cows bolted as he came near, their eyes showing white. Many never saw a human unless he had a rope in his hand or was on a horse, and they were naturally skittish. These were range animals that spent most of the year in the high pastures of Cal Blake's lease land and were used to fending for themselves. They were brought down to the home ranch for feeding in the winter, but rarely handled. The older cows no doubt nursed grudges about former roundups and doctorings, plus recollections of previous calves being taken away and returned bruised and sore each spring, definitely not memories inclined to dispose them toward a human being.

So far, so good. It was an incredibly stupid thing for Daisy to do, but it looked like she was going to be okay. The cows hadn't even noticed her. He'd just ride up and politely ask her to leave, maybe escort her to make sure she got out all right. He might as well prepare for an argument, too.

In the distance, he saw another rider enter the field from the opposite side. Jeremiah Blake, Cal's brother, and manager of the Diamond Eight up at Elk River. Jeremiah began loping toward them, and a knot of thirty or forty cows swung to watch him approach. Then they seemed to spot Daisy for the first time and lurched toward her, first at a fast walk, then breaking into a shambling trot. The lead cow bellowed furiously and Ben spurred his horse into a gallop. So did Adam, he noticed from the corner of his eye. Adam was coming up on the inside, trying to catch the knot of cows that had broken away; Jeremiah was approaching with the same intention.

Goddamn! Ben spurred the gelding again and got a burst

of speed out of the big quarterhorse. The cows were running now, but Daisy seemed completely unaware, still nonchalantly trudging up the hill.

"Daisy!"

She didn't turn. No wonder. Between the calves and the cows, what was one person yelling?

"*Daisy!*"

She hesitated, then turned and Ben would have given anything to spare her the horror of that moment. Two riders trying to head off a phalanx of angry-looking cows headed straight toward her and another rider—him—bearing down on her as fast as he could make his horse travel.

Adam had caught up to the lead cow but so far he wasn't having any luck turning her. It was unfortunate that Jeremiah had entered the field from the opposite direction, because his actions had the effect of causing the cows to bolt from the middle, rather than letting themselves be trapped between two hat-waving, yelling cowboys.

Ben's only option was to grab Daisy and haul her up onto his horse. Either that or make a stand by her to try to hold off or divide the cows, not an option he preferred. Neither did his horse, he was sure. The cows were no more than thirty yards away from Daisy and traveling full out now. A few more seconds and—

"Daisy!" He leaned over to the left, indicating what he had in mind and she held up her arms. He came in from the north, veered toward her and hauled on the gelding's reins, slowing enough so he could bend down, grab her around the waist and pull her up against him and the saddle.

Somehow, she managed to get one arm around his neck and hung on for dear life. He turned away from the cows, and the big horse responded smoothly, galloping uphill with two people on his back and most of the weight to one side—with Daisy hanging off and Ben doing his damnedest to hold on to her.

The cows gave up, as he'd hoped they would, faced with an uphill run. He heard Adam and Jeremiah hoot and holler, and with a quick glance over his shoulder realized they'd gained control of the situation. He stopped the horse and let Daisy go.

She dropped to the ground like a sack of oats and Ben was off his horse in a second, reaching for her hand, wishing he hadn't let her go the way he had. She sat up. Her hand trembled. "Are you all right?" he asked hoarsely.

She looked up at him with big scared eyes and then she released his hand and flopped back down on the grass, covering her face. *"Omigod!"* She let out a wail and her shoulders began to shake. Ben stood up, not sure what he should do now.

He heard a rider approach and walked around to the other side of the gelding, who was standing patiently nearby, sides heaving.

"Everything okay?"

"Fine." Ben waved, and Jeremiah loped toward the ranch and the business at hand: branding.

Ben turned back to Daisy. He felt sorry for her and at the same time he was damn mad. "What the *hell* were you doing in that field anyway? Those cows were upset." She stared at him in shock, then covered her eyes again. "Yeah, yeah, taking pictures for the paper. You could've been killed, you know that?" He slapped his hat against his thigh and jammed it back on his head. His own knees felt a little weak. "Dammit, you scared me half to death!"

She took her hands away and gazed up at him. "What about *me?*" she wailed. She put her hands over her eyes and started sobbing again.

Ben got down on one knee beside her. "Here." He

clasped her forearm and shook her gently. "Get up. You'll feel better when you stand."

"I c-can't stand up," she said, freeing her arm. "My legs are like—like noodles. What happened anyway?" She half sat and frowned at him. "Why did they ch-chase me like that?"

He shook his head, not sure what to tell her. Her eyes were red, her nose was red, her face was dirty and there was grass in her hair. She'd lost her hat and there was no sign of the damned camera. Her eyes were the bluest blue he'd ever seen.

"Come here." Standing, he offered his hand again. This time she took it. She swayed and he caught her, gripping her upper arms, bare skin beneath the short sleeves of her T-shirt. He noticed she'd scraped her elbow. "You know, if you were any kind of real cowgirl, instead of such a *girl*—"

"I'm not a girl!"

"How old are you—twenty-one?"

"I'm twenty-five. Nearly twenty-six—ooh!" She swayed and went even paler, half closing her eyes, and grabbed his shirtfront to steady herself. Ben was shocked to hear that she was in her midtwenties, no girl at all. She just looked about eighteen.

"If you were any kind of cowgirl," he repeated, "number one, you'd wear long sleeves to protect yourself when you're doing ranch work. Number two, you'd have enough sense to stay away from cows that are madder 'n' hell about being separated from their—"

"Ben," she interrupted, wiping her eyes with the backs of both hands. "Never mind all that, okay? I did the wrong thing. I'm sorry." Her lower lip started to tremble and she whispered, "Thank you for saving me." Ben felt a sudden urge to step forward, to take her in his arms properly, to lean down and—

"Promise me you'll never do something that stupid again." His voice was gruffer than he'd intended.

Her eyes held his and he could sense her indecision. "I'll probably do something stupid again, but it definitely won't be that," she said finally. "I promise."

They stared at each other for a few seconds, and Ben felt his blood sink to his boots and slowly start to rise, burning all the way... *Promises.*

"So." He cleared his throat. "You ready to go back and rassle some calves?"

"I guess I'd better," she replied softly. "Although, frankly, I'd rather go home and have a stiff drink."

"Too early for a stiff drink," he said, smiling. "Besides, you don't want everyone thinking you're a coward, do you?"

"Even if I am?" She managed a tiny smile, too, which made him feel a whole lot better. She had grit; he had to give her that.

"You're not. Believe me, you're no coward. Now, do you want to walk or ride?" He turned to the gelding, who was observing them with interested eyes, ears flicking back and forth as they spoke.

"Can't we both ride?"

Ben looked at her, surprised. "I guess we can." He picked up the reins, then swung into the saddle and kicked his left foot free of the stirrup so she could put her foot in. He grabbed her arm to help her up, then felt her settle behind him.

"Hang on, now," he warned. *"Tight."*

"I am," he heard, her voice muffled in his shirt. "Ben?"

He turned his head. Her face was inches from his. "You never called. You said you were going to call me."

"Yeah, well." The gelding moved restively and Ben held him back. "Something came up." *Which was a lie.*

"I suppose you want me to find that camera," he said, shifting to look at her again. "If it hasn't been tromped into the ground by fifty of Cal Blake's best cows."

"Yes, please." Her voice was small. She was shaken up, all right. Who wouldn't be? "And Ben?"

He raised one eyebrow.

"Maybe my hat, too, if you see it. It belongs to Emily."

Ben nodded and shook his reins, urging the gelding on. He had to admit he was gratified to hear her small gasp and feel her arms tighten as the horse began to gallop. Her face, her arms, her whole body was snugged up against his back, and he was thinking that riding double with Daisy Sutherland was a mighty nice feeling....

Course, riding double with any woman at all would've felt that way. It had been a while. Nope, Casper Desjarlais had nothing on him in the fool-for-women department.

CHAPTER FIFTEEN

FORTUNATELY THE FIELD was somewhat distant from the branding area and not many people gathered at the Rocking Bar S ranch that morning had witnessed her predicament—or her rescue.

Ryan and Rosie had. They were all eyes when Ben dropped her off at the calf chute and trotted away without a backward glance.

All in a day's work.

"Wow! That was just like in the *real* rodeo!" Ryan exclaimed.

Daisy smiled ruefully. *Felt* like it, too; her ribs were sore where Ben had grabbed her and she was sure she'd bruised her bottom when he let go. Her legs had been so weak, she'd hit the ground hard. And she hadn't even begun what she'd set out to do today—*rasslin'* calves, as Henry put it.

"What happened to you?" Emily demanded when Daisy hobbled to the branding area. Emily had already started, teamed up with a handsome cowboy named Jesse Winslow, who offered to show Daisy some tricks of the trade.

"Little adventure," Daisy muttered to her friend, indicating with hand signals that she'd fill her in later. Daisy wasn't keen on the entire crew knowing how foolish she'd been.

"Okay, now you just grab on to the rope and lean on this little critter here." The cowboy illustrated the best way to hold down a two-hundred-pound calf that didn't want to be held down, and Daisy tried to follow suit. The trick, it seemed, was to use gravity, a knee on the calf's neck with her partner stretching the back legs out so it couldn't kick. If it came to a tussle between the greenhorns—she and Emily—and the calves, the calves usually won and Jesse, ever patient, would demonstrate again.

Daisy found herself partnered with Brian, a high school senior who'd been helping out at the Rocking Bar S brandings for three years. He manfully took the rear, where he not only had to hold the back legs steady but was exposed to the nastier parts of the process—the branding and castrating. She had to endure the dehorning, ear-notching and vaccinating at her end, arguably less nauseating. But it was all over in about a minute, and the dazed calf was on its feet being shepherded back to the calf corral, soon to be turned in with the cow herd to "mother up." By then, a roper would be dragging the next calf to the fire. And so it went.

Daisy was fascinated. Not only by the smooth, efficient process of roping, throwing and branding, but the good humor and camaraderie of the crew, which ranged from Amanda, an elderly local rancher, through assorted teenagers and friends, to the eight-year-old Rosie Garrick, helping her pal, Ryan, at the calf chute gate. Amanda wielded the branding iron, alongside the ranch owner, Cal Blake—a privilege reserved for the most experienced, Daisy had discovered.

She knew she was going to get a great feature story out of this. She planned to run a pared-down version in the *Times* since most readers, even town dwellers, would be familiar with a relatively common event such as branding. She didn't think she'd mention her near disaster in the cow field in either one.

At noon, someone rang a cowbell, and Henry Hilton

called a halt for what he referred to as "dinner." As far as Daisy could tell, the majority of the calves had been branded and turned back into the field with their mothers. Some cows had actually moved away from the fence to begin grazing quietly.

"So, what happened to you?" Emily asked when they walked to the ranch house to wash up.

Daisy tried to explain and Emily giggled. "You mean you had to be rescued just like those guys who get dumped off bulls at the rodeo?"

"Something like that," Daisy admitted. They strolled across the back lawn of the ranch house toward the trees, where a huge outdoor buffet had been set up in the shade. This must be some of that famous ranch cuisine she'd heard about, Daisy mused. She'd heard that cooks and ranch wives competed to put on the best spread for the branding crew and their helpers. There were tables groaning with salads and rolls, fried chicken, pitchers of lemonade and five-gallon buckets of ice full of beer and cans of iced tea. A half-barrel barbecue pit was already smoking away with grilled meats of various kinds, mostly beef, manned by a Chinese cook in a big white hat that read Only A Fool Argues With The Cook across the front.

"Oh, well, it could've been worse," Emily cheerfully went on. "At least you got rescued by a handsome cowboy."

"You got your eye on Ben Goodstriker, too?" Daisy asked with a smile. Her friend had always been an inveterate flirt and Daisy hadn't missed the looks she'd exchanged with Jesse Winslow over the prostrate calves that morning.

"No. I can see you do, though," she said, giving Daisy a nudge and a little wink.

Daisy ignored her. They loaded their plates and meandered toward the trees, searching for a place to sit down.

If she sat on the ground, she wasn't sure she'd make it up again, but her throwing partner, Brian, produced lawn chairs for her and Emily, then parked himself nearby. They were joined a short while later by Jesse and Young Ben, who Daisy now knew was Ben Longquist, brother of Trevor and Jill. Ben's niece, Laverne, also sat with them, as well as Ryan' and his twin brother, Rosie Garrick and Henry Hilton.

"How you gals holdin' up?" Henry asked before taking a big chunk off a chicken drumstick he held in one gnarled fist. The food was as delicious as it was plentiful.

"Fine." Emily looked at her. "Right, Daisy?" Daisy nodded.

"Well, we're nearly finished up here, so if you gals got other things you'd rather be doin' this afternoon, ain't none of us gonna complain if you decide you've had enough. You've done real well for a coupla greenhorns."

Daisy was relieved. Emily would probably stay, but she wanted to slink off to Tamarack, have a nice, hot bath and nurse her bruises.

"Daisy?" She glanced up. Ben held out her camera, which looked none the worse for wear, despite a few scuff marks on the case.

"Oh, thank you!" She put down her fork and took the camera from him. "What about the hat?"

He shook his head. "Trampled. Looks more like a paper plate from last month's picnic than a hat. Listen," he added in a low voice, "you okay?"

"I'm fine. Thanks." Her voice quavered a little; she kept thinking of what might have happened if he hadn't seen her in that field.

"Hey, Ben!" someone yelled. "You going to the dance next weekend?"

"Guess I have to," he said, then turned his attention to loading his plate.

"Who you goin' with?"

Ben looked up, frowning. "Marie, I suppose."

There was a short lull in conversation while Ben carried his plate of food thirty feet away, to where a clump of cowboys sat under the trees. They were eating silently, as though they were in a bunkhouse, not sitting sociably under the cottonwoods with all the greenhorns, including Daisy and Emily. What had happened between his cousin and Wayne Petrenko hung over the community like a cold fog. No matter how popular or well liked Ben was, Daisy realized, he couldn't escape what was on everyone's minds these days: his cousin had killed a police officer.

"How about you, Emily?" Jesse Winslow broke the awkward silence. "If you don't have a partner, I'd be proud to take you."

Hoots and hollers followed from all the other cowboys Emily had flirted with that morning.

Emily blushed prettily. "Sure, Jesse. I'll look forward to that."

Daisy had a feeling her best friend genuinely liked the big, handsome cowboy who'd shown them how to handle calves that morning.

"Are you going, Daisy?" Nina Blake, a slim woman with a beautiful smile, set two meringue pies on the table to another chorus of appreciative whistles. "I suppose you're covering the dance for the newspaper." Daisy had met Nina briefly when she and Emily had gone into the house to wash up.

"Yes," she said, studying her plate to locate the last forkful of potato salad. "Gordon Bass asked me to go with him."

Ben, Daisy noticed, gave her a long, cool look from his position on the other side of the lawn.

"Who's Gordon?" Emily asked. "Is he that RCMP guy from Glory?"

Daisy nodded. She hadn't actually accepted Bass's invitation yet, but what the heck, everybody else seemed to be making an announcement about their dates for the dance.

"Well," she said, mustering some energy and desperately wanting to change the subject, "this morning doesn't seem very much like what you see at a rodeo. On television, anyway."

"There isn't much about rodeo that relates too closely anymore to what goes on at a modern ranch," Cal Blake commented quietly. Daisy had noted that the ranch owner, a tall, serious-looking man, didn't talk much. But when he did, the cowboys listened.

"Calf ropin' is more like what you seen here today," Henry Hilton agreed, pushing back his hat and producing a toothpick from his shirt pocket. "It sure ain't chasin' down a little calf and knockin' him off his feet."

"What about bronc riding?" Daisy was curious about Ben's event.

"All show," Henry said, nodding toward Ben and Adam Garrick. "Them boys'll tell you. They know all about roughstock, even raise 'em. Why, those horses are more trained athletes than some of the cowboys. They sure as heck know what that little eight-second bell is all about and they're listenin' for it."

"It looks so cruel, though," Daisy continued, thinking she'd make some notes on this when she got in the car. It seemed too formal to take her microcassette recorder out of her pocket and switch it on. "What about that horrible leather strap that's cinched around them?"

"That strap!" Jesse Winslow gazed around the group for support. "Man alive! That strap gets *all* the attention, don't it? That's the bucking strap and it's loose, not tight, and it's lined with lambswool, for cryin' out loud, not barbed wire. It wouldn't put a scratch on your pretty face."

"What's the point of it, then?" Daisy asked stubbornly. "It seems to make the horses buck like crazy."

"That's what it's designed to do," Adam Garrick offered. "If they didn't buck, they'd run blind and probably hurt themselves and the cowboy. Ever notice how the horses quit bucking when the strap's released?" Daisy recalled seeing exactly that on television: the second the strap was released, the horse stopped bucking and looked around for the gate that led out of the ring.

"As a grazing, running animal, a horse's natural instinct is to do anything, including buck and kick, when something touches its vulnerable belly or flanks. That goes back to wild horses getting attacked by wolves or mountain lions. All the strap does is remind them there's something touching them where they don't want to be touched. So they buck."

Emily was admiring the desserts on the buffet table. "Who made that pie? You, Nina? It looks fantastic. So," she challenged the crowd. "Just to get this straight, is there *anything* in the rodeo that's the same as what happens on a ranch?"

"Chuckwagon!" Ryan Webster sang out, to general laughter, holding his hot dog high in the air.

CHAPTER SIXTEEN

"TRY IT, John. J-O-N-N. You might be surprised." Daisy saw Ellin cast a sly look at the teenager, who was hunched over a keyboard at the desk used by Bunny McPhee when she was in. Daisy had decided to send her and Fairlie to the sour gas emission hearings in Glory next week, and Bunny was taking time off to research the issue. Fairlie, as usual, wasn't answering his phone—not that Daisy had any photo assignments for him this week, anyway. He was probably up in the mountains searching for the Lost Lemon Mine.

"Could be the start of a whole new life full of challenge and excitement—hey, Daisy!" Ellin had just noticed her. "How ya doing?"

"Mmm?" Daisy slung her bag down and picked up the spike of messages sitting in the middle of her empty desk. "Any coffee yet?"

"Just made. Ben Goodstriker called yesterday. Twice. Maybe he doesn't know we're closed Monday. Messages were on the machine when I came in this morning. Weren't you waiting to hear from him?"

Daisy nodded, not wanting to appear too enthusiastic. She'd spent most of Sunday in bed, snoozing and nursing her bruises, then had gone to Lethbridge with her parents on Monday. "Thanks."

She glanced at the teenager. "John, I thought you had an exam this morning."

"After lunch. English. No problem," he said, with a cryptic grin at Ellin. "I'll ace it."

"Oh, ho!" Ellin retorted. "Maybe if you change your name, you will."

"Could you develop some pictures for me later this afternoon?" Daisy interrupted. She hoped she had some decent shots of the branding. "If you have time. When are your exams over?"

"Friday. Chemistry."

"So, you got a summer job lined up?"

The teenager turned red, which emphasized his spotty complexion. "N-not yet." Whenever he was put on the spot, John had a slight stammer.

"You want to work here? Full-time? I could probably even give you a bit of a raise."

"S-sure." He threw Ellin a triumphant look. "Reporting?"

"Yeah. I think you could handle more reporting. In fact, why don't you see what you can get on that ball tournament slated for the August long weekend? Find out which teams are entered, who's sponsoring, schedules, whatever. Talk to Bob and see if he's started selling ads for that issue yet. You could be our sports reporter, John. How about it?"

"Gotcha!" The teenager beamed and reached for the phone. "S-so, what's this about n-new ch-challenges if I change my name, Ellin?"

She cracked her gum and returned her attention to the invoice she was typing out. "Luck, Johnny-boy. You ever hear of luck?"

Daisy flipped through the slips of paper until she came to the message from Ben. He'd called just after two and then again at half-past four. It was almost noon now on Tuesday, and she still had her notes from the village council meeting last week to write up. Nothing much there—

grant to this year's Strawberry Social, put on in late June by the Friends of the Library, new streetlights to go up at the campground on the edge of town, vandalism to the flowerpots on Frank Street.

Emily was back in Calgary, full of their branding adventures and thrilled about coming back for the rodeo dance next Saturday. Daisy's father and mother had driven to Blairmore early this morning for a golfing foursome with her aunt and uncle, who were retired and living in the mountain town. The council meeting? Yes, she needed to write that up but she could do it later.

Daisy felt strangely despondent. Restless. And, to be honest, the last thing she felt like right now was a mug of Ellin's coffee.

She dug through her bag and handed John three rolls of film. "These are from the branding, John. There are a couple of other rolls in the darkroom in-box you could print up, too."

"Okay. I'll do them after my exam."

"Fine. No rush." Daisy slung her bag over her shoulder again. "Anything important comes up, Ellin, give me a call. I'm going to run a few errands."

She went to the drugstore on the corner to buy stamps at the Canada Post counter and pick up some vitamins, then headed across the street to the Treasury Branch, where she'd opened an account when she'd first arrived in Tamarack.

When she came out of the Treasury Branch, she paused to find her sunglasses in her bag, briefly checking her appearance in the dark shiny window of the building. At the sound of brakes, she turned.

Ben's pickup was idling at the curb, his dog hanging happily out the open passenger window, barking at her.

"HEY, THERE!" Ben grabbed Dodger. "Settle down, pal." He didn't blame the dog for getting excited....

"Hi!" Daisy stepped up to the window with that little waggle of the fingers, the high school sophomore being propositioned by the town bad boy. Except he just had this beat-up five-year-old Chevy. *She* was the one with the chrome-plated classic convertible.

And she wasn't eighteen.

"I'm taking a run out to the reserve. Want to come?" She put her hand on the door handle right away and Dodger cocked one ear and glanced at him. *Hey...is this allowed, pal?*

"Hold it." He got out and came around to the passenger side. Daisy was grinning like a crazy woman, for some reason—which, he had to admit, he liked. He'd been a little worried after Saturday. She was very quiet when he'd returned her camera at lunch. But she hadn't slacked off after her escapade and, according to Henry, for a greenhorn she'd done a decent job with the calves.

"You don't want to sit with my dog," he advised, grabbing Dodger and tossing him into the truck box.

"I don't mind."

"You mind," he said. He tipped the blanket, lying folded along the top of the seat back and waiting for just this kind of occasion, onto the seat and did his best to ignore the pert shape of her backside as she climbed in.

The truck was tidier than it had been last week when they'd driven Junior to Florence's. Nothing rolling around, not even chew toys or coffee cups. He'd wiped off the dash and the dog drool on the inside of the windows. She'd probably realized that he and Dodger were the main occupants of this vehicle, but he was glad he'd cleaned up, anyway.

"Poor boy!" He saw her look through the rear window while he studied his side mirror, waiting until a Purolator van drove by, his hand resting on the stick shift. Dodger's face was right up against the glass, peering into the cab, eyes bright. Nothing bothered that mutt.

"Yeah, poor dog." Ben saw a woman come out of the Treasury Branch and stare at them. He noted Daisy's smile and tiny wave. "Friend of yours?"

"Janet Parrish," she said. "Emily's mother. She was in the bank when I was there a few minutes ago." The Treasury Branch system was a form of government-backed credit union, unique to Alberta.

"Sure seems interested." Ben observed in his side mirror that the woman continued to gaze after them as they drove away.

Daisy craned her head to peer behind them, then turned to him. "Actually, I've noticed that you seem to attract a lot of attention in this town."

"Me!" He gave her an incredulous look. "I've lived around here all my life. I think she's keeping an eye on *you.*"

"Whatever for?"

"So she can tell your folks you're playing hooky?" He shot her an amused glance. "And maybe who you're playing hooky with?"

"Don't be ridiculous. Who I see is my business!"

"Small towns are nosy places...."

"Speaking of nosy, how's Junior?"

"He's okay." Ben was pondering this simple piece of luck. He hadn't planned to call her again, not after two messages she hadn't returned. Payback for his lousy phone habits?

But he wanted to take her out to the reserve, introduce her to some people. If she was going to continue with this little investigation of hers, he'd let people know that he was backing her. Phoning her to set up this trip was one thing; coming across her on Main Street was better. More natural. "You eat yet?"

She shook her head. "No. I just got to work, actually, but I always have supplies in my bag." She held up her canvas tote. "Granola bars and an apple. You?"

"No. We can pick up a couple of burgers on the way out of town."

"Where are we going?" She didn't seem worried. "Specifically, I mean."

"Maybe back to the crime scene, if you want."

"Oh, yes! I haven't been back since it—well, since it happened. Maybe seeing it again will set my mind at ease about a few things."

"Like?"

"Oh, I don't know." She frowned, as though trying to remember. "I got so many weird impressions that day."

Ben pulled off the highway into the parking lot of his favorite diner. Trixie's wasn't much to look at, with its dented aluminum siding and faded awnings flapping in the wind, but you couldn't beat the fries. There was a lineup at the take-out window, no surprise considering the time of day.

Ben ordered three cheeseburgers—one for Dodger—an order of french fries, one of onion rings and two strawberry shakes, then drove to the side of the parking lot to wait for their order to come up. Nice to see she wasn't one of these gals always on some diet. She even liked strawberry shakes—his favorite.

"So," he began cautiously, "how are you feeling since Saturday?"

"Bruised. Sore. A little wiser." She was smiling.

"About cows?"

"Maybe. I know how to 'rassle' a calf now, too. Didn't know how to do that a week ago."

A black pickup pulled up beside them and Casper got

out. Ben saw Casper's eyes widen when he realized who was in the passenger seat.

"Hey, Ben." He grinned and nodded at Daisy. "How's it goin'?" Dodger jumped up on the side of the truck box and started growling and snapping.

"Hey!" Casper sounded surprised. "Quit that!" Ben opened his door and ordered the dog to be quiet, then slammed it again. Dodger was annoying him lately. It was one thing to be a decent watch dog, quite another to go after people who'd known him since puppyhood.

"Casper, this is Daisy Sutherland. Don't know if you two have met. Daisy? Casper Desjarlais, old pal of mine."

"How do you do?" Daisy said, rather formally.

"Ma'am." Casper acknowledged her greeting and turned nervous eyes to Ben. As usual, Casper looked like he had something to hide. Ben was used to it and never paid him much mind. Florence always said all the Desjarlaises were born shifty. "Where you two off to?"

"Something to eat, then heading to the rez for the afternoon."

"Oh?"

"Daisy wants to take another look at that spot where Arlo was killed. Doesn't think it makes much sense."

"*What* makes much sense?" Casper frowned.

"The circumstances. You know—that the two of them shot each other dead like that." Ben shrugged. "What can I say? She's a reporter. It's her business to poke around."

Casper shook his head. His eyes were bloodshot and his clothes looked as if he'd slept in them.

He wiped his upper lip with the back of his hand. "How's Marie?"

"Doing okay, I guess. She wants to go to the dance next week, says Arlo would've wanted her to."

"I'd be happy to take her." Casper stood straight, squared his shoulders.

"I'm taking her."

"Fine, fine, you take her then," Casper said testily. He leaned on the side of the door, his face close, eyes narrowed. Ben wondered why Casper was ignoring Daisy, after all the big talk in his kitchen a while back. "What about the kid?"

"What about him?"

"He talkin' yet?"

"Not yet." Ben glanced toward the diner, where the orders were displayed on a neon board as they came up. Theirs had just been posted.

"Could be he's messed up for good, eh?"

"He'll be fine, the doc says. Takes time."

"You got to believe that, anyway, eh? Poor kid!" Casper's concern was to his credit. Ben hadn't seen much of him in recent years and had no idea how he felt about Arlo's family. Now he was asking after Marie, giving her money. Just went to show that the unlikeliest guys could have feelings.

"Our stuff's ready." Ben opened the door, smiling at Daisy. "I'll be right back."

"Here." She shoved a handful of cash toward him, which he ignored.

Casper followed him to the pickup window. "I'm worried about you."

"Me?" Ben laughed.

"You don't want to get involved in this—this mess about Arlo and Wayne."

Ben threw three tens on the counter and pocketed his change. "Get a grip, Casper. I'm just humoring her. Keeping her out of trouble. If I don't, she's just going to keep bumbling around here in town and at the reserve, making people mad. Let her do her reporter thing. Doesn't mean squat. Nothing's going to bring Arlo back," he finished bleakly.

"Exactly. What's done is done."

"Hell, I know that. You know that. But *she* doesn't. It's not as if anything I could say would stop her, anyway. I've already tried." For a second or two Ben thought he might mention the box of gallbladders supposedly found in Arlo's truck. He'd heard the news from Morris Jack, not always the most reliable source. Tamarack was a small town. If anything was really happening in the way of on-going poaching activity, someone else was bound to say something, sooner or later. Time enough to fill Casper in when he had some hard facts.

"Flea market doing well?"

"Couldn't be better. Busy time of year."

Ben wouldn't have thought so. It was hardly spring-cleaning season and too early for the fall trip to the dump. Still, flea market folks were nuts about a bargain, so time of year probably made no difference. "I'll be over soon with some of Arlo's stuff."

"You do that. Listen, this Daisy—you got something goin' with her?" Casper hitched up his pants and gave Ben a sweaty grin.

"Nah." Ben loaded up the food, paper bag of burgers and fries in one hand, shakes in a cardboard tray in the other. "City gal. Not my type."

Casper hit Ben lightly on the shoulder and laughed. "Good! Wouldn't want to muscle in on a pal. I might ask her to the dance myself, since you're gonna be tied up with Marie." He winked and Ben had that strange impulse to take a poke at him again. Lucky his hands were full.

"You do that, Casper," he said easily, turning to leave. Should he tell Casper that Daisy was going to the dance with a cop? Nah. Let him find out on his own.

He'd said Daisy wasn't his type. That was for Casper's benefit. Just what *was* his type, Ben wondered as he walked back to the truck. It'd been a long time since he'd been involved with a woman. Two years? At least. Most of his experience to date had been short-term, mainly buckle bunnies. Now, with Arlo getting killed, he had Marie and the kids to look out for, plus Florence to keep an eye on. He didn't have time for a relationship....

"So that's your old pal Casper, huh?" She took her shake as soon as he got in the truck, after tipping Dodger's cheeseburger into the back. She peeled the paper off her straw. "I don't think I like him."

He stared at her. "You and my dog both. Why the hell not?"

She drank some of her milkshake through the straw, then peeked in the paper bag while he started the vehicle. He didn't feel like eating lunch in the parking lot, not with Casper right next to them and all kinds of other folks he knew sitting in their vehicles, no doubt speculating about him and his lunch date.

"No reason." She shrugged. He noticed she'd left her money piled on his dash. "For one thing, I didn't like the way he looked at you."

And at you, Ben thought, signaling left to pull onto the highway. A couple of quarters fell off the pile onto the floor.

"Casper's okay. Talks big but he's a small player." Ben reached for his shake, which Daisy handed him. "He's harmless."

She licked ketchup from her fingers. "Seems like it," she agreed, nodding, "but you can never tell with that type. A lot of resentment there."

"Resentment?" Ben was astonished. "Casper's a happy man. He's got it made here, which is why he never leaves. Big fish in a small pond. Buys here, sells there, some petty crime now and then, nothing he's ever gone to jail over. Friends. Hell, he's even got his own little gang out there

at Pekisko, plays Robin Hood to a bunch of underem-
ployed bow-and-arrow boys.''

''Fun game for someone who's never grown up,'' she
said innocently and, exasperated, he shot her a dirty look.

She held up her hands and laughed. ''Fine. Okay. Forget
it. He's a wonderful guy. Talented, a joy to be around.
You know your friend.'' She took another bite of her
burger. Daisy was right. Casper never *had* grown up. Neither had Arlo.

Ben signaled to pass a logging truck on the narrow road
and as he accelerated, more of her money fell on the floor.
''Put your money away. Lunch is on me.''

She gathered up what was left on the dash, a couple of
loonies and a few quarters, and dropped it in his glove
compartment, in with the DC charger for his cell, a pair
of new cotton work gloves, a Robertson screwdriver and
an unopened cello-pak of triple A batteries.

''So!'' She sucked noisily at her shake and gave him a
bright smile. ''Do I get to meet the chief?''

CHAPTER SEVENTEEN

"I DON'T KNOW." Daisy peered doubtfully into the ditch, riddled with dried mud patches in the bottom—puzzle pieces with clumps of dusty grass growing through. It had been foaming over with muddy water the last time she'd seen it. "Somehow this all seems so different."

Sun baked the back of her neck, and the silence, except for the grasshoppers and the occasional ping of Ben's truck engine as it cooled, was huge. They were deep in a backwoods area of the Pekisko Reserve, which stretched for nearly twelve miles in a narrow valley that ran between the hills bordering Highway 22 and the Livingstone range to the west and north as well as the mountains of the Crowsnest Pass to the south. Her shins were scratched from tramping through saw grass in the ditch and beyond, into the dense alder and willow thickets that lined the road allowance. All they'd found was a rusted-out muffler, a cruddy half-buried woolen sock, two squashed beer cans and a sunfaded ball cap, kid-size, with Calgary Stampeders stitched across the front. Ben had picked it up, knocked some of the mud off and mused aloud, "Some kid's sorry this flew out the window, I'll bet," before tossing it back in the grass.

What had they expected to find? Daisy wasn't sure. Now that she'd driven here with Ben, she was doubly astonished she'd been able to locate this spot on her own, with only John Spears's cryptic directions.

Fifteen feet away, Ben leaned against the front bumper

of his truck with his arms crossed, as though giving her plenty of room to recall her memories of the crime scene. It had been almost a month ago. Who could remember all the details?

"Wayne's car was here," she said, stepping forward and gesturing at the area covered by the cruiser. "And his door was open."

"Passenger door?"

"No, driver's door. There were a couple of cruisers, Mounties who'd already arrived. Here and here and—" She moved up the road and indicated a space across the road, the car that had arrived last "—here, I think."

"Ambulances?"

"There was only one. It left just as I got here." She looked up at Ben, suddenly feeling cold in the afternoon sun. "I knew something wasn't right then. It wasn't speeding. Of course, the road was muddy but they just had their lights on, not the siren. I knew whoever was inside was probably dead. Even if the injuries were minor, I'm sure the ambulance would've been speeding toward the hospital." Glory had the nearest hospital. Pincher Creek had one, too, and Blairmore.

"Either that, or no one was hurt," Ben added.

"Right." Daisy was conscious of the toll this must be taking on him. "Except we know now that wasn't the case. Also, John told me that the code for officer down had gone out on the police radio. He'd heard it."

Ben looked around slowly, as if he was imagining the scene Daisy had described. "Where was Arlo's truck?"

"Right here." Daisy walked to the side of the road where she'd seen the pickup. "The driver's door was open, too."

"What about the canopy? Was it closed?"

Daisy frowned. "I don't remember. I wasn't paying a lot of attention to that. I noticed a few other details, like his upholstery wasn't in the best shape and he had one of those deodorizer things hanging from his rearview mirror.''

Ben smiled grimly. ''See any rifles? Fishing rods? Arlo often carried a .22 in the rack behind the seat. Not that it's legal, but Arlo was known to do it, anyway, especially out in the backcountry like this.''

''That rings a bell, but…'' Daisy shook her head. ''I really couldn't say for sure.''

Ben walked down the road, pausing at the place his cousin's truck had stood. They'd been here for half an hour and hadn't seen one other vehicle. Remote country, to say the least. Daisy wondered who'd stumbled across the crime scene just after dawn that rainy day, who'd called the police. Maybe Wayne had managed to alert his colleagues— but hadn't Bass said he'd died instantaneously?

Daisy joined Ben. ''The ditch was brimful of water. Rain was pelting down. My uncle's car was leaking, and water was getting in the back window.'' She laughed nervously. ''I was worried about that. I swear I can't see how the cops could make out anything in the way of clues that day. Everything was a mess of mud.''

She hesitated. Ben deserved to know everything. He was trying to help her. By bringing her here to the reserve, he was showing the world he didn't think she was crazy— well, not about the shoot-out, anyway. Just associating with her, he was taking a risk in the community. So was she, in a way. The other day, her mother had mentioned that people—some people—were talking about how the Sutherland's daughter seemed to have more sympathy for a cop killer than for one of Tamarack's finest.…

''There was a big puddle right here by Arlo's truck.'' She sketched the area with the toe of her sneaker. The ground was hard-baked now. She swallowed. ''It was…pink.''

"Blood."

"Yes. I distinctly remember that." Daisy's voice was hoarse. "When I got home, I threw up."

Ben's eyes met hers.

"It made me sick."

He nodded. Daisy ached to put her hand on his arm, to comfort him somehow, but she sensed that he wasn't a man who accepted comfort. It was all right for him to take care of everyone else—from his cousin's widow to poor Junior who couldn't talk, to his grandmother up there in the bush when she needed groceries or her wood chopped, to *her* when she stepped into a field full of stressed-out cows—but he steered clear of being on the receiving end of comfort or care.

"I've seen some terrible stuff in this business, Ben, and it never gets any easier," she explained in a low voice. "I have nightmares...." Daisy held her breath. Recalling the pool of bloody water brought back snatches of other crime scenes she'd witnessed, the neglected babies, murdered street people, other horrible images.

Ben stared at her, then at the bone-hard ground in front of the truck. "I guess that would mean Arlo bled quite a bit," he finally said. She was glad he didn't ask about the nightmares. "Possibly even survived for a little while. Maybe he'd gotten out of the truck. Maybe the door was open and he'd fallen out when he was hit." Then he frowned and shook his head. "No, there were no windows broken, beyond the cracks on the windshield, which had probably been there for months. I didn't see any blood in the truck when I picked it up. He must've had the door open or been out of his vehicle altogether when he was hit."

Daisy and Ben pondered this, and Daisy finally spoke. "Which doesn't exactly sound like somebody worried about being arrested."

Unless he didn't know he had anything in his vehicle.

"I don't suppose details like that are mentioned in the police report."

"I haven't seen it yet. It's supposed to come out this week."

"What about the bullet that killed Wayne, the one presumably from Arlo's gun? Or rifle. What kind was it?"

She shook her head. "Gordon Bass wouldn't tell me."

"The cops handed over three fishing rods and two rifles when I picked up the truck," Ben said slowly. "Both registered. One was a .22 single shot and there was a box of ammo in the glove compartment, unopened. No ammo for the .357. I'd be curious to know where his rifles were in the vehicle and what caliber of bullet killed Wayne."

"I'll show you the report when I get it. They're sure taking their time for such a cut-and-dried investigation."

"You sound a little cynical," Ben said.

"Who? Me?" Daisy tried for a laugh but didn't quite succeed. "When you're a reporter, you've got to depend on the police, but it's not always an easy relationship. They don't really trust us and we don't really trust them."

Ben gave her a strange look, and she remembered that she'd told everyone at the spring branding she was going to the dance with Gordon Bass. Ben must think she was a hypocrite of the first order.

"Ben?" She couldn't get sidetracked. "Think about this for a minute. What if Arlo didn't *know* he had that stuff in the truck. That would account for him getting out to meet Wayne. Otherwise, wouldn't he just try to hightail it out of there, maybe lose Wayne on those winding roads?"

"I don't know," Ben muttered. "Wayne knew this country pretty well, too." He stared toward the mountains, then looked at her, and Daisy felt an odd tingling in her toes. She was having a hard time with her feelings about this man, ever since the cow incident. Even before, if she was ruthlessly honest with herself, which she was doing her darnedest not to be. On the one hand, she was aware that she was attracted to him in a way that was—well, the word might be *inappropriate*. Conflict of interest and so forth. On the other hand, she realized how much he was doing to help her. He'd never given the slightest indication that he had any feelings about her at all, beyond a certain annoyance at her questions. She already knew he thought she was an idiot for going into that field on Saturday.

He was doing her a favor. All she *should* feel was straightforward gratitude.

"Maybe it's even simpler than that, Daisy. Maybe there was no box of gallbladders at all."

THE PEKISKO RESERVE, home to 173 souls, was strung out along the Pekisko River, which fed into the Horsethief River south of Tamarack, which, in turn, ran through the town of Glory, twenty-five miles to the northeast. The Horsethief ran into the Bow, and the Bow ran into the South Saskatchewan, and the Saskatchewan drained into Hudson's Bay, at Churchill, Manitoba, many thousands of miles away.

The Catholic church, Saint Jerome's, was on a hillside, set apart from the other reserve buildings, with a small rectory beside it. There were no other churches. Houses were built here and there, wherever the builder had decided to pour footings. There was no zoning to worry about and everyone had a septic tank and a private well.

A store, run by Eunice Weaselfat and her extended family, had a pump outside that served anyone who needed gas, standard grade only. There was a separate pump for diesel. In the ambitious eighties, the band council had started a business selling tax-free gas at reserve pumps, but too few off-reserve customers made the trip several miles out of their way over potholed gravel roads to save five dollars on a fill-up. Plus there'd been no end of trouble employing reliable qualified mechanics, so the service station had fallen into disrepair and now consisted of a large boxlike building set back on a paved lot dotted with dandelions, where band members parked their snowmobiles and RVs in the off season. The gas pumps had long since been removed by the oil company.

Other business ventures had met with more success. A partnership arrangement with another band had led to the Spindrift Moccasin Company, down the road toward Lundbreck, a cooperative venture that produced "genuine" Indian moccasins, made out of factory-tanned steerhide and rabbit fur and decorated with matching leather instep medallions beaded in Taiwan. Some members of the band had private businesses, sometimes with outside partners, guiding and outfitting for hunters and European eco-tourists eager to sample whatever Alberta's Rocky Mountains had to offer. The Rattlesnake Trading Post, another come-hither for tourists, stocked a few dusty crafts, snack foods and sun-faded postcards. One or two houses had signs in their windows boasting *Wir sprechen Deutsches;* whether they did or not, Ben had no idea.

Most folks living on the reserve were either seasonally employed or not at all. Talk of building a casino had never gone far, after the embarrassment with the service station, blamed mostly on the George family. They were a large group who elected the chief every term, it seemed, and ran the band government. Besides, the big money in casinos was over. Who would drive out to Pekisko to gamble? Especially now that any town in Alberta could hold a plebiscite and, if favorable, build its own casino.

Alcohol caused enough trouble without bringing in gambling, too, many said. Besides, there was plenty of government money coming in with welfare and settlement claims. And if the cash tended to stick to the hands of the families that first came in contact with it and didn't always get spread around to all 173 members the way it should, well...that was another story.

All of which, in Ben's opinion, left too many young people with too much time on their hands and either too much money—if they were a George or related to one— or too little. Both ways spelled trouble.

CHIEF WINSTON GEORGE and his wife, Doris, lived in a prefab, what most folks called a double-wide trailer but what was known in the newly image-conscious industry as a "manufactured home." The sorry-looking lawn, sparse and dry, was fringed with native perennials, mock orange, buckbrush and wild sage. A bed of hot-pink petunias right in front of the house under the picture window struck a discordant note, Daisy thought. There were two SUVs in the driveway, as well as a late-model pickup.

Chief George answered the door in response to Ben's knock. He was a tall handsome man in his sixties, with a shock of white hair and a spreading belly that did nothing to undermine the immediate impression of good sense and awesome physical strength. Daisy noted his hands, the size of baseball mitts. He glanced at her when he first opened the door, a look intended to sum her up instantly.

"Ben! Good to see you, son. Come in, come in." The chief held the door wide, and Ben and Daisy stepped inside. The living room was dominated by a large television revealing an afternoon talk show, muted, in one corner, surrounded by a matched living room set, chesterfield and two chairs plus a recliner, all in an overstuffed style popular about ten years before.

"Chief George, this is Daisy Sutherland," Ben said at the door and the chief nodded pleasantly. No indication that he'd complained to her father about her....

Daisy offered her hand. "I'm pleased to finally meet

you, sir. My father speaks highly of you.'' The chief took her hand in a brief, warm clasp, but Daisy didn't miss the daggerlike look he shot at Ben.

"Daisy and I are out for a drive this afternoon," Ben said, appearing somewhat ill at ease. "I'm introducing her to a few people and showing her around the district as she's relatively new.''

"Grew up in town, though, didn't you?" the chief, broke in, turning to her. "That's not far.''

"Yes. But I haven't lived here since high school.''

"Long time ago, eh?" Chief George winked at Ben. "Maybe six or seven years?''

At least he'd gotten her age right.

"Yes, but I've never been out here before," Daisy went on doggedly. Which wasn't entirely true... "Well, not since—''

"Daisy's been looking into that incident with Arlo and Wayne," Ben interrupted. "She wants to do more of an in-depth write-up for the paper.''

"So I understand. Matter of fact, I've been meaning to return your calls, but I've been caught up with one thing and another—band business, you know. This is a busy time of year," he finished blandly.

Somehow she didn't believe a word he said. How busy could it be if the chief had time for TV afternoons with Maury Povich? He'd been avoiding her. He'd complained to her father. He hoped she'd just go away.

"You need more, you'll have to talk to the RCMP. They're in charge of that particular business," he continued, then addressed Ben directly. "You wanted to see me about something, son?''

The change of subject was as chilly as the air-conditioning which, until now, had felt very welcome.

"As a matter of fact, I did.'' Ben shifted his weight and

turned to her. "Uh, Daisy, do you mind waiting for me in the truck? I'll just be a minute."

Daisy knew why he'd sent her out; the chief might speak more freely to Ben than he would when Daisy was there. The request made sense. It was an irritating fact of life around here that no one wanted to talk to her. But when Ben returned to the truck ten minutes later, he didn't volunteer anything about what he and the chief had discussed.

And that didn't make any sense at all.

CHAPTER EIGHTEEN

BEN DROPPED HER OFF at the *Times* just after four and Daisy finished up her notes from last week's village council meeting by six. She'd left space for council news and, with her father's editorial, which he'd put on her desk, that week's edition was complete, including the new "Police News" column, which detailed various B and Es in the district, speeding tickets issued, public mischief, drunk driving arrests and the like. Daisy wasn't sure what her dad would think of *that* when he saw it, but in her view, she was hardly cutting new ground, considering the number of weeklies that ran similar features. Plus it was a lively addition to the *Times.*

Ad lineage was down, which was slightly worrying although the *Times* had a more than healthy split of around sixty-five percent advertising to thirty-five of editorial, better than the industry average of sixty-forty. Owen Sutherland was still nominally in charge of sales, but his longtime ad manager, Bob Roberts, who worked from home, did most of the selling these days. Bob hadn't mentioned anything to her about losing any advertisers.

Roberts did display ads for his clients. Ellin, as Daisy's newly promoted production manager, was in charge of the classifieds and oversaw the layout generally. Despite her airhead impression, she always did a good, careful job.

Daisy shrugged. Maybe a midsummer drop in advertising was normal. She'd ask her father. Tomorrow morning, she'd take the computer disk to Lethbridge, where the paper would be printed, with a courier delivering the completed product in the afternoon. By noon on Thursday, most of the good citizens of Tamarack would have copies of the *Times* in their hands, hot off the press.

Wednesday was really a better day for a weekly newspaper to come out—to take advantage of upcoming weekend sales and community events—but the *Tamarack Times* had always been published on Thursday and…well, that was just the way it was.

Daisy glanced at Owen Sutherland's editorial, the usual hearty boosterism, this time in the form of support for the proposed municipal park on the edge of town. The cautious rider, of course, was the need to secure plenty of government money up front to support the project. Daisy knew next week's paper would have a full complement of letters for and against, with queries as to whether RVs would be allowed to overnight in the park and how council intended to deal with the teenage vandalism that would ensue, not to mention bonfires and noisy parties with underage drinking.

On the way home, Daisy swung by the small house behind the hardware store where Wayne Petrenko had lived. Even though she hadn't really considered the dwelling for herself, she couldn't help a twinge of disappointment when she noticed that it was occupied already, by a family with children.

When she saw Albert Valentine, owner of both the hardware and the bungalow behind it, in the yard, Daisy pulled over and stopped. The small building, white-painted with red trim, was set well back on the lot behind a picket fence and tidy caragana hedge. It was barely recognizable as the run-down cottage with overgrown bushes and peeling paint Daisy remembered when the house had been occupied by Miss Birch.

"I see you've got a new tenant," she said, getting out

of the convertible. Daisy and Emily had been on the high school track team with Mr. Valentine's granddaughter, Lorna Gagliardi.

Mr. Valentine looked over his shoulder, as though to check on the accuracy of her statement. "Yes. Yes, I have. Say, Daisy," he said quickly, "you weren't thinking of the little house for yourself, were you?"

"Oh, no!" Daisy waved a hand nonchalantly. "I'm thinking more along the lines of an apartment or something. Of course, I'm welcome to stay at Mom and Dad's as long as I like but—" She raised one shoulder in a shrug.

He joined her at the curb. "Nice young woman," he said, nodding toward the house. "Two kids. No man around to give her a hand, so I stopped by to help put up the swing set for the youngsters."

"It was—such a shock, wasn't it, that Wayne was killed like that? How long had he rented from you?"

"Terrible business." Mr. Valentine briefly raised both hands, palms up. "Just under a year. Good tenant, too, always paid on time." Mr. Valentine gave her a sad look. "I knew Wayne ever since the Petrenkos adopted him, little gaffer of two or three. He was hell on wheels back then. Can't say as I always expected he'd turn out to be such a fine citizen."

"Didn't he work in your store once?" Daisy asked. "In high school?"

"You remember that, do you?" Mr. Valentine rubbed his whiskered chin thoughtfully. "Oh, my, yes. I had to let him go not long after I hired him. Such a shame…"

"What happened?" Sometimes straightforward was the best way, Daisy had found.

The hardware man glanced back over the fence. There was no one in sight. "I don't mind telling you, since your family's so close to the Petrenkos and of course his dad knew. Maybe your dad, too, for all I—"

"Knew what?"

"Why that some of the cash had gone missing. I think young Wayne was dipping his fingers into the till to tide himself over until payday. I had a chat with Bill and it was all made good, but I couldn't keep Wayne on. Heavens, no." Mr. Valentine shook his head. "It would've sent the wrong signal to the rest of my employees, wouldn't it?"

"Stealing?"

"Borrowing is more what he thought it was, I'm sure. But, yes, you're right, an old-fashioned person like myself might call it stealing." Mr. Valentine wiped his hands carefully with a rag he was carrying, then stuffed it in the back pocket of his overalls. He beamed suddenly. "But, it all came out okay, didn't it? Eh? Fine member of the Royal Canadian Mounted Police in the end. Couldn't ask for more."

Daisy surveyed the yard, the big cottonwood with the tattered rope swing hanging from a heavy branch that had been crudely sawn off and left to weather. She had a sudden feeling about the place that sent a shiver down her spine. "He must've been lonely here, all by himself."

"I don't believe he was. He had plenty of visitors. Maybe a few too many, if you know what I mean—" Daisy didn't "—but there was never any trouble. A landlord like myself hates to see trouble around his place but you're not going to see trouble when you rent to a policeman, are you?"

"Of course not." Daisy opened the door of the convertible. "How's Lorna doing these days?"

"Fine, fine! She's married and has two little boys. A nurse, married to a doctor. She lives in Red Deer."

"That's wonderful. Say hello to Mrs. Valentine for me, will you?" Daisy got in the car, feeling vaguely depressed. All her school friends, except Emily, it seemed, were married and mothers already. Or, they had fabulous careers and lived far away....

"Will do, Daisy. And Daisy—" He came closer, leaning on the window frame. "I'll keep an eye out. There aren't many apartments in town. I would've mentioned the little house before but I never thought you were serious about staying. There's not much in Tamarack for a young woman like yourself, my dear. A town of loose ends and dead ends, the missus likes to say, but then she's always pined for back East where she came from. So, when that young woman happened along with the two youngsters..."

"No, no, the house would've been too big anyway. Thanks for considering me, though." She smiled and waved as she drove away.

Fingers in the till. Too many visitors of the wrong kind. Living in this out-of-the-way forgotten little house in the middle of downtown, all by himself.

Was there a woman in Constable Petrenko's life? Daisy had never heard of one. Still, she had no doubt he was the type who'd considered himself a red-blooded, macho type, as most cops did. There'd been local stories going all the way back to high school....

Which reminded her of Gordon Bass. As soon as she got home, she'd phone and accept his invitation. No one else had asked her; she wasn't counting the garbled message on the *Times*'s answering machine from Ben's friend, Casper, which she'd accidentally deleted before she'd realized he was inviting her to the dance, too.

Suddenly Gordon Bass didn't look so bad. Besides, who knew what she might be able to winkle out of him if she managed to catch him in an off-duty moment?

Did the Gordon Basses of the world *have* off-duty moments?

THE BENEFIT DANCE was being held on the outskirts of town, in the clubhouse at the new nine-hole golf course, a recent addition to the town amenities and another huge source of civic pride, Daisy had discovered. Her dad had a standing eight-fifteen tee-off every morning at the Mountain Pines Golf Club, unless he'd arranged a date with a buddy at an eighteen-hole course somewhere else in the district, say Glory or Blairmore.

Daisy had told Bass that they could meet at the clubhouse, since it was hardly a real date, but he insisted on picking her up at her parents' house, anyway.

Marian Sutherland seemed to think it *was*. She began to glow as soon as Bass showed up on the doorstep.

"Now don't forget to give our check to whoever's in charge of collecting for the junior rodeo," she reminded her daughter as Daisy slipped a light cardigan over the sleeveless sundress she'd decided to wear, lacking suitable western garb. Daisy had no doubt Emily would show up in full cowgirl plumage. "Lucas Yellowfly, isn't it?"

"Yes. Thanks, Mom." Daisy took the check for one hundred dollars, which the Sutherlands were donating to A Good Cause, and kissed her mother on the cheek. The Sutherlands were going to a retirement party for a local dentist, or, Daisy knew, they'd have gone to the dance themselves.

"Have fun, you two!" Marian closed the door behind them, positively twinkling. Son-in-law material—her mother's mental forecast was woefully transparent.

Daisy was a little embarrassed, but apparently Gordon Bass was the type of man who expected every woman with an eligible daughter to feel that way. He didn't seem to notice anything unusual.

"You're looking very pretty this evening, Daisy," Bass said as he started his vehicle, a late-model Nissan Pathfinder. "My compliments."

"I'll call you Gordon instead of Staff Sergeant Bass

because this is a social occasion,'' Daisy said, wanting to be really clear with the persistent RCMP officer. "As I said, this isn't a real date. I'm working."

"Gotcha!" he said with a smile and a wink.

"Allow me to say that you're looking quite unpolice-manlike yourself," she added, smiling back. "And that *is* a compliment." Indeed, in a dress shirt, black jeans and hand-tooled cowboy boots, Gordon Bass was a very attractive man.

Excellent. She hoped he'd have lots of willing partners this evening because Daisy had a job to do. Notes, quotes. Pictures to take. Duncan Fairlie had told her he couldn't make the rodeo dance, due to some mysterious business he had in Calgary. Luckily, Daisy enjoyed taking photos. On dailies, photographers were an entirely separate breed from reporters. Not so on weeklies. Duncan Fairlie was turning out to be practically part-time, anyway, with all the days he booked off. Now John Spears was on the payroll full-time for the summer and Bunny McPhee had been bumped up, albeit reluctantly, from part-time society reporter to nearly full-time regular reporter. It helped, too, that her dad was doing editorials again. Daisy felt she was getting close to a regular staff for a weekly paper. All she needed was an assistant for Ellin, and she intended to hire one temporarily from the pool of high school students out for the summer.

The dance was scheduled to start at half past nine, but the parking lot was already crowded when they arrived, ten minutes early. Music and laughter wafted out of the building, the doors of which stood wide open. The sun had gone down half an hour before, but the evening air still held the day's heat.

"Hi there, Gordie!" A good-looking blonde in tight jeans and a sequined top greeted Bass as they went up the steps. She waved before disappearing into the dim interior. Several smokers lounged at the top of the steps.

Gordie?

"Lonny Harris," Bass said in response to Daisy's raised eyebrow.

"Friend of yours?" Looked like there'd be no trouble palming off the handsome RCMP officer…

"She's a waitress at Wiley's. I've had a few beers there," he said with an easy grin, dropping two tickets in front of a vivacious auburn-haired woman at the entrance desk. "How's business, Virginia?"

"Excellent! Nice to see you, Gordon. And you must be Daisy Sutherland." The woman offered her hand and Daisy shook it briefly. "I'm Virginia Yellowfly. Lucas has me on cash tonight." She leaned forward with a smile and said in a low voice, "We've been *really* busy."

Daisy rummaged in her bag and found her mother's check. "Here's a donation from my parents. They're at Dr. Warshawski's retirement party."

Daisy got Virginia to pose for a picture, dropping the check through the slot of a locked metal cash box. It was positioned on the table next to several small piles of fives and tens, as well as an ice cream bucket full of loonies and toonies. Tickets to the dance were ten dollars each, almost straight profit. The hall, Daisy knew, had been donated and she'd heard that the band, the Sheep Creek Rovers from Glory, were performing for a minimal fee. "I think we'll have a sell-out crowd. Adam and Lucas are going to be very pleased. Ben, too."

"Is he here?" Daisy ventured casually, not sure why she asked. She *knew* he'd be here.

"I saw him earlier." Virginia looked over her shoulder, through the wide doorway into the hall behind her. "Marie's here, too, and Laverne, Marie's daughter. This whole small-fry rodeo was a Goodstriker idea, you know, partly because Laverne is such a great little rodeo gal. The news about her dad was so—so *shocking*." Virginia frowned.

"Wasn't it?" Daisy would have asked a few questions if Gordon Bass hadn't been hovering. "I've seen the girl in action. She's very good." Which reminded Daisy to interview Laverne for a human interest piece on the upcoming junior rodeo.

She was aware of Gordon's hand on her elbow as they moved into the hall. Whether it was because folks knew he was a cop or because he had such a prepossessing air, the crowd tended to make way for them. She wasn't complaining.

Daisy snapped a few more pictures once they got inside, using her recorder to tape the names of the people she photographed.

People, Daisy—she could hear her dad now—a weekly newspaper is about *people.*

And speaking of people… Where was Ben?

CHAPTER NINETEEN

SHE TURNED TO BASS. "I'm going to go up near the stage to get a few shots of the band."

He waved her off, already talking to one of the high school teachers, and Daisy skirted the crowd, taking photos as she went. She saw Casper and smiled in what she hoped was a noncommittal, friendly manner. How weird was that, asking her out via the *Times*'s answering machine? And totally unexpected after he'd ignored her at the diner a few hours earlier. Fortunately he seemed tied up, busy with a group of native youths, probably in their late teens or early twenties, dressed in buckskin and beads. Presumably the "Robin Hood gang" Ben had mentioned. She waved to Mr. Valentine, who was there with his wife.

On stage, the Sheep Creek Rovers—two guitars, fiddle, drums and keyboard—were tuning up, getting ready for the evening's performance. Canned music played on the club sound system, intermittently audible over the laughter, the conversation, the clink of glasses. The bar was already doing a raging business.

Daisy got a few pictures of the musicians and then turned to scan the crowd. Her plan was to do a candid photo montage for the centerfold of next week's paper.

"Daisy!"

Emily approached, dragging her date behind her. She wore a cleavage-revealing peasant blouse topped with a bright embroidered vest, a wide-cut denim skirt and high heels. Daisy guessed Emily had decided the high heels worked better with the outfit than cowboy boots.

"You remember Jesse?"

"You bet I do. Hold it!" Daisy got a quick picture of her and Jesse Winslow, handsome in a typical cowboy way—big hat, fancy, western-yoked shirt, jeans, boots and a rodeo-style belt buckle the size of a satellite dish.

"How could I forget someone who introduced me to my very first calf, close-up and personal?"

The tall cowboy grinned.

"That outfit's terrific, Em," Daisy continued. "Very western."

Her friend glanced down at her full skirt and wiggled her hips a little. "I know," she said, with typical Emily Parrish modesty. "So, where's your man?"

"My man?" For a minute, Daisy didn't have a clue what she meant.

"Your cop. Didn't you come with the staff sergeant from Glory? Or did you decide to chase down Ben Goodstriker, after all?"

A male throat was cleared nearby. "Chase down Ben Goodstriker?"

Ben was at her elbow and must've heard every word!

"For a picture!" Emily blurted, thinking a whole lot quicker, thank goodness, than Daisy was. "Good thing you're here. Come on, Daisy. Get one of all three of us."

Daisy dutifully snapped Emily between the two men, hoping her cheeks didn't look as fiery as they felt.

There was a garbled announcement over the sound system, and the band played a crashing introductory chord and then swung straight into their first tune of the evening. Emily and her date disappeared onto the dance floor, leaving Daisy and Ben standing near the stage.

"You wanted a picture of me?" He sounded skeptical.

"Of course." Daisy was having a hard time meeting his

eyes. "You're one of the main organizers of this event, aren't you? That makes you news," she finished lamely. In an effort to change the subject, she asked, "Where's Marie?"

"She's here." He glanced around the room. "Somewhere. She came with Laverne and a friend."

"Laverne? I thought *you* were bringing her."

"That was the plan. But it turned out she'd already decided to go with Ed Sawchuk."

"Her boss?"

Ben nodded. "He's been good to her since Arlo died. Helped out a lot. He drove her and the girls in."

Good to her. Daisy digested that one, feeling awkward standing there alone with Ben when everyone else seemed to be dancing. Maybe she should move along, too....

"Here you are!" Gordon Bass emerged from the crowd on the dance floor and touched Daisy's shoulder. "Ready to dance?" He gave Ben a hard look, which Ben returned, Daisy noticed.

Hard to believe, considering how exasperating she found him, but she was actually relieved to see Bass. As she followed him onto the dance floor, though, she couldn't help feeling she'd missed an opportunity. She should've asked Ben to dance. Why not? Instead, she'd been what her father would've called "miss-ish" and had gone completely stiff, like a stick of last summer's chewing gum. Ben remained leaning against the wall, watching her. She wished he wouldn't.

Gordon spun her in a fancy turn and ended up with his back between Daisy and the stage, blocking her view. Deliberate? So Marie had declined to accompany Ben and he had arrived on his own. Gordon whirled her again, and she spotted the blonde who'd spoken to him earlier heading Ben's way. Daisy didn't think Ben would be alone for long.

As VIRGINIA YELLOWFLY had anticipated, the dance was a roaring success. Besides Tamarack residents, Daisy saw townsfolk she recognized from Glory and many from the Pekisko Reserve.

She saw Henry J. Hilton sitting at the side of the dance floor with a pretty woman who, Emily told her, was the Blakes' nanny, a woman from the Philippines who'd been Nina Blake's nanny when she was a girl and who was the light of Henry Hilton's life. Letty didn't dance, so Henry happily ignored one polka after another, content to sit beside his lady love. Daisy thought they made a sweet pair. She spotted Adam Garrick dancing with a young woman she didn't recognize—Jill Longquist, Emily informed her—and Daisy wondered if she owned the black horse Ben was training.

She'd lost track of Ben during the first hectic half hour of the dance, then he suddenly appeared—no Lonny Harris in tow—just as she'd finished dancing with Jesse, while Emily danced with another cowboy she'd flirted with at the spring branding. Emily spread her favors around; it was a cardinal rule of hers. Daisy'd lost track of Gordon Bass again, but that was not weighing heavily on her mind.

"Dance?" Ben held out one hand.

Daisy hesitated briefly. Then, responding to the challenge in his eyes, she moved forward. As easy as that. She held her breath as she adjusted her steps to his. Had she even touched him before now? You could hardly count the madcap rescue on Saturday. Now she was dancing with him, excruciatingly conscious of his right arm around her, his hand holding hers. He was a good dancer but she hadn't expected less. Emily maintained that all cowboys were good dancers, and Emily, at least, possessed enough experience to make generalizations.

"I've got things to say to you," Ben said quietly.

"Things?" *Omigod.* Daisy felt faint. It was hot in the clubhouse, even with the doors open.

Ben glanced down. "I've been hearing this and that around town."

"About you and me?"

He looked bewildered and she could have kicked herself. "You and *me?*"

"Oh, never mind! It's just that my mother told me she's been hearing some gossip."

Ben frowned, then gazed over her head and cleared his throat. "No, it's got to do with what was in the back of Arlo's truck."

"Oops, sorry!" Ellin Brodie and her partner, a red-faced, balding young man who worked at the co-op store in Glory, careened into Daisy on the crowded floor, pitching her heavily against Ben. She felt his arm tighten around her shoulders as he steadied her and then, as quickly, loosen as she regained her balance.

Ri-ight! Here she was thinking *romantic* and he was being polite by dancing one dance with her, maybe trying to work in some business because he didn't know what else to talk to her about.

Well, at least the incident had given her a chance to recover from her conversational gaffe. Before Ben could continue, the music wound down and Gordon popped up in front of them. "I'm back. My date, my dance, right?"

Daisy was prepared to argue the point, but Ben nodded quickly and relinquished her hand. He disappeared into the crowd.

TEN MINUTES LATER, right after someone had made an announcement about a car in the parking lot with its lights on, the power went out.

There were squeals and then laughter when someone shouted, "Hey, you were supposed to turn off your *car* lights!'' The drummer banged out a roll and there was more laughter. The lights came back on, as if on cue, and a young man tapped Gordon on the shoulder and the two of them left. Bass returned a few minutes later. ''Somebody ripped off the cash box while the lights were out,'' he told her grimly. ''I'm going to check into this. Do you mind?''

''Of course not! Can I come with you?''

''There's no story here, Daisy,'' he said firmly. ''The cash box has already been found. I think it's a prank.'' He strode in the direction of the outer corridor, where Virginia had been stationed earlier.

Gordon Bass wasn't the editor of the *Times*—she was. Prank or robbery, when something happened in this town, it *was* a story. Daisy tore after him, but at the door she was hailed by Mr. Valentine.

''Daisy! I've run into a lead on an apartment,'' he said, putting his hand on her arm. Gordon Bass had disappeared.

''Oh?''

''Upstairs over Len's butcher shop on Main Street. It's not big but it would probably do.''

''Er, thanks,'' she said, with a longing glance in the direction Bass had taken. ''I'll look into it next week.'' An apartment over a butcher shop wasn't really what she'd been hoping for.

''A word to the wise, my dear,'' Mr. Valentine went on, coming closer and lowering his voice. ''I see you've been dancing with Ben Goodstriker.''

Daisy's eyes narrowed. ''Yes, I have. He's an excellent dancer.''

''That may be,'' Mr. Valentine went on confidentially, ''That may well be. I do feel, though, that I've got a duty to warn you that some folks in town might be taking your, er, friendship the wrong way. There's been quite some talk about you digging into this business between his cousin and Constable Petrenko, eh?''

Daisy dearly wanted to tell him to butt out, but she was too polite. After all, she'd known him her whole life.

''D'y'see what I'm getting at?''

Daisy shook her head. ''I'm afraid I don't, Mr. Valentine.''

''It's just that it doesn't *look* good, if you know what I mean. Now, I've got nothing against the Goodstriker family in general, although I have to admit I never thought much of the deceased.''

Daisy sighed, resigned to hearing him out. Now she'd never get anything on the so-called prank. Gordon Bass certainly wouldn't supply her with details.

''You should be aware of what people in town are saying. For your parents' sake.'' He beamed. ''That's all, my dear. Now you go ahead and enjoy the dance!''

Daisy hurried away, but before she reached the end of the hall, Bass reappeared, striding toward her. ''I'd like to catch whoever thought it was funny to flip the main switch and then grab the cash box. Poor Virginia! She was having fits that all the profits from the dance were gone.''

''Who found it?''

''Monty Watkins, the young fellow who came to get me.''

''Where?''

''In the kitchen, sitting on the counter by the coffee machine. It doesn't seem to have been tampered with. Somebody's idea of a joke. Don't quote me, it's hardly news. Okay, now where were we?''

They'd come to the door, and Daisy saw Mr. Valentine smile at Bass and wink approvingly.

So a full-of-himself RCMP staff sergeant was preferable to a community-minded ex-rodeo rider who happened to be related to an alleged murderer....

Or was it because Gordon Bass was white?

"DAISY!" Emily grabbed Gordon's sleeve. "Hurry, you two, they're getting up a square dance and we need more couples."

"I've never square-danced in my life!"

"You just follow what everyone else does," Gordon said. "Nothing to it." Daisy would have guessed he'd never square-danced in his life, either, but would he admit it?

They joined Emily, Jesse and an older couple Daisy didn't know. The band was playing a medley of square dance tunes, old conkers like "Turkey in the Straw" and "Little Brown Jug."

"We need one more couple," Emily announced, ever the organizer, then started waving frantically at someone in the crowd.

Ben and Lonny Harris joined the circle. Daisy thought Ben was as surprised as she was. And that *woman*—she was everywhere! Shouldn't Ben be spending some time with his cousin's widow? Daisy hadn't seen her on the dance floor, but that was understandable. Even though Arlo had been behind the kiddie rodeo idea, Marie might well have believed it was too soon after his death to be dancing.

Daisy felt a surge of energy. Maybe she *could* square-dance, after all. How hard could it be?

"All right, folks! Circle to the left, then circle to the right…"

Daisy was between Gordon and Jesse. That call was easy enough to follow. At the end of the maneuver, Ben and Lonny were opposite each other.

"Swing your partner, couples promenade—"

Daisy linked arms with Gordon, then, watching the others carefully, advanced to link arms with Ben.

"Know what you're doing?" he murmured.

"No. Do you?" she retorted, holding tight as they continued around the circle.

His hip brushed hers. "Dance-wise, yes."

What was *that* supposed to mean? Now she was paired with Ben while his partner stood on the opposite side with Gordon as the other couples changed places.

"Chief George tells me a few of the young guys on the reserve seem to have a lot of money lately," Ben said in a low voice, leaning toward her while they marked time by clapping lightly.

"Oh?"

"I asked if he'd heard anything about poaching. No sign of it on the reserve, he says. Some illegal hunting, maybe. Small stuff."

"For cash?"

"Poaching the odd animal out of season would only be for food. A deer or an elk, and no one's going to pay much for that."

"And no one's going to shoot black bears for the barbecue."

"Exactly."

"Where else would they get money? Are they working?"

"No. A few odd jobs for Casper Desjarlais, the chief says. There's reserve money, too, of course, but that's a sensitive subject with the chief."

"Sensitive? Why?" Daisy found it odd, carrying on a conversation like this with Ben while trying to pay attention to the dance moves.

At that moment the caller sang out something else that sounded quite complicated and Daisy got thoroughly mixed up, stumbling around as helpful hands tried to put her right. By the time she got sorted out, she was on the other side of the circle, paired with Gordon again.

They performed some kind of mixed-up turn in the middle, then there was a shout and the lights went off again. Oh, for Pete's sake!

Someone had closed the outside doors, and this time the room was pitch-black. She heard Gordon swear. Pranksters? This was getting ridiculous. Daisy held her hands high so she wouldn't bump into people and began to edge toward where she thought the wall was, where she'd left her bag with her camera. She'd lost interest in square dancing. Dancing of any kind. In fact, she was feeling slightly claustrophobic....

"Oops, sorry!" She ran into someone and before she could step back she felt strong hands grip her shoulders.

Then someone's mouth was on hers.

Omigod! Daisy's first impulse, which was to scream, instantly gave way to something even scarier.

She knew who this was—she *knew*. And all she wanted to do was kiss him back.

CHAPTER TWENTY

DAISY WENT UP on tiptoe as an arm slid around her shoulders and a hand slid up behind her nape to hold her head angled to his. The magic lasted ten, twelve, perhaps fifteen seconds, and by the time she'd made up her mind to put her arms around him, too, he'd pushed her away and was gone.

Ben!

She reached for him but only succeeded in grabbing someone else's shirt—Jesse's?—and let it go again. She wanted to call out but managed to restrain herself, pressing her lips together, still feeling the salt-sweet sting of his mouth on hers.

Then the lights came on and the lead singer made some wisecrack, causing the crowd to break into laughter. When Gordon returned, she was standing at the side of the stage, her camera bag slung over her shoulder, her brain still whirling.

"Caught him!" he exulted, his eyes alight. "Alan Poundmaker from the reserve. He and a couple of his pals. I'm going to charge them with mischief."

"Oh, Gordon! Why would you? They're just kids fooling around."

"Kids? Alan's nineteen. Old enough to know better. Grabbing that cash box was no joke, even if they didn't take anything." He looked around the room, his gaze lingering on the buffet table that had been set up just before the lights went off. A committee organized by Lucas Yellowfly had provided sandwiches and cake for the function. "So—anything happen while I was gone?"

ON MONDAY Daisy left Tamarack just after one, intending to catch Laverne and Marie before they went to Laverne's dance class. A talented girl. Dancer as well as barrel racer and roper and, according to her mother, straight A student, as well.

Daisy had tried Ben's number, too, not quite sure what she was going to say to him. She got a wrong number once, and then, as usual, his phone rang and rang. No answer. As she drove by, she studied his house. His pickup wasn't there. Since the dance, she'd thought of very little other than the way he'd kissed her and disappeared. She'd searched for him at the buffet, then Casper Desjarlais had asked her to dance, saying he'd seen Ben leave just after the lights went out the second time.

After he'd kissed her.

She'd agreed to one dance with Casper. After all, he was kind enough not to mention that she hadn't even responded to his invitation. Besides, she wanted to ask Casper what he knew about illegal hunting in the area. He astonished her by flat-out suggesting she should ask her boyfriend—by whom she realized he meant Ben—who could tell her a thing or two about poaching.

Daisy intended to get to the bottom of that, too.

She pulled around by Marie's trailer, catching a glimpse, through the trees that separated the two residences, of another vehicle just driving away. Black and shiny, sun on chrome. Probably the annoying Casper… Thank heavens he was leaving.

Marie seemed more cheerful than Daisy remembered. They'd spoken briefly at the dance, when she'd introduced Daisy to her boss, and then, this morning, on the phone.

"Do you mind if I don't join you?" She indicated that

Daisy should sit at the kitchen table and went to the hallway to rap sharply on a door. "I need to take a shower before we leave. Laverne? Ms. Sutherland's here."

"Not at all." Daisy accepted a glass of lemonade that Marie poured from a jug in the refrigerator. She set another glass down opposite Daisy, presumably for the girl.

"Where's Junior?"

Marie shot her a surprised glance, then put the jug back in the fridge. "Around somewhere." She shook her head. "He's so quiet. I'm worried. The doctor says it's just the shock...." Marie's eyes met hers, tortured. "Arlo's death and all."

"Of course." Daisy paused. "Do you think that bullying incident has anything to do with it?"

Marie shrugged. "Who knows? Maybe. Maybe that horse he saw Ben put down, too? He's like a shadow these days. Doesn't want to play with his friends. Not even Stevie out at the reserve, who's been his best friend since kindergarten. He hasn't been to Stevie's place since his birthday last month—"

"Stevie's birthday?"

"No, Junior's." Marie wearily pushed her thick black hair from her face. "Junior turned nine the day before his father died."

"I'm sorry," Daisy said. "I didn't know that."

"He won't hang around when visitors come," Marie said with a sigh. "Just wants to go up in the hills and stay at Granny's."

"I met her with Ben once. She seems very pleasant."

"Pleasant?" Marie snorted. "Not a word I'd pick. But then we've never been very close. She's good to the kids, I'll give her that. And there are new pups up there. I think that's the main attraction right now. Junior's crazy about animals, just like Arlo."

Laverne appeared in the kitchen, a slight version of her

mother, paler skin but eyes just as huge and dark. Her shoulder-length hair hung loose and she looked as though she'd just woken up. Like Marie, she wore a haunted, haggard expression.

"Is this a good time to talk, Laverne?"

"Sure," the girl said quietly.

"Please call me Daisy." Daisy had noted that Marie had referred to her more formally. "And I'd really like to get a couple of pictures of you with your horse—what's his name?"

The girl brightened. "Brownie," she said.

"How old is he?"

"Eighteen. He's old for barrels, but I've had him since I was seven." Her dark eyes were soft. "He's my pal. I couldn't ever get another pony while I've got Brownie."

Her mother smiled. "Not much chance of that on our budget, honey. Old Brownie's part of the family, isn't he?" The girl nodded. "You be ready in forty-five minutes—is that long enough?"

Marie addressed the question to Daisy, who glanced at her watch. "No problem. We'll just talk a little about Laverne's rodeo experience and her plans for the future, and then we'll get a few shots of Brownie to go with the story. Half an hour, tops." She was dying to know where Ben was, but decided it wasn't exactly professional to ask.

Might as well get started. "How old were you when you first got interested in rodeo, Laverne, and what's your favorite event?"

"Ben took me to the Little Britches Rodeo in High River when I was six, and I got Brownie right after that. Ben and my dad gave him to me. My dad taught me to throw a rope and he practiced with me all the time. I really miss him," she added in a low voice. "Ben helps me, but it's not the same as your own dad," the girl finished in a whisper. Her face crumpled slightly but she quickly recovered.

"Is roping your favorite event? You were pretty good with those calves last week." Daisy felt sorry for the girl but she wanted to steer the conversation away from the sad topic of her father's death.

"I like barrels best. We're real good, Brownie and me." In barrel racing, the horse and rider galloped around three barrels then raced for the finish line. It was timed, the only rodeo event dominated by girls and women.

"Brownie's really fast," Laverne added proudly. "We've had lots of seconds and thirds. Maybe we'll win a first this year."

Fifteen minutes later, Daisy closed her notebook and reached for her bag. "Well, I think I've got enough. I know your mom's in a hurry to leave. I'll phone you later if I need some more details."

Laverne led her to the pasture behind the barn, the pasture Ben had turned the black horse into the first day she'd come out to the ranch. As they walked by his house, Daisy could hear loud music playing. Heavy metal. "Is Ben home?" she blurted, surprised.

Laverne shook her head. "No. He's fixing the spring up on the hill."

The spring? "But I can hear music coming out of the house, can't you?"

"Yeah," the girl replied. "That's just the hitchhiker Ben picked up."

"You're kidding! He's got a hitchhiker staying with him?" Daisy stared at the house, then hurried to catch up with Laverne. How weird was that?

By the time Daisy had shot half a roll of Laverne and her horse, a quiet-mannered bay gelding, she'd managed to weasel directions on how to get to the spring.

She could have asked Marie and maybe she should have but…well, Marie was busy. She was taking a shower.

EARLY MONDAY MORNING, Ben drove to the flea market in Lethbridge with a load of Arlo's stuff. He still hadn't gotten around to checking Arlo's account with the bank in Glory, and now Marie had discovered a safety deposit box key in Arlo's sock drawer—more surprises—but he figured there was no real rush on that either. Harold was starting to cut the timothy the next day and their haying crew was booked for a couple of days after.

As for Saturday's dance in Tamarack, a resounding success according to Lucas… He tried not to think about it. The rodeo was in good hands, with Lucas and Adam Garrick taking care of the details.

One of the best ways to put anything out of his mind was to spend some time up at the spring on the hill, the source of the ranch's name. Every year about this time, between branding and his first hay crop, Ben spent an afternoon or two digging it out, making sure the fence he'd put up to keep the cattle out was okay, just generally reflecting on life.

Fame? Fleeting. Money? Hard to come by. Women…always a mystery.

Before reaching the spring, he took a side trip to look at his small herd of bucking mares, pastured on high range for the summer. They would be, he hoped, the foundation of a future business raising rodeo roughstock. The bunch included three home-bred yearlings and a two-year-old, all by Moses, the champion bucking stallion he and Adam had co-owned, an old battler that had died two winters before. Seven of the mares had new foals, all of them from Piece of Cake, his new stallion. Ben had high hopes for that stock. It would be years before he knew if he had any winners and more than that before he'd know if any of his mares had reliably passed on the traits necessary in a bucking horse. Strength, heavy bone and overall soundness, as well as athleticism and unquenchable spirit. If you could find a good foundation mare or stallion, a hit-or-miss proposition, you could build a herd.

Bucking horses spent their first five or so years as wild and free as possible. No halters, no saddles, little contact with people. Antirodeo protesters had some points, Ben would be the first to admit, when it came to roping calves at top speed, for instance, and a few other less than defensible rodeo events, the kind of spectacle that had no real place on a ranch. But one-ton bulls and bareback broncs? You couldn't feel sorry for two thousand pounds of bull over two hundred pounds of cowboy, and you sure couldn't feel sorry for a bucking horse, which lived a life as close to the mustangs of the old days as possible in today's world. Thoroughbreds, which were trained and ridden as two-year-olds—practically babies with young bones and soft ligaments—fared far worse, in Ben's view. During their working lives, as mature and proven bucking stock, rodeo horses were treated like the solid gold they represented to their owners. Abuse? A roughstock owner would sooner kick his dog.

With the morning trip to Lethbridge and the snap decision to visit his stock first, Ben didn't arrive at the spring until after two o'clock, later than he'd planned. While Dodger sniffed around for rodents, Ben waded out into the clear, cold water, wearing a pair of old running shoes and cutoff jeans, and got to work. The sun was hot on his back. He was half-finished digging it out, tossing aside junk that had blown in or washed down the hill over the past year, when he heard an engine in the distance. Harold? He stood, shading his eyes.

Well, well. Speaking of mysterious women...

He winced when he saw the Thunderbird scrape over a

high spot. Her uncle Leroy wouldn't like that. The track, not much more than a faint rutted and rocky trail, was traversed maybe half a dozen times a year by a pickup, his or Harold's, when they came to check on the spring or on the series of waterholes and creek below.

She could have driven a little slower.

"Hi!" Daisy parked the convertible next to his pickup and walked toward the pond through the gap in the barbed wire gate.

"Howdy." He leaned on his spade handle for a few seconds, watching her approach, then set to work again prodding the bottom for sticks and other debris. A plastic Safeway shopping bag—how did things like this find their way to his spring? He tossed it onto the bank. The water wasn't deep, maybe midthigh in a few places.

"Ben." She stood on the edge of the bank, her arms crossed. "I think we need to talk. Are you listening?"

He bent down to catch a handful of cold water to splash on his face and chest, then leaned on his spade handle again, aware of the cold rivulets running down his over-heated skin. "I'm listening."

"Did you kiss me at the dance?"

He straightened. "Yeah, I did."

She threw her arms up in the air. "Why? Why didn't you *say* something? Why did you take off? Why did you kiss me in the first place?"

"You'd really like to know?" He was kind of glad she was on the bank and he was in the middle of a cold spring-fed pond fifteen feet away.

"Of course I'd like to know!"

"I wanted to."

"You wanted to!"

"And I didn't think I'd get another chance."

She stared at him.

"It was an impulse, okay? I just decided I wanted to kiss you, that's all. And I had the chance—"

"That's all!" she shouted. "That's *all!* You're impossible, you know that?" She threw her hands up again and began to pace back and forth. "And didn't we have a conversation earlier that never went anywhere? During the square dance? Weren't you telling me what you'd heard from the chief? I looked for you later and you'd disappeared!"

Ben nodded, relieved. She obviously wasn't going to pursue that kissing business. She just wanted to know why, naturally enough. It had been an impulse, like he'd said, and he'd tried hard to regret it since—with zero success. Feeling himself tied up in a knot every time he saw that damn Glory cop waltzing her around and grinning at her hadn't helped.…

Once a competitor, always a competitor, it seemed. When he'd ridden broncs, though, it had been him, the horse and the clock, not other cowboys. Or cops.

"And what's this about you having a hitchhiker staying at your house?"

"What about it?" He started digging again.

"You mean you just let some stranger stay in your house when you're not there?"

Ben kept digging. "Why not? It's just temporary."

"He could rob you blind! Take all your furniture—"

"Don't have any furniture."

That stopped her.

CHAPTER TWENTY-ONE

"NO FURNITURE," she repeated.

"That's right."

Dodger barked, distracting them both. The dog dug frantically behind an Oregon-grape bush, probably after a marmoset or ground squirrel. Ben could see him, dirt up to the eyeballs from snuffling in the hole he'd made.

"I heard music playing in your house."

"I have a sound system," he admitted.

"Fridge and stove? Washer and dryer?"

"Dishwasher, too."

"Table and chairs?"

"Nope. I eat at the island counter in the kitchen or in front of the television."

"So you have a chair," she said flatly. "And a television. That's furniture."

"And I have a bed and a pool table."

"Nowhere else to sit? Don't you ever have visitors?"

"Two kinds. One kind uses the pool table, and the other kind, not quite as often, uses the bed."

From where he stood, he could see her blush. That was an adorable trait she had. He didn't know many women who blushed anymore. Especially tough-talking women of nearly twenty-six. Of course, he knew very well that she wasn't as tough as she let on.

He resumed his digging.

"I'll pretend I didn't hear that," she said loftily. "That is a totally disgusting, sexist remark. There are plenty of women who play pool.'' She paused. ''So, what's this I hear about you poaching?''

Ben seated his spade deeply in the bed of the pond. ''What the *hell* are you talking about?'' he demanded.

''Casper said if I wanted to know about poaching, I ought to ask you.''

''You asked him about poaching?''

''Well, you were gone. I asked him if he'd heard anything—''

''*Sonuvabitch!*'' Ben stabbed at the pond bottom again, narrowly missing his canvas-clad foot.

''What's that supposed to mean? You *do* know something about this poaching business you're not sharing with me?'' She actually sounded hurt. Ben shot her a quick glance.

''My source isn't reliable. Why spread rumors? I asked the chief but he hadn't come across anything and he's pretty well informed, so...'' Ben shrugged. ''I figured, that's it.''

''You know what, Mr. Goodstriker?'' She had her hands on her hips. ''I think for a grown man with a lot of experience and responsibility, you can be pretty damn gullible.''

''Gullible!'' Ben was outraged. Even standing in spring-cold water, she sent his temperature through the roof.

''Okay, *trusting,* then.''

''Calm and sensible is more the way I look at it.''

''You would.'' She put up her left hand and ticked off various points on her fingers. ''One, you won't ask tough questions. I can just imagine you beating around the bush with the chief. Two, you believe everything these people tell you when they *do* say something and that includes the chief, whom I don't trust a bit—''

She wouldn't.

"—and, three, there's a difference between not knowing and not telling."

"Are you saying the chief wouldn't tell me the truth?"

"I'm saying he's not going to tell you everything he knows just because you ask."

Daisy was uncomfortably close to a notion that had crossed Ben's mind: the chief didn't want any extra government or police attention on the reserve. He had his own reasons, Ben suspected, reasons that might have to do with how band money seemed to get spread around—or not. And, as a matter of principle, who'd want to draw extra trouble when it could be avoided? As far as the chief was concerned, the incident between Wayne and Arlo had been cleared up to everyone's satisfaction. Everyone except Daisy Sutherland.

And now, since he'd shown up on Chief George's doorstep with her in tow, maybe Ben Goodstriker.

Ben sighed and started digging again.

"Am I right?"

"You may have a point," he admitted.

He had to hand it to her; she didn't crow. He prodded the bottom of the pond for a few minutes in silence, then added, "Anyone else I should be careful of?"

"Casper Desjarlais. He's a creep and a slimeball. I don't trust him."

"You only talked to him once."

"Twice. And I danced with him—"

"*Danced* with him!"

"Just to get some information."

Ben grinned. "And that makes you—"

"A good reporter," she said briskly. "He invited me to the dance, too, you know, but Gordon Bass had already asked me. Frankly, I didn't like the man the minute I saw him."

"You've made that clear. But Casper's harmless. I told

you that. I've known him since we were kids.'' Ben couldn't believe he was defending Casper, especially now that he knew Casper had actually asked Daisy to the dance, as he'd bragged he would. ''He doesn't have the imagination to be a serious slimeball. That takes smarts and connections. Casper doesn't have either. He's a petty crook and a lousy businessman. You should see his so-called flea market operation.''

''You went there?''

''This morning. He said he'd sell some of Arlo's gear for me. What a joke! Vacant lot between a storage facility and an auto wrecker. Maybe a dozen folks with junk piled on card tables and tailgates, wandering around buying each other's trash. Casper sitting there on a lawn chair, under a sun umbrella, wearing a tie and a sports jacket and taking his cut from those poor slobs. Couple of his pals from the reserve hanging around, smoking and drinking beer.''

Ben laughed. ''I swear, if you offered Casper a shoeshine, he'd follow you anywhere.'' He shook his head and picked up the spade again. ''Pathetic, that's what it is.''

''He seems to have money. He drives a new vehicle.''

Ben shrugged. ''You never heard of credit? Probably making payments to some loanshark that'll go into the next century.''

He started wading toward the bank. ''Damn, it's cold in here!''

She stepped back a few paces from the grassy edge. ''I'm sorry, I guess I interrupted your work.''

He tossed the spade onto the bank. ''I'm finished for now. I like to come up here to think. It's too noisy for that today. How'd you find me, anyway?''

She looked uncomfortable. ''I asked Laverne for directions.''

''Oh, yeah?'' Ben grinned. ''Ask a kid all the tough reporter-type questions, right? That's your department.

While I just swallow everything people tell me, hook, line and sinker.''

"Maybe I was a little hard on you.'' She smiled and he felt like reaching for the hand she offered and pulling her into the water with him. Surprise her. Cool off, play around, laugh a little, maybe kiss her...

Instead he climbed up onto the bank himself, grabbing a small willow for balance. His cutoffs were wet and his shoes made ugly slopping sounds. He kicked them off, then bent down to pour out the water.

"It's just that I feel a bit frustrated,'' she said, jamming her hands into the pockets of her short denim skirt. She was wearing a lime-green T-shirt and sandals on bare feet. Toes painted bright blue today. "We don't have any leads—''

"We?''

"Okay. *I* don't have any leads. You believe your cousin wouldn't poach or kill a boyhood friend, no matter what, and yet we've been told there was contraband in his truck, giving him a motive.''

"Not told. Get that straight. I heard about it, that's all.'' Ben forced his wet feet back into his sneakers.

"Gordon Bass acted like it was true when I mentioned it. He got quite official on me and threatened all kinds of things if it got into the paper.''

"What kinds of things?''

"Oh, you know. Shut me down, that sort of bluff.'' She laughed. "All garbage, of course. He kept talking around it, making sure I knew he wasn't confirming anything, so to speak, so I took that as an admission it was true.''

"Do you like him?''

"*Like* him?'' She looked astonished, her eyes very round and blue.

"I mean, you went to the dance with him.'' Ben wanted to get out of his clothes in the worst way, but he couldn't seem to leave this thing between her and Bass alone. Like probing a cracked tooth.

"I went to the dance with him mainly because I wanted to see what I could pry out of him."

"He like you?"

"Sure, he likes me! Everybody in town likes me!"

"You get anything out of him?" Stick to the topic, Goodstriker, he told himself, shifting from one wet foot to the other.

"He played cop the whole time. Even said he was going to charge Alan Poundmaker with mischief for throwing the main switch and fooling around with the cash box."

"Alan Poundmaker, huh?" Ben mused softly. The boy was one of Casper's little band. He'd worked in an auto repair shop in Glory for a few months after leaving high school two years before, but as far as Ben knew, he'd been pretty much unemployed ever since. Unemployed but not short of cash. But then, Alan was a distant cousin of the chief's, on his mother's side. The Georges and anyone related to the Georges were never short of cash.

"Oh!" Daisy clapped a hand to her mouth. "I forgot. You were asking about Arlo's truck, so I got John to print up some contact sheets from the roll of film I took that day. We only used two pictures and— Where are you going?"

Ben stopped and turned back to her. "I'm getting out of these wet clothes. I've got some jeans and boots in the truck. I'd appreciate it if you didn't peek."

He wished he had a camera to capture her expression. She wouldn't look—not that he gave a damn if she did— because for all her bravado, deep down she was a nice Tamarack girl and nice Tamarack girls didn't peek when guys changed.

"The pictures are in the car," she blurted and hightailed it toward her vehicle.

Ben laughed. He pulled a T-shirt out of the pile of clothes on the floor of the pickup and shrugged it on. He glanced around—instinct—then kicked off his wet sneakers, dropped his cutoffs and quickly stepped into dry jeans. He didn't bother with underwear.

He was just pulling up his zipper when he heard, *"Peek!"* and he spun around. Daisy was bent over laughing by the tailgate of his truck.

"Damn! You scared me," he said, starting to laugh, too. He'd kept such a good lookout toward the front of his truck and toward the Thunderbird, but he hadn't thought of her sneaking up behind him.

"You have a nice bum, Mr. Goodstriker," she managed to tell him, coughing in her fit of laughter.

"I do?" He grinned and grabbed her shoulders, giving her a playful shake. "And you need yours paddled, Ms. Sutherland. Hasn't your mother ever told you not to sneak up on strange men? You don't know what could happen."

"Maybe she has," Daisy gasped helplessly. "I don't remember. Why, what could happen?"

He was so close to her. As close as when they'd danced. She stopped laughing and so did he. The air was heavy with the scent of pine and sagebrush. The shadows were long and the entire hillside was bathed in a warm, golden glow. It had to be four o'clock, maybe later. He felt like a kid in the middle of the school holidays. Warm, green days of summer. Endless blue sky. With the responsibilities of school and growing up an unimaginable distance away…

"Anything." He barely recognized his own voice. "Anything could happen." He ran his thumb down the curve of her cheek and saw her swallow and her eyes darken.

"L-like what?"

"Like this," he said. He hauled her roughly into his arms and he covered her mouth with his.

Had it only been Saturday since he'd kissed her? Two days ago? He pressed her against the rear quarter panel of his pickup and felt his blood begin to burn when she squirmed.

Then, when she reached up and wrapped her arms around him...

Oh, man, this was crazy! This wasn't part of his plan. Not for her and especially not for him.

CHAPTER TWENTY-TWO

DAISY STUMBLED and clutched at Ben's shirt. He responded by shoving her against the hot metal of his truck and wrapping his arms around her.

His kisses...*oh!*

She *knew* he'd been the one to kiss her at the dance the other night. But why did he run off? If he felt this way about her?

Daisy gave herself up to the delicious sensation that flooded through every pore. There was no question of fighting it. She'd been attracted to him—terribly, *inappropriately*—almost from the day she'd met him. She'd never dreamed he'd been holding back all this—this *passion....*

"Damn it, Daisy! This isn't right." Ben raised his head suddenly. She couldn't breathe, let alone say anything in response.

He stared at her for thirty seconds, then muttered "Oh, hell" and began kissing her again.

Then his darn dog started barking and Ben took a step back as though startled, and looked around wildly. *Oh, hell* was right, Daisy thought, pulling down her rucked-up skirt and plucking the perspiration-damp T-shirt from her overheated skin.

"What do you mean this isn't right?" she asked, making a tent of her shirt at her waist and flapping it back and forth. Hoo-boy, it was hot. "It seems very right to *me.*"

"We're—we're just working together, that's all," he said, running one hand through his hair. It stood up in dark clumps. "On this harebrained scheme of yours," he muttered. "Remember?"

She was going to ignore that. "Why? Why do you say 'that's all'?" she demanded. "Who makes the rules?"

"I do. This isn't a social relationship. I told myself right at the beginning that I wasn't getting mixed up with you, no matter how tempting the prospect might be."

"Mixed up?"

"You know what I mean."

Daisy stepped close to him and put her hands on his shoulders. "Kiss me again, Ben Goodstriker, and then tell me you aren't getting mixed up with me."

Ben dragged her into his arms. "I've got plans." He pressed his lips against her eyes, her eyebrows, her hair. "And they don't include *you*." Yet he fastened his mouth on hers and Daisy sagged against him, her entire body feeling about as substantial as the fabric of her damp T-shirt.

He kissed her deeply, then groaned and wrenched his mouth away, holding her close. "Goddammit, Daisy, this is no good!"

"You're crazy. It's *good*," she whispered. "It's very good. Kiss me again." Her brain was reeling and she thought she'd faint from the heat—of the sun and of Ben's kisses. He kissed her once more, briefly, and held her away, staring into her eyes. She was tired of arguing with him. Why didn't they just take this discussion to a nice grassy bank and—

"Now what?" she ventured in a thin voice.

"Exactly," he said grimly. "Now what?"

His hands were hard on her shoulders, almost hurting. Daisy lowered her gaze and licked her lips. "Exactly," she repeated stupidly, and looked up at him again. It struck her that there was really nothing else to say. She wanted him. Badly. *Now*.

"I'm furious—with myself." He shook his head, as though bewildered. "I don't get it. What's *happening* here?"

"Sex," Daisy said simply. It seemed pretty clear to her.

He grimaced. "You're right. Sex. That's what it's about, isn't it? Sex. Nothing more."

"I—I guess so." Now Daisy was confused. Was he talking to her—or to himself?

"You don't understand." He shook his head. "I have obligations, plans. I have a carefully thought-out agenda for the next few months. Year, maybe. My plans involve Marie—all of Arlo's family. My ranch. My horses. My future. I have made no allowance for—for diversions. For *sex*. For someone like you in my life. I have—hell, why am I telling you all this?" He let go of her shoulders and turned away, running his hand through his hair again. Then he whistled and Dodger ran up, shaking his head and snorting dirt out of his nostrils and mouth.

Ben quickly fastened the barbed wire gate, then tossed the dog into the box of his truck. He dug deep in the pocket of his jeans, producing keys, which he held high. "Let's go back to the ranch." He paused. *Where there was a bed, if nothing else. And a pool table.* "Maybe we should discuss this."

He got in his truck.

Discuss. I like that, Daisy thought as she put the convertible into gear and lurched after him. *What's to discuss?* He was driving like a madman and all she could see of his pickup was the trail of dust behind it. Was he that ardent? Or was he trying to leave her behind?

Ouch! She touched the brake as the convertible hit a rock and heaved to the left. Damn. If she hadn't had some consideration for Uncle Leroy's pride and joy, she'd have gunned it herself.

Oh, well. Slow down, Daisy Jean. Take your time.

She knew where the ranch was.

WHEN SHE GOT TO Ben's house, he was waiting outside beside a mangy young man with a backpack. The hitch-hiker. She'd forgotten about him.

"This is Cedric," Ben explained in response to her look of inquiry. His face was impassive. Controlled. As if the recent events at the spring had been strictly a figment of *her* imagination. "Friend of my sister's kid. He's got an appointment in town and I thought you might give him a ride in," he continued smoothly.

Daisy examined herself in the her rearview mirror, glad she had her dark glasses on. She touched her lower lip lightly, aware that Ben was watching her closely. Her hair was a mess. "Sure," she said. "Can I use your facilities before I go?"

Ben nodded, jaw tight, eyes wary. "Go ahead."

Daisy got out of the convertible. "Cedric, why don't you put your gear in the back and wait for me? I'll just be a minute."

"Okay." The boy—he might have been eighteen or nineteen—threw his pack in, got into the front passenger seat and began playing air drums between his knees and the dash of the Thunderbird.

Ben opened the door of his house and Daisy walked through a small vinyl-tiled foyer into the kitchen. Clean, uncluttered, no pictures on the wall, no dishes in the sink. A calendar by the phone featured a large sleepy-looking Hereford bull, displaying an extraordinary amount of tenderloin and testicle.

"The bathroom's down here," Ben said, indicating a short hallway that had another door in it, possibly a laundry room.

"Can I see your living room?" She quirked an eyebrow. If he wasn't going to mention what had happened at the spring, neither was she. "I've never seen a living room with no furniture."

He cracked a smile. "Sure." He led the way through the kitchen into an area that in anyone else's house would be a dining room. There was nothing in it; the walls weren't even painted. On the other side of the dining room was a good-size living room, with a big river-rock fireplace, a twenty-six-inch television, a well-worn Naugahyde recliner chair with a pile of magazines beside it and a floor lamp. Nothing else—if you didn't count the wicker dog basket by the fireplace, complete with Black Watchtartan-covered cushion and well-chewed rims.

"You haven't painted in here."

"Yeah." Ben looked around his living room as though she'd just pointed out something interesting. "I've been meaning to get around to it." He shrugged. "One of these days, I guess."

She noticed another hallway off the living room. "Is that where the bedrooms are?"

"Yeah. Three bedrooms, a bathroom, a linen closet with towels, toothpaste, soap—you want the whole tour?"

"No." She turned back to the kitchen. Actually, she was curious about the pool table.

Ben was waiting for her when she'd finished with the bathroom. "I'm sorry about—well, what happened up there." He gestured toward the hills that rose behind his ranch. He looked tired, a man with too much on his mind. Daisy felt a flash of sympathy for him, for all he'd been through in the last month. But did that have anything to do with their kisses at the spring? Or at the dance, for that matter?

"I'm not sorry," she said.

"I can't explain—"

"Then don't," she interrupted. "Okay? We're both adults. It's stupid to think about this too much."

He didn't smile. They walked outside and Ben reached down to pat Dodger. Daisy got in the convertible and started it, turning on the radio full blast.

"Aw-ri-ight," the teenager said with a grin, rocking in his seat. He gave Ben a thumbs-up. "Thanks, dude, 'ppreciate it. See ya later."

"No problem." Ben nodded.

No problem. Maybe not for him! Daisy shifted to Drive when the engine whined hysterically and she realized she'd accidentally put the transmission into Neutral in her haste to make an elegant, if speedy, departure. She hoped Ben hadn't noticed.

What did all this about Marie and Arlo's kids and his ranch and his horses and everything have to do with having a relationship with *her?* Even a casual relationship that happened to involve sex?

Was that what she wanted? A brief, hot affair with a sexy stranger, no strings attached—she guessed Ben still qualified as a stranger, since they'd never dated, never gotten to know each other. But was that true? She had the feeling that, for her, there were already plenty of strings attached to Ben Goodstriker.

Dammit. Daisy didn't know *what* she wanted.

She spent half the drive back to town feeling hurt that he'd dismissed her the way he had, and the rest of the time plain frustrated that the hitchhiker had been there, putting a wrench into her plans—hopes?—for one of the few pieces of furniture Ben owned.

She dropped the boy off at Wiley's, where Ben had arranged a dishwashing job so he could replenish his cash before he hitchhiked up to Jasper to look for summer work—she'd heard the whole story on the way into town. After that, Daisy circled around the block twice, intending to go into the *Times* but not quite able to make up her mind to stop and park. It was nearly five o'clock. She should write up the piece on Laverne for this week's paper and leave her film and a message for John to do a contact sheet of the photos she'd taken of the girl and her horse when he came in tomorrow morning. Daisy thought she'd pick out a few nice ones and give them to Laverne.

Then what? Dinner with her parents loomed, as it did every night. Another casserole, even tighter jeans—and what had she done about finding a place of her own? Zilch.

Daisy pulled a U-turn around the cenotaph at the top of Main Street and fumbled in her bag for her cell. "Mom? I won't be able to make supper tonight. Where? Oh, I don't know, I'll grab something somewhere. A—a friend's. Yes, I have my key. Don't wait up for me." *Please* don't wait up for me.

Nothing ventured, nothing gained…

Actually, she had a lot of reasons to go back to Ben's ranch. What about the contact sheets of the crime scene she'd brought to show him? She'd been distracted when he changed and had left them in the back seat of the convertible with her other stuff.

Then there was the poaching business Casper had mentioned. She hadn't found out about that, either.

And hadn't he said they needed to discuss what had happened at the spring? Well, they hadn't discussed anything yet, had they?

It was fourteen miles from Tamarack to Meadow Spring Ranch. Daisy gave herself until the ranch turnoff to decide how she was going to tackle that particular item.

BEN WAS HUNGRY. He'd missed lunch coming back so late from Lethbridge and then going straight up the hill, intending to dig out the spring in one afternoon.

Forget that. He still had a couple of hours' work there, but now he had to concentrate on haying for the next week or two. Harold had managed to put a crew together, mostly high school kids but they'd have to do.

He pulled a cold beer out of the fridge and made himself a pepperoni, mustard, pickle, lettuce and Havarti on rye, which he carried into the living room to eat in front of whatever was on TV.

Golf. He sat through three holes of some PGA tournament before he finished his sandwich and flipped off the set.

Golf! He hated golf. Sure, Tiger Woods was a hell of an athlete, no question, but he was sick of the guy's face on television and in the newspapers and besides, what kind of sport was that? The only serious physical risk was dropping dead of a heart attack from boredom. Or getting struck by lightning. He didn't see what all the fuss was about a bunch of middle-aged white guys chasing a little white ball around a hundred acres that would be better seeded into timothy or canola or running a few feeder cattle.

Maybe he was being unfair. He was still reeling from kissing Daisy Sutherland up there at the spring. It wasn't as though he hadn't felt chemistry with a woman before, but nothing like the explosion Daisy had set off. It was scary. A little quiet afternoon golf on television wasn't going to help that....

He needed a shower. A cold shower. And a distraction. Maybe he should go to Glory for a meeting with Lucas and the junior rodeo committee. Or, his preference, he could check over his mowing equipment again. Or change the oil in his pickup. Lucas and Adam and their wives had the rodeo organized. They didn't need him. Now that there was some real money, thanks to the dance, the junior rodeo was all set to take place in two weeks. Laverne had a good chance of getting a ribbon, maybe even top spot with old Brownie. Arlo would have been proud.

Ben put his plate in the dishwasher and peeled off his shirt, throwing it on the kitchen counter. Yeah, he'd better have that shower. Damn if he'd ever thought he'd require cooling off after spending nearly two hours in a spring-fed mountain pond, but that was before he'd met a certain newspaper reporter.

She'd been giving him sleepless nights since he met her. He recalled the day she'd come out to the ranch, all chirpy and nosy as hell, camera strapped around her neck, toenails painted some weird color, asking questions he didn't want to hear, let alone answer.

Now he was in it right up to his neck.

Come to think of it, she'd been giving him restless nights since *before* he met her—since he'd seen her at Wayne's funeral. Ben stepped under the spray. He soaped off and then ruthlessly turned the faucet gauge to C, full blast.

He heard Dodger bark in the kitchen. Damn! Should've let the dog out—why hadn't he thought of that? Man, this was turning out to be one helluva day.

He distinctly heard the click of the bathroom door opening. *Shit!* "Who's there?" he yelled, pushing the shower off. Junior? Marie?

"Just me."

Ben slammed open the shower door so hard it bounced off the bathroom wall, forgetting that he was stark naked except for a washcloth and he had that in his hand.

Daisy Sutherland, her cheeks flushed bright pink, was reaching for the clasp on the wisp of a bra she was wearing. She'd already dropped her T-shirt. As he watched, thunderstruck, the bra followed and then she unfastened the snap on her skirt. Cold shower or no cold shower, Ben felt the temperature rising all over again. And not just his temperature...

"Oops," she said, and removed something from her

pocket, which she tossed to him. He automatically caught it, then opened his hand. A condom packet.

Her skirt fell to the floor, and all she had on now was a minuscule thong. Bright blue. To match her toenails.

"Daisy—" He sounded like a crow with a bad cold.

"I just wanted to see if it was really true that you couldn't possibly get mixed up with me. That you had so much other important stuff you had to think about…"

"Come here!" Ben reached out and grabbed her.

"Oh, you're freezing!" She smiled but he could see that beneath all the big talk she was scared. *Just like him.*

"Cold shower'll do that," he growled, pulling her full against him.

"N-not on my account, I hope."

He didn't bother answering. He just started to kiss her. Yeah, as he'd thought earlier, what a helluva day this was turning out to be.

CHAPTER TWENTY-THREE

FLORENCE HEARD the rifle shot just after she finished her breakfast, cooked oatmeal with raisins, brown sugar and evaporated milk, a meal she'd eaten nearly every day of her adult life. The boy wasn't so fond of porridge; she kept a box of cereal for him. But she rarely had ordinary cow's milk—no refrigeration—and the boy didn't care for the tinned stuff.

She heard the second shot ten minutes later, when she'd washed her bowl and spoon and gone out to open the chicken coop and feed the hens. Junior was still sleeping. He'd spent the night with her, something he was doing a lot since school let out, almost as though he hated to be home.

The day was cool this early, the air fresh. Welcome after all the heat they'd had. It was too hot for so early in the summer. Too hot and too dry. Not many bugs, though, which was good for people, but maybe not for birds and for Jupiter, the toad. Florence glanced to the southwest. The shot hadn't sounded that far away. A heavy caliber. It wasn't somebody after fool hens, that was for sure.

It wasn't hunting season but that didn't mean much. Florence had been known to snag a deer out of season herself, if her smokehouse had room and her stomach was empty. Hunting for food was a way of life. No game wardens were ever going to change that....

When she returned, Junior was sitting up in the bunk

Henry had built in the corner when Ben came to live with them. He rubbed his eyes when he saw her.

"You want eggs for breakfast?" she asked. "The stove is hot."

He nodded sleepily and lay back down again. His dark eyes caught and held hers, and he grinned. *He hadn't heard the shot.* He was a good-looking boy, just like his father. His sister, who was a beautiful girl, didn't resemble Arlo at all—why would she? Florence wasn't the only one who could count....

Not that it mattered now; the dead couldn't talk.

She got out a small cast-iron frying pan, put it on the woodstove, then cracked two new eggs into a Pyrex bowl, added salt, pepper, a dash of tinned milk and stirred the mixture with a fork. "Might be a nice day to pick some strawberries," she said, looking quickly at the bunk as she poured the eggs into the pan.

Junior nodded and stretched and smiled at her again, and Florence felt a sudden prickle of understanding, of insight. A fierce desire that things work out—whatever those things were. She rarely knew. No one did.

"Here, now, Junior. Wash up. Your eggs are ready."

IT LAY ON ITS BACK, like a man fallen down drunk never to rise again, mouth agape, filled with flies, molars glinting bone-white. The carcass had been partially skinned, probably because it was a cinnamon, a color sport of the ordinary North American black bear, *ursus americanus,* and someone had thought they'd take the hide.

Florence had noticed a golden eagle and half a dozen ravens flying over the aspens but had paid them no mind, believing the ravens to be harassing the eagle, as ravens and crows often did.

But the two dogs barked and barked until Florence made her way, grumbling, up the ridge, warning Junior to stay back. Dogs were a nuisance in the berry patch. A feeding bear might run off when a dog barked. But if the bear gave chase, instinct sent an untrained dog straight to its owner with possibly disastrous consequences.

This bear wasn't a danger to anyone. It was half-grown, a scrawny yearling not long out of hibernation and freshly killed. It hadn't been feeding on the hillside; there were too few berries at this time of year for a hungry young bear to bother with. There was no doubt in her mind that the animal had died from the shots she'd heard that morning. The black jellied mass spread through the grass and lichens was evidence of a gut shot that had allowed the animal to run a short distance before collapsing, and then, below the right ear, the entry wound of the bullet that had finished it off. Where the skin had been peeled back on the belly, she could see a knife slash. She had seen two similar kills last fall on her trapline, both times the same belly wound and the paws removed.

This bear was missing the front paws only, and the glint of raw bone in the mass of blood, hair and tissue made her grimace and step back. She gripped her half-filled margarine tub of wild strawberries, wishing vaguely—was it the flies? the stench?—that she'd brought the plastic lid with her.

"Bounder! Ringo!" The dogs were avid, eyes bright, tongues lolling, teeth sharp. Oh, they were brave now. And within a week, with the ravens and the coyotes and other scavenging creatures, there wouldn't be anything left but hair and bones drying in the sun. "Come *here!* Come away!"

This was nothing for the boy to see....

She heard a terrible cry and turned to see him fallen on his knees behind her, eyes blind with terror, small red berries scattered everywhere.

DAISY WOKE UP, wondering for a moment where she was. Soft light, the lowering rays of the evening sun, streamed into the room beneath half-lowered blinds. Bed, dresser, open closet door revealed shirts, hats, boots, belts... She was in Ben's bedroom.

She turned to glance over her shoulder. He was awake, facing her on his pillow, smiling.

She yawned and smiled, too. "What time is it?"

He reached for his watch on the bedside table. "Eight o'clock."

"I must have fallen asleep." She yawned again and blushed at his steady gaze. They'd made love in the shower and then he'd carried her into the bedroom and they'd made love again.

"Thanks for coming back," he said and stretched out his left hand to trace her profile with his finger.

She smiled up at the ceiling. Ben's room was painted, at least, a nice coffee color with creamy white trim. Hardwood floor, a carpet near the bed. No pictures, no doodads, but it looked like an ordinary bedroom. "I guess that cold shower was for me, huh?" For no reason, she felt inordinately pleased with herself.

"Yeah." He ran his finger gently over her nose and chin again. "Didn't work, though."

She was silent for a moment, then turned to face him fully. "You must think I'm pretty bold."

He shook his head. "No. This is what I wanted. Just chickened out, I guess, when I got home." He met her eyes. "I'm glad you didn't."

"Oh, Ben!" Daisy felt as if she'd melted into a million puddles. She leaned forward and kissed him. He pulled her into his arms and kissed her properly.

Then they lay close together, smiling at each other. "What's on your mind, Daisy?"

"How do you know something's on my mind?"

He laughed. "You've got that look. I can see the wheels turning."

"Okay." She glanced down, traced his strong collarbone with her thumb, then met his gaze again. "I don't get it, Ben. What's this about having a 'plan' and me not fitting into it? Not that I'm asking to," she added hastily, "I—I just thought this was, you know, a *good* thing."

"As in 'just sex,' right?"

Daisy nodded uncertainly. "Well, sort of—"

Ben sighed and drew her a little closer. "It's never really 'just sex,' is it?"

She rested her head on his arm and looked up at him, not sure what he meant.

"I don't feel it's fair to either you or me to act as though a relationship—and that's kind of what this is now, isn't it?—" she nodded "—has much of a chance. It doesn't. First and foremost, I've got Marie to worry about."

"Marie?"

"Yes, Marie. Now that Arlo's gone, I feel responsible for her and the kids. She lives here in the yard, in my old place. I've been thinking, hell, maybe sometime down the road, maybe a year or two from now, I might ask Marie to marry me—"

Daisy sat up. "*Marry* you?"

Ben didn't seem to share her dismay. "Yeah. Why not? There was a time when—" he grimaced slightly "—I was pretty hot to marry Marie myself, but that was years ago. Before she and Arlo got married."

"You mean you were *in love* with her?" This was getting stranger and stranger.

"Hell, cut me some slack here. I was nineteen." Ben said dismissively. He didn't seem to take her astonishment as seriously as she thought he should. "She was eighteen. Everybody was in love with Marie back then. Me, Arlo, Wayne, Casper—all kinds of guys. Hey, come here!"

Ben pulled her down and she nestled against his chest. *I'm here, not Marie or anybody else,* she told herself, ever the pragmatist. *That's what counts....*

"So, answer me this. Are you in love with her now?"

"No, I'm not." Well, *that* was a relief! "But I like Marie, I always have. Good marriages have been based on less."

"Says who?"

"Well, they have." Ben gave her a crooked grin. "I'm no expert, but I'm sure it's true." She reached up and he grabbed her wrist when she tried to cover his mouth with her hand. "Listen! Ever since Arlo and I were in rodeo, I've known that if anything happened to my cousin, I'd look after his family. It's an understanding we had. Now he's dead, and I feel just as responsible for them as if he'd been hooked by a bull or got killed in a highway accident."

"That's very generous of you," she said. And she meant it—to a point. Daisy wasn't too worried about competition from Marie. What Ben didn't seem to take into account was that Marie might have something to say about his plans for her future. No modern woman was going to accept a marriage of convenience just because her dead husband's cousin had an outdated sense of chivalry. Women didn't need looking after, not the way Ben seemed to think they did.

Still, the whole concept was touching. She nestled closer, inhaling the warm scent of his skin and the musky, rumpled aftermath of sex in his bed. She'd only brought two condoms....

"I suppose you came here to ask me about that poaching business, too, didn't you?" Ben said, appearing to ignore her wandering right hand, which was exploring the smooth bumps and hollows of his firmly muscled chest.

"Yes!" She pulled back, suddenly remembering some

of her reasons for returning to the ranch. "What is *that* all about?"

"It happened a long time ago, and it wasn't really poaching." Ben looked pensive. "Arlo and I went camping one year in Banff National Park with Casper and Wayne. I was about sixteen. Wayne had his dad's car so we had wheels. While we were fishing, we came across a mountain sheep that had been killed by a train. Big ram. Apparently, it was pretty common in the parks, animals getting onto the train track and getting hit. I'd heard about it from a retired guy in Glory, someone who used to be a conductor on the freights."

Ben paused, then went on, frowning. "The whole thing was really my fault, because this trainman had also told me that trophy animals were worth a lot, mainly to American hunters and they'd pay big money for a full-curl ram. You know, for their rec room wall. I mentioned what I'd heard. We ended up skinning out the front quarter and packing out the cape and head. Wayne stuck it in his parents' locker at the butcher shop." Daisy recalled that years ago her parents had rented a freezer locker at the butcher's, too. It was a common practice in small towns, where not everyone owned a home freezer.

"Anyway, next thing I knew, Wayne and Casper said they'd found a buyer, I have no idea how, and they were going to sell it to some guy from Idaho." Ben paused.

"How much?"

"Plenty." He seemed reluctant to go on. "A lot more than any of us had ever seen before."

"How much?" Daisy pressed.

Ben looked at her. "Eight thousand dollars."

"That much?" Fifteen years ago for some poor dead animal's head? *Ugh.*

"That's peanuts. A trophy head in today's market brings upward of fifty thousand dollars."

"Maybe that's the kind of poaching we're talking about!" Daisy broke in excitedly. "Maybe it's where those boys out at the reserve are getting their money!"

"Too risky. Fish and Game watch for that sort of thing, and I wouldn't be surprised if the RCMP kept tabs on it, too. Besides, the biggest trophy heads are in the parks, not around here."

Daisy shook her head. "I can't believe Wayne was involved. I wonder if his parents knew."

"Of course they didn't. Not unless they happened to check their locker and unwrap that sheep's head before we got rid of it. And, don't forget, the sheep was already dead, so it wasn't exactly illegal. Borderline, maybe. Arlo and I got fifteen hundred bucks each, mainly to keep our mouths shut, I think. It was a lot of money to kids who'd never seen more than fifty bucks at one time. Casper and Wayne pocketed a bigger share because they'd found the buyer. That was their reasoning, but I've always suspected they made a lot more on that deal, maybe even got a higher price than they told us."

"This happened more than once?"

"Twice that I was involved in. Then Arlo and I got busy trying to break into rodeo and that was it for us. Wayne and Casper might've done it a couple more times, I don't know. Train kill isn't exactly easy to find, unless you have an insider feeding you information, maybe an engineer or a conductor. Then, a year or two later, Wayne decided to go into the RCMP and a month after that Arlo and Marie got married."

"Were you surprised at his choice of career?"

"Not really. Sometimes reformed bad guys make the best cops. They know what to look for." Ben smiled grimly.

"But they might be more tempted to backslide, too." Daisy hadn't thought about that angle before—but it fit with what she'd heard. The drug or alcohol problem, the fingers in the till at Mr. Valentine's hardware, the too many visitors of "the wrong kind"—even the stories she'd heard way back about Wayne's reputation with one or two girls who disappeared to "live with an aunt" in Calgary or somewhere for the remainder of the school year. Her sister, Karen, would know more about that; maybe she'd ask next time she called home.

"Do you think Arlo might've gotten back into it? In later years?"

"I considered that when I first heard about the bear gallbladders. But I don't think so. For one, it wasn't exactly easy finding those animals on the rail lines and it was hard work packing them out. Most illegal trophy poachers don't rely on a freight to do their work for them. They go out there, often in the national parks, and hunt to order. That happens, but not with Arlo. He was no hunter, much as he loved the bush. Plus, you need contacts if you're dealing contraband. Arlo didn't have any. He never even ran up a long distance bill. Casper? Doesn't have the smarts. Wayne? Well, Wayne was a cop, wasn't he? He was on the other side of the law."

"What if he was working both sides? Mr. Valentine said he had a lot of unsavory visitors. Well, what he said was 'visitors of the wrong kind'. He seemed to think I'd know what he meant by that."

"That could be Indians," Ben scoffed. "Albert Valentine isn't exactly known as a bleeding heart liberal."

Daisy remembered his warning about dancing with Ben. She wondered what he'd think if he found out she was in bed with him right now. Correction, she *knew* what he'd think. And he'd feel it was his duty to inform her parents as soon as possible. Something she intended to do herself.... She wondered, too, if her parents—or Ben—were ready for a "guess who's coming to dinner?" scenario. She knew she was.

"Anything else?" Daisy asked, moving her hand slowly down his ribs.

He caught her hand and squeezed her tight against him. "Hold on, Daisy. Later." He grinned. "Didn't you say something about pictures?"

The contact sheets! Daisy jumped up, then realized she was stark naked and grabbed a shirt of Ben's from a nearby chair and shrugged it on. "I left my bag in the kitchen. I'll be right back."

Why the modesty, she didn't know. He'd already seen her totally naked, wet and dry.

She brought the envelope with the contact sheets and handed it to Ben. He turned on the bedside light. Propped against the headboard, he began to study the series of photographs. Daisy had looked them over earlier and didn't see anything unusual. Most were terrible, with the side mirror of the Thunderbird in the way or the rain blurring the details.

"Look at this," Ben said, indicating a shot of Arlo's truck. "See here?" He put his thumbnail on the portion of the rear window visible behind the driver's seat. "These look like rifles in the rack behind the seat. Two. I don't think they're are fishing rods—" the picture was very indistinct "—they'd be in the back. I wish I knew what kind of ammo killed Wayne. And look at that," he continued softly.

Daisy looked. "What?"

"It's open." Daisy saw that the back door of the canopy was ajar, angled away from the Fiberglas sides. The hinges were on top.

"Maybe it didn't close properly," she suggested.

"Could be, considering the condition of the thing. But check out the back of the truck."

"What? The tailgate's down?" She didn't know what she should be looking for.

"Nobody drives with the tailgate down."

"Which means that somebody opened it and left it that way."

"I'd say so," Ben finished. "I doubt Arlo would've fiddled with the truck after he'd been shot. Nor do I think he'd return a rifle to the rack behind his seat if he'd just used it to shoot someone. But maybe he went into his truck to get something *before* he was shot."

"Or maybe somebody else opened it."

They both considered that possibility in silence. Who? The cops? The first person on the scene? Wayne? Then Ben put the contact sheets on the bedside table and reached for her.

"Let's think about it later," he said. "All this talking makes my brain hurt."

"Mine, too," she said, adding, "Hey, I only brought two condoms."

"What do you take me for?" he growled, stroking the curve of her left breast. "I might not have been a Boy Scout but they aren't the only ones who're prepared, you know."

"No?" Daisy giggled.

"No," Ben said, opening the drawer in his bedside table.

CHAPTER TWENTY-FOUR

DAISY ENTERED the welcome coolness of McPherson's Furniture and walked toward the sales counter. The place had been updated recently with glass-and-steel doors, new light fixtures and what looked to be a recently installed oak floor. She had distant recollections of worn vinyl and factory lighting. Definitely no air-conditioning. But then she hadn't been inside the store since high school. Emily had had a part-time job at McPherson's during their final year.

"Is Mr. McPherson in?" It seemed that Jack McPherson still employed high school students. The gum-chewing, frizzle-haired, eyebrow-pierced receptionist showed a lot of youthful leg as she got up from her word processor and addressed Daisy with a friendly smile. "May I tell him who's calling?"

"Daisy Sutherland. *Tamarack Times.*"

"I'll see if he's in," she said and walked toward the back of the store.

Daisy glanced at the five other customers—who included, she noticed, Ed Sawchuk and two women from the nearby Hutterite colony, dressed in their long print dresses and headscarves—and did a quick survey of the store. Maybe she could bring Ben here to buy a few things for his house....

"Daisy!" Mr. McPherson emerged, accompanied by the teenager, who promptly sat down and started frowning at the word processor. "What brings you in today? I heard you were looking for an apartment. Maybe a nice dinette set?" He waved a hand toward a display area. "We've got them on summer special right now."

"A summer special?" Daisy took the opportunity to introduce her concerns. "Gosh, I should've read about that in the *Times* but I noticed you didn't have your usual half-page ad in last week."

He looked as though he'd just remembered he had stomach trouble. "Ach, gir-r-l," he said in his heavy brogue, an accent Daisy was sure he cultivated, as it had been forty years at least since he'd left Scotland. "Business hasn't been so good." He shook his head. "No. What with all the new stores opening and folks going to Lethbridge and Calgary to shop…"

"You seem fairly busy today," Daisy interjected, gesturing around. She smiled. "I'm sure Mr. Sawchuk here knows you've got the best prices in town."

Marie's boss had approached the counter and was inspecting a sheet of paper handed to him by Randall Bream, Mr. McPherson's longtime assistant manager. He looked up. "I'm a busy man. I haven't got time to dawdle around the malls in Lethbridge. McPherson's suits me just fine."

Daisy was encouraged. "See that? Now, if more people in town knew you had a sale on, you'd probably be even busier, right?"

"I suppose you're wanting an ad, girl."

"Not my department, Mr. McPherson. But I did notice you hadn't advertised this week, and I thought I'd drop in to see if it was an oversight."

"Well, not exactly." He shot a pained glance at Sawchuk, then leaned forward and lowered his voice. "The truth is, I've been hearing things. So has Mrs. McPherson. We're awful proud of Wayne Petrenko in Tamarack, y'see? He was a kid with a lot of strikes against him and he turned into a fine young man that this town was very proud of—weren't we, Ed?''

"No question." Ed Sawchuk was frowning over his sales slip.

"And that Arlo Goodstriker. Ver-r-ry bad news, he was." Mr. McPherson shook his head. "It worries me and Mrs. McPherson that you've been asking so many questions about this terrible incident, almost as though you'd like to see that half-breed cleared. If he didn't shoot Wayne, who did? The cops know what they're doing, Daisy! Trust me. Trust *them*. Ye reap what ye sow. Goodstriker got no more than he deserved, y'take my meaning?''

Daisy wasn't sure she did. "Are you saying he deserved to die? He had a wife and two kids, you know—''

"Not that he ever cared much for them!" Ed Sawchuk interjected bitterly. "He was a born loser who couldn't hold a job for more than a week. Couldn't be bothered working like the rest of us. Lots of folks tried to help him out—''

"Even you, Ed," McPherson broke in helpfully.

"Even me." Sawchuk scowled. "I gave him a job driving truck for my gravel pit and what did he do? First week he got drunk and drove the truck into an embankment. Cost me over a thousand bucks to get it fixed. Goddamn liability, that's what he was. If he hadn't got himself shot like that, I'd have had half a mind to do the job myself.''

"Not to reflect badly on the family," Mr. McPherson said hurriedly. "Oh, no. Marie's a fine woman. She did what she could. If it wasn't for her, those kids would've gone to bed hungry most nights.''

"I don't believe that," Daisy said flatly. "Ben wouldn't allow it.''

"Yes, Ben's a good man, for an Indian, but he's always had a blind spot where that cousin of his is concerned.

Why, there was a time I thought Ben might be the one to marry Marie.'' Jack McPherson gave her an exaggerated wink but she didn't respond. She was still seeing red from his ignorant comment about Ben's Indian blood.

''All the young bucks were after her back then, eh?'' McPherson looked to Ed Sawchuk for confirmation and got a black look in return. ''Wayne, Arlo, even Casper Desjarlais. Ain't that right, Ed?''

''She's a *beautiful* woman.'' Sawchuk scrawled his signature on the sheet of paper in front of him and pushed it across the counter. ''Too good for that bum she married. See that this is delivered right away,'' he snapped.

''Very good, sir. This afternoon, sir.'' Bream stepped back to answer the jangle of the wall telephone, still an old-fashioned Bakelite model, Daisy noticed, part of the original decor.

''Truth is, I golf with Bill Petrenko,'' Mr. McPherson confided, leaning toward Daisy again and glancing at the other customers. The Hutterite women were standing in front of the television display, all twenty sets tuned to the same channel, which featured motocross racing. ''The wife plays bridge with Alice, d'ye see? Alice Petrenko is in a terrible state. Mrs. McPherson's been giving me the dickens for keeping my ad in when there's so much upset in the community. I've even had complaints from folks on the reserve. And believe you me—'' his expression was gloomy ''—*nobody* likes that new column in the paper telling the world who got a speeding ticket last week and whatnot.''

As Daisy recalled, Jack McPherson had been cited as picking up a fine for driving over the speed limit in a school zone. He shook his head and placed his meaty paws on the counter. ''Nooo. My hands are tied, dear girl. I can't afford to put off the few customers I've got left. I decided

I'd just, er, drop the ad for a few weeks. Let things cool down, so to speak.''

''If business is bad—'' although Daisy didn't believe for a moment that it was ''—you need to advertise more, not less. I hope you change your mind soon. Your ads are a hit, and they've always been so regular, something for readers to look forward to every Thursday.''

''I know,'' Mr. McPherson said sadly. ''I *know*.'' His ads, a product of his and Bob Roberts's creative genius, always worked around a play on the *f* sound in *furniture* and *McPherson* and tended to run along the lines of ''phine phurniture at phantastic prices!''

Juvenile, Daisy had always thought, but, hey, whatever worked.

Whatever worked was no longer working. She hoped her father would have better luck convincing the old Scot to reconsider. It was depressing to think that her parents were right: the editorial content of the paper directly affected the advertising. Petty and small-time, but true. And it happened in big papers, too. You weren't likely to read a big exposé about, say, a corrupt developer cutting costs and building substandard condominiums, as long as said developer kept the weekend Real Estate section plump with ads. Daisy had done just such a series of stories once, only to see them deep-sixed by her editor.

''I don't like to speak poorly of the dead, but believe me, Miss Sutherland,'' Ed Sawchuk said in a low voice as he jammed his wallet in his rear pants pocket, ''it was Marie Goodstriker's lucky day the morning Constable Petrenko ran into her husband on that back road. Wayne did her a *favor*.''

Daisy stared after him as he left the store and got into a shiny black vehicle, some kind of late-model SUV.

''Don't mind him,'' Mr. McPherson said with a nervous smile. ''Ed wouldn't hurt a fly. One of those quiet types.

Never says a word but he has his convictions. Why, I believe he was sweet on young Marie, too, at one time.''

And maybe still is. Daisy picked up her bag and cast a quick glance at Sawchuk's order, which lay on the counter while Randall Bream was on the phone: patio set and sun umbrella to go to Meadow Springs Ranch. Prepaid.

That order wasn't going to fill up Ben's empty backyard.

DAISY DECIDED to stop in at Wiley's after she left the furniture store. It had occurred to her that if Gordon Bass lifted a few glasses at the tavern, Wayne probably had, too. She figured cops typically kept an eye on establishments like Wiley's. Maybe Lonny Harris knew something that might shed light on what had happened between Wayne and Arlo.

It was just after eleven o'clock and the tavern wasn't busy, so Lonny brought Daisy's coffee and the butter tart she'd ordered and sat down at the table with her.

''Wayne? Sure, I knew Wayne as well as anybody.'' The waitress lit a cigarette and thoughtfully blew the smoke away from the table. ''We went out for a while when he first came back but nothing came of it.'' She picked at a fingernail, then took another drag of her cigarette and laughed. ''He worked crazy hours. Crazier than me!''

''So he wasn't on traffic?'' Daisy wasn't sure where she'd got the idea that Wayne Petrenko was a traffic cop.

''He worked traffic, crime, everything the cops usually do. I know he had a special interest in detective stuff.''

''He did?''

''Oh, yeah. He loved talking about going undercover. I don't know how much of it was just big talk but I think he'd actually done some in the past, back East. But out here? Nah. Just the regular cop stuff.''

''Were you surprised he was never promoted?'' Daisy

didn't want to offend Lonny, although the waitress didn't seem too torn up over Wayne's death. "I mean, constable is the lowest rank, isn't it?"

"Isn't corporal lower? Or is that the army? Anyway, Wayne told me he'd been an undercover detective, which is a step or two up, back East, but something went wrong and he got sent to Alberta until things cooled off. I never really knew what he meant by that. Maybe a drug bust. He was in some kind of trouble, I gathered that much. He said he had something going here that would clear his name, but I always thought it was just a lot of hot air." She reached forward to drop ash in the glass ashtray she'd brought to the table with her. "That's guys, eh? A lot of b.s., some of them. Trying to impress you. In one ear and out the other, for me."

This was news about Wayne's past; but Lonny probably knew what she was talking about. What kind of undercover stuff had he supposedly done? She needed to make some calls, find out. Gordon Bass wasn't about to tell her. "Do you know if he saw much of Arlo Goodstriker?"

"That's the crazy thing, eh? He did. They were the best of friends, from what I could see. I couldn't believe it when I heard they'd shot each other." Lonny's eyes watered a little, maybe from the smoke, and she shook her head and stubbed out her cigarette. "I liked Arlo. People called him a loser, but he had a heart of gold. Thought the world of Marie and the kids. That doesn't spell loser to me. Dreamer, though. He was always telling me he was going to hit the big one soon and buy his daughter a new horse. I guess he meant the lottery."

"Wayne have any bad habits?" Daisy was just fishing. Nothing seemed to go together. If Lonny had said Arlo and Wayne had hated each other, it would've made more sense.

"Oh, just the usual—smoking, gambling and chasing

women," Lonny said sarcastically. "That's why we broke up. He cheated on me. But he was generous and he always had money. He bought stuff for my kids and took me to Vegas twice. We had a hell of a good time," she said, her eyes soft. She seemed to have been fond of Wayne, despite the womanizing and crazy hours.

"Well, I got a customer," Lonny said, getting up and taking her ashtray with her. A couple of truckers had just walked in. "If you think of anything else, just call me."

"Thanks, Lonny," Daisy said. "I appreciate your help. How's Cedric working out?"

"Fine." She winked. "You tell Ben he's doing just great."

Tell Ben.

The whole town must know by now that she and Ben were sleeping together. How news traveled so fast in a small town was a mystery and a miracle to Daisy, but it did. People didn't need to buy a newspaper to know what was going on.

Of course, it was hard not to notice the Thunderbird, and it had been parked at Ben's place until well after midnight three of the past five nights. At least Marie would have noticed, plus any visitors she might have had. Then yesterday, the day after her parents had gone on their long-postponed trip to Saskatchewan, Ben had surprised her by coming to town and spending the night with her. He'd left before dawn, supposedly to get back to the ranch before his haying crew arrived, but Daisy thought he was really more concerned about her reputation with the neighbors. The neighbors would certainly have been aware that she'd had company overnight—and who it was—no matter what time he left.

Ben's plans for himself and Marie hadn't been mentioned again. Daisy was in love. Head over heels. It was scary, the way she felt. She'd been in love before, several times, starting with the crush she'd had on the high school football captain, Benny Lorimer—whatever happened to him?—and most recently with a stockbroker she'd met at a New Year's party two years ago, although that hadn't lasted past St. Patrick's Day.

This was different. It had felt different from the minute she'd met him. Deeper. Hotter. He wasn't much for talking and she'd never dreamed she'd fall for the strong, silent type. But she had. As he said, she talked enough for both of them. Nor had she introduced Ben to her parents yet, as a potential suitor, but that was next. Daisy was quite sure her mother was already planning a full-dress RCMP wedding.

Gordon Bass, for all his charm and good looks, hadn't done a thing for her on any level that mattered.

Daisy didn't discount Ben's declaration about his plans for his future, a future that didn't include her, but she fervently believed that she could change those plans, given half a chance.

When Daisy got back to the car, there was a piece of paper on the front passenger seat and a brown bag on the floor in back. She looked around. The doors to the car were unlocked; why bother locking them when the top was down? Daisy reached for the paper and turned it over. The message, badly spelled, sent chills through her: We found this. If you want to know more, meet us at Sawmill Road and we will show you everything. The note was signed *Chip and Dale*.

That made no sense. There was no Chip and Dale, except in Disney cartoons. Daisy opened the back door and reached for the bag on the floor, her heart pounding. It was heavier than she'd expected. A bomb? No way. She choked back a scream. Inside the bag was a bear paw. Dull, black, desiccated, its long shiny claws had sunk into the fur, almost hidden. She gagged, then dropped the bag and got in the driver's seat.

What should she do? She wanted to talk to Ben, but he was out haying. Her dad was in Regina. There was no point in talking to anyone at the office. She considered Gordon Bass for a moment, but decided against him. He'd just order her to turn everything over to the police, and then he wouldn't tell her anything more. Just like the business with Arlo and Wayne or the prank at the rodeo dance.

It was the middle of the day. Realistically, what could happen? She'd drive out, meet up with this Chip and Dale and let them show her what they'd found. They were probably a couple of locals. Maybe they wanted to do the right thing but didn't want to go to the police. Maybe they'd heard about the bear gallbladders in Arlo's truck, as Ben had, and knew she'd been asking questions around town. Maybe they were on the wrong side of the law themselves, out hunting deer illegally, and had stumbled on the black bear poacher's lair—where else would they have gotten this paw? Perhaps they'd come to her because they didn't want to draw attention to themselves and have to answer a lot of difficult questions if they went to the police.

She was a reporter, after all. She was supposed to be nosy and to protect her sources. They were leaving it to her to follow up on this. Write her story or go to the police. Or both.

Or not do anything at all.

That wasn't an option. Daisy started the convertible and called Ellin. No answer. Probably out for lunch. The machine came on but Daisy disconnected. She wasn't going to leave anything about this on a machine that anyone could overhear. She'd try Ellin again in half an hour or so. She called Ben, thinking she'd leave a message for him, but his phone just rang and rang. His machine must be off.

Oh, well. She had two-thirds of a tank of gas and her

canvas bag with camera, notebook, cell phone, water and granola bars. There was a jacket in the trunk and running shoes she'd exchange for the sandals she was wearing when she got to the rendezvous.

She was set.

CHAPTER TWENTY-FIVE

WHEN DID HE start to worry? Ben wasn't sure.

And what *had* they decided that morning, before he'd left her sleeping in her own bed? He was in a fog, exhausted from long days spent working in the fields and then up half the night making love. His impression was that she'd drive to his place after she'd finished up at the paper, cook him dinner and have it ready when he came back from the hay field.

She liked playing house. She already had the colors and furniture picked out for his living room, and they'd had a friendly scrap about whether he ought to paint his walls Cloudy Morn or Perfectly Peach. He didn't know why he'd fought his attraction to her the way he had—maybe for all the reasons he'd told her—but forbidden fruit was all the sweeter, they said. And it was definitely true.

Ben shrugged off his disappointment that she wasn't there when he came in, dusty and tired, at nine o'clock. He checked his answering machine but discovered that he'd turned it off the day before and forgotten to turn it back on once he'd cleared all his messages. Damn technology!

He hadn't realized until he'd seen the dark, empty windows of his house just how much he'd looked forward to having her there, banging around in the kitchen, singing along to the radio. Harold took his haying responsibilities very, very seriously, and with the weather forecast indicating change, he'd insisted they use every possible minute of daylight. At this time of year, that meant going well into the evening.

Ben cleaned up, wondering if he'd ever be able to take a shower without remembering that first time, hot and hasty against the Fiberglas surround, warm water pouring over both of them. Then he fixed himself a frozen pasta dinner and ate it at the counter, trying to read the sports section of the *Herald*. The Bruins had won the Stanley Cup, the CFL was well underway and, so far, the Eskimoes were waxing the Stampeders every time out—which reminded him of the muddy cap they'd found in the ditch two weeks ago. The Grey Cup was going to be in Calgary this November, at McMahon Stadium. He gave some thought to picking up a few tickets, one for him, one for Harold, one for Junior and maybe one for Daisy. She struck him as a woman who'd like football....

Damn, where *was* she? He couldn't stand it any longer. He got up and dialed her parents' house, but the phone just rang and rang. The answering machine didn't kick in. Then he called the *Times*. No answer there, either. He left a message, in case she was working late and had just stepped out to the washroom.

But if she was working late, why wouldn't she have called, as she'd done several times when they'd been separated for a whole day? Man, he was starting to act like some fretting husband! You'd think they were on their honeymoon. Well, in some ways, he supposed they were.

He tried her cell. He got a message saying "The customer you have dialed is not available," which meant she didn't have it turned on.

Worry turned to anger, and Ben spent five minutes cussing her out for not having her damn phone on. Then he started thinking about Gordon Bass and wondering if she was with him.

Hadn't she gone out with Bass to see if she could get

information from him? Hadn't she danced with Casper to see what she could find out about poaching? Maybe she'd gone to bed with *him* just to learn about—about what? But he couldn't work himself up about that. She knew everything he did about Arlo and Wayne—more. And the past five days had nothing to do with anything except him and her. Frankly, Ben was tired of her obsession with what had happened out at the reserve. He had too much other stuff to think about—including her, now—to keep playing reporter games.

Still, he couldn't put it out of his mind. What if she was off on some harebrained chase to do with *that* business? Ben's blood ran cold.

He went to the phone again. "Morris? Listen, where did you hear about those bear gallbladders you mentioned to me a couple weeks ago? Come on, you old bastard, think!" Ben waited impatiently while Morris Jack recounted some rambling story about going behind the pool hall to take a piss and talking to someone back there. "Casper? You heard it from other guys, too? Okay, Mo. Thanks."

Ben pushed down the receiver button and dialed Information. He wasn't even sure where Casper lived these days. "Tamarack. Casper Desjarlais." When the operator gave him the number, he dialed it. No one home there either.

JUNIOR SCUFFED through the long grass that grew between the lane and the river. He wasn't sticking around home while *he* was there. Junior hated him coming around to see his mother.

Maybe he'd go to Granny's. When Ben came back from town, he'd ask Ben to take him to Granny's. Or he'd go over the hill by himself, walk if he had to. It wasn't late.

He knew the way through the woods; his dad had showed him lots of times.

He didn't want to ask his mom to drive him. He knew she didn't like Granny for some reason.

'Cept Ben was real busy today. Maybe he wouldn't want to drive him, either. Ben was worried about Daisy. Before breakfast, he'd been over to talk to his mom, said Daisy wasn't answering her damn phone.

What if *he*—no, Junior didn't want to think about that.

The sound of an engine got louder and louder behind him but he didn't turn around. Good. *He* was leaving.

Junior jumped when the horn tooted right beside him and Ringo barked like crazy.

"Hey!" *He* pushed open the passenger door and was leaning across the seat. "Come here, kid. I want to talk to you."

Junior considered playing deaf as well as dumb, but in the end he walked slowly toward the open door.

"Smart boy." *He* laughed and got out the driver's door, coming around to the grass where Junior stood. "I see you got a new patio set. Nice, ain't it? You and your mom and sister prob'ly have picnics outside now, have some lemonade, enjoy the sunshine."

Junior scowled and took a step backward, suddenly afraid. What was *he* trying to do?

"No, come here!" *He* grabbed Junior's arm and pulled him toward the road. Ringo barked but his tail was waving. He was no guard dog, that was for sure. Junior dug in his heels and started to cry.

"Hang on there, pal. Don't worry, I'm not gonna hurt you. Now you listen to me. I got news. You know how everyone's hunting for Daisy?"

Junior looked up, stunned. *They were?* He nodded slowly.

"Well, guess what?" *He* grinned into Junior's face. His

breath stank of garlic and beer. "*I* know where Daisy is. Little bird told me. And guess what else? She wants to see you."

Junior hung back, frowning. *Me?*

"Yeah, she's in big trouble and she wants to see you. How 'bout that? Get in." He pulled on Junior's arm, half dragging him toward the open passenger door. "I told her I'd bring you. You gonna get in or am I gonna have to throw you in?"

Junior considered. He liked Daisy. Daisy understood things, kinda the way Granny understood. She'd helped him when those bullies beat him up. She might need him. It was true; Ben was looking for her. She *was* lost. He got in the truck and stared out the back window. Were they going to take Ringo too?

No. *He* slammed the door and threw a rock at the dog. "*Git!*" Then *he* ran around and climbed behind the wheel. Clicking the automatic door locks, he put his foot on the gas. "There! Nothin' to it, eh? Don't be scared, I won't hurt you. If I wanted to hurt you, I'd a done it before, wouldn't I?" He looked at Junior and made a face. "Poor dumb cluck. Brains scrambled, ain't they? That head's no more good to you than a busted-up pumpkin rottin' in the sun—hey!"

He spotted his cell phone on the dash, grabbed it and punched in some numbers. "I better call your ma and tell her, eh? See? Everything's ok." He winked. "She was worried where you went, taking off how you do all the time. You shouldn't do that."

Junior glanced out the window. They were nearly at the highway. Tamarack was right. Granny's was left.

"Marie? I picked up the boy. Saw him walkin' on the road on my way out. Don't worry, I'll take him up to Florence's for you, no problem. Okay?"

Granny's? Junior looked over as he threw the phone down on the seat between them.

"Never mind, kid. I told her Granny's so she won't worry, that's all. Put your seat belt on, don't you know nothin' about safety?"

Then *he* laughed, that big wet laugh Junior hated so much. Following instructions, he fastened his seat belt and held on to the door handle as they turned.

Toward Tamarack.

Daisy would help him. Daisy would know what to do.

BEN COULDN'T SLEEP. He told Harold he'd be late, then he called the *Times* office as soon as it opened.

"Ellin? Could I speak to Daisy?" he asked, clearing his throat a little to dispel the tightness.

"Funny, I was just going to call you, Ben. I haven't seen Daisy since yesterday morning, when she went over to McPherson's to check on an ad. She had an appointment with the dentist this morning at half past seven, and I just got a call from him to ask why she didn't show up." It was eight-fifteen now.

"McPherson's, huh? That's the last place you know she went?" Ben tried to keep the worry out of his voice. Daisy was an adult; she didn't need to report in to him. Maybe she'd gone to see Emily in Calgary, on a whim. Maybe she went for a drive and ended up having to spend the night somewhere. Maybe—maybe what?

"Ben, I'm worried. It's not like Daisy to miss an appointment. Or not call in. I wonder if she's—if she's fallen down and got hurt or something. She's alone in that house. Maybe I should get in touch with the Petrenkos? They live next door."

"Never mind. I'll go over there right now and let you know. She's probably just fine, got busy with something else and forgot about the dentist. Hey, who wouldn't?" He tried hard for a light note. After all, he wasn't *married* to Ellin's boss. "And, listen, if you hear from her, you give her supreme hell for not calling both of us, okay?"

Ben put down the phone and checked his messages. Nothing. Then he grabbed his truck keys and ran to his pickup, changing his mind at the last minute and heading over to Marie's to tell her that if she heard from Daisy or saw her, if Daisy came to the ranch while he was away, she was to call his cell and let him know immediately.

Then he got in his pickup, Dodger beside him, and high-tailed it for town.

THE SUTHERLANDS lived in the nicest part of Tamarack, on a slight knoll overlooking the Rockies. Big yards, green lawns out front, even in this drought, clipped caragana hedges and towering Norway maples and ashes behind freshly painted fences. The houses were mostly wood and stucco, but some, like the Sutherlands', had been built on a grander scale. The red brick had been manufactured in Lethbridge, using St. Mary's River clay around the turn of the last century, the foundations faced with stone.

Ben had never imagined he'd be sleeping with a daughter of one of the town's most prominent families. Or, if he'd ever had such thoughts—and, okay, maybe he had once or twice—he would've figured on a quickie in some scabby motel at the edge of town. Or a tumble at the buffalo wallow during a grad year bonfire celebration. He wouldn't have guessed he'd be invited right into her bedroom.

This morning, he didn't care who saw his truck parked in the driveway.

He went to the front door, then the back. Of course they were locked. But a basement window on the east side had a catch missing, and it didn't take Ben more than five minutes to lower himself into the basement, make his way through the cobwebby gloom past the furnace, past the laundry room, past a motley collection of rusty outdated tools hanging on the wall, to the stairs.

He searched the first floor, then raced up the stairs to the bedrooms, half listening for the sound of a police siren. Most of the women in this neighborhood didn't work "outside the home," as the expression went, and he was pretty sure everyone knew the Sutherlands were away on vacation and that Daisy wasn't home for some reason or other, if only because her car was missing. A strange pickup parked outside for more than five minutes would warrant a quick 911 to the forces of law and order.

He paused at her bedroom, the bed unmade, the sheets still rumpled from their lovemaking the morning before. He knew in his heart that she hadn't slept there last night. The house was quiet and cool; even the dog was gone. But he knew that. Her parents had taken the spaniel with them.

No one had seen her since she'd gone to McPherson's.

Ben let himself out the same way he'd let himself in and made a mental note to suggest Owen Sutherland get that latch fixed.

Randall Bream was just opening up when Ben got to the store at nine.

"Daisy? She was here yesterday morning," Bream said as Ben followed him inside. He watched the assistant manager hurry to a wall panel behind the counter and switch on all the lights. "She was right here—" he patted the counter in front of him "—talking about Jack advertising in the *Times*. The boss didn't run his regular ad for, uh, several reasons." The assistant manager coughed somewhat apologetically, but Ben was too distracted to care why.

"Where'd she go from here?"

"I don't know. Why not ask her? Isn't she at home or

at work?'' Bream regarded him curiously, adding, ''Ed
Sawchuk was in at the same time.''

''He was?'' Maybe he should track Ed down and see
what he remembered.

''Yes, he, uh, he'd just purchased a patio set for your
cousin's family, and he wanted it sent out right away. We
put it on a truck yesterday afternoon. I hope it got there
in good shape.''

Ben didn't have a clue whether it had or hadn't and
didn't care. He wondered briefly why Ed Sawchuk was
buying Arlo's family lawn furniture, but Bream's next
words caught his attention. ''—before Daisy left, she mentioned she might go over to Wiley's for lunch or drop in
at the pool and take pictures of the Water Lily class. They
were having some kind of exhibition.''

''Thanks, Randall.'' Ben headed back to his pickup.
He'd try Wiley's because it made the least sense. Why
would Daisy even think of having lunch in a smoky, dark
truckers' joint?

The bar and grill didn't open until ten, but Ben banged
on the back door and Lonny let him in. She came early
sometimes to do the books for the owner, an elderly balding alcoholic named Bud ''Call me Budweiser'' Campbell,
who lived in the trailer park in Glory and never arrived at
work until after the lunch rush.

''Ben! Where's the fire? I've never seen you in such a
hurry for a drink!''

''Hell, Lonny.'' Ben felt a bit embarrassed. Maybe he
was overreacting. ''It's Daisy. I don't know where she is
and I talked to Ellin at the office and *she* doesn't know,
either, and—''

''She was in here yesterday just before lunch. About
eleven. Had a coffee and one of Rick's butter tarts and
asked me a few questions.''

''What about?''

"Oh, this and that. She wanted to know more about Wayne, what kind of guy he was, whether he saw much of Arlo."

"Goddammit!" Ben turned away in frustration. He felt like punching the door jamb, but as he'd learned ten years ago, that didn't get you anything except a sore hand. "I *knew* she was still chasing that story!"

"She's a reporter," Lonny said philosophically. "She's got a bee in her bonnet. Hey, I heard you two have a thing going—hold on, I'm coming!" she yelled toward the front of the establishment where another customer was banging on the door. "Back door, front door. Damn, you'd think this town didn't have a liquor store to tide a fellow over till the bars open."

It didn't; the nearest liquor store was in Glory.

Ben went to the counter and poured himself a cup of the coffee Lonny had started. *A thing going.* It was a lot more than that. Daisy's disappearance had scared him more than any bull ever had. He'd face ten rank bulls in a rodeo ring before another morning like this one. He didn't know what to do next. Should he phone in a missing person's report to the Glory RCMP detachment? No, then he'd probably have to talk to Bass and he'd just as soon avoid him if he could. Besides, was she really missing just because she hadn't called her office or showed up at his place last night to make his supper and warm his bed? This whole—what, romance? between Daisy and him was still so new. Maybe he was going haywire because of the way he felt about her.

"You can give me a cup of that red-eye or whatever you're pourin' there." Tiny LaPointe slapped his hat down on the counter and straddled a stool. He wiped his face wearily. "I thought I'd get me a wakeup shot of rye from Lonny, but I changed my mind. What're you doin' here, Goodstriker? Waitin' tables?"

"He's looking for Daisy Sutherland," Lonny said, proceeding to right the chairs that had been stacked on the tables overnight and arrange the salt and pepper shakers and serviette dispensers. "She's gone missing."

"Missing?" Tiny opened his bleary eyes wide. "She still drive that fancy Thunderbird? I saw it parked this morning on the Old Sawmill Road when I drove down from Castello Mountain."

CHAPTER TWENTY-SIX

DAISY AWOKE in the dark. Her mouth felt as though it had been stuffed with rubber bands and it hurt to swallow. She touched her legs. Her arms. At least she was all there. But where?

She half sat up, trying to penetrate the blackness by widening her eyes as much as she could. She felt around, discovering that she was on some sort of rough wooden bunk or pallet. But who had brought her here?

Chip and Dale, obviously. The two men, dressed in the camouflage fatigues so de rigueur among the men-playing-survival-games class, had arrived at Old Sawmill Road about twenty minutes after she did. She hadn't thought about the fact that no time had been mentioned in the note; she'd just driven out there, following the old Alberta road map she'd found in the car. Did that mean the men had watched her leave town?

Chip and Dale had disguised themselves with ski masks, too, looking perfectly ridiculous, but they'd seemed pleasant enough, producing three Red Robin take-out coffees when they got out of the truck. The taller one—"Chip"— handed her a paper mug with a lid.

She'd thanked him. She was going to play along, she'd decided, no matter how silly this was. The men both tossed back their coffee, which was only lukewarm, and the short one told her the ski masks were because they didn't want anyone to know who they were. As if *that* was hard to figure out. He said they'd take her to the place where they'd found the bear paw and she could look around, take pictures, whatever she wanted, and then they'd bring her back to her car again and they'd leave separately. They had their reasons, they'd more than hinted, to "Stay below the radar."

All fine by Daisy. Their truck, the color heavily obscured by dried mud, had two mud-splattered all-terrain vehicles in the back. Daisy recalled sipping the coffee as she watched them unload the ATVs, thinking how oversweet it was, and wondering why their equipment was so muddy when there'd been no rain in the district for weeks. Mind you, she knew that a muddy four-by-four vehicle was a sought-after fashion statement for a certain kind of guy.

Now the too sweet beverage made sense: it had been drugged. She shuddered to think how long she might've been unconscious if she'd swallowed the whole dose of whatever they'd given her. While they were busy unloading their ATVs, she'd thrown most of it away.

The men had obviously brought her to this place and left her. She was in some kind of shelter. A cabin? A cave? Whatever it was, it stank. The odor was terrible—rotting garbage, old blood and something worse. *Death.*

All of a sudden Daisy felt completely overwhelmed. She leaned over the bunk and retched, as much from fear as from the odor in the room. There was nothing in her stomach and the effort wore her out. She lay back on the hard pallet, sweating, her heart pounding in her ears. *No one knew where she was.*

She hadn't tried Ellin again and Ben's machine was off.

What time was it? Daisy couldn't even see the dial on her watch. It must be the middle of the night. But even in a closed-up cabin, surely there'd be enough light leaking through windows, door jambs, from the moon and stars to provide reflection for a watch dial....

Her cell phone!

Daisy felt cautiously around on the bunk, her hand coming in contact with rags or other soft, disgusting materials that made her think of spiders and mice. She resolutely barred the images from her mind or she knew she'd go mad and kept feeling around until her fingers closed on firm canvas.

Oh, thank heavens! They'd left her bag, which meant she had water, she had a little food, and—most important of all—she had her trusty cell.

Daisy fumbled until she found the On button. She'd check the time and then she'd call for help. She wondered what Chip and Dale were using for brains, leaving her the phone. She didn't have a clue where she was, but at least she could let someone know where to start. Old Sawmill Road. Her car was there, parked well off to one side. She had no idea if the road led to wherever she was now, since she'd ridden behind Dale on one of the ATVs. She'd forgotten that, but now she remembered hanging on to him, her mind swimming, vision blurring. What had they done with her when she'd finally passed out? Tied her to the vehicle so she wouldn't fall off?

The LCD display lit up with an electronic sound that Daisy had formerly found annoying but that now sounded positively cheerful. It was 3:37 a.m. No wonder it was so dark. She'd been unconscious since the middle of the afternoon, over twelve hours.

She punched in Ben's number, fingers trembling in her hurry to hear his voice—he must be frantic! There was no ring and she stared at the message on the tiny greenish display frame, the dim light standing out like fireworks in the utter blackness: No service area.

She was somewhere, possibly a dip in the hills or behind some mountain, where radio signals didn't reach.

Daisy turned off her phone to conserve her battery and

lay back down. She pulled her knees up to her chest, and tried hard not to think of spiders.

She'd committed the cardinal sin of the lone investigative reporter: she'd told no one where she was going. She hadn't arranged for backup. How could she possibly have forgotten to call Ellin? Why hadn't she tried her from the car, when she was waiting for Chip and Dale?

The smell in the cabin nauseated her. She thought of all the horrible crime scenes she'd witnessed in her role as reporter. She'd been an observer; now she was a victim. Just like those two babies. No matter what Oliver had told her, Daisy felt responsible for the suffering they'd gone through. One had died—would he have died if he hadn't been abandoned by the kidnappers, thanks to her article? Maybe not. Oliver had said he would've, but what did he know?

The baby girl had lived. Hot tears rose and Daisy covered her face with her hands. She thought of the infant being returned to frantic parents who'd lived through the nightmare of their child disappearing....

She cried until she slept. For hours, mercifully, because when she woke, she could see a little more. There were pinpricks of light, possibly around boarded-over windows, enough to get her bearings. Enough to make out a few shapes, to know that, yes, she was in a cabin of some kind. The pallet she lay on was built along one wall, well away from the door, which she made out as a dark oblong between what she took to be two small windows.

On the far wall were rows of shelves. In front of them were poles of some kind, maybe ropes, strung across the width of the cabin and there was something on those poles. Something dark. Black. Substantial, but not too big, attached to the poles at intervals.

Daisy felt in her bag for the penlight attached to her car keys. Why had they left her bag? That didn't seem to make any sense, unless they knew she couldn't reach anyone with her phone....

Which meant they were very, very familiar with this place.

Well, duh. Of course they were. Chip and Dale aren't just traveling woodcutters in some fairy tale. Helpful woodsmen who innocently provided tips to the press. They left you here for a reason....

She located her penlight and shone the feeble light down—at a dry dirt floor. No spiders or mice that she could see, but she wasn't going to check the corners. She eased her legs over the side of the bunk and stood up. A little wobbly, but otherwise okay. Just very thirsty.

She tried the old-fashioned latch on the door. It was solidly barred from the outside. What had she expected? The windows were nailed over, too, on the inside and maybe the outside as well, considering how dark it was. Beside the door was a bucket of water sitting on an over-turned wooden box. She scooped some in her hands and smelled it. It appeared to be fresh so she splashed a little on her face and hands. She had a water bottle in her bag that she'd use before she'd drink this. They must be coming back for her—sometime. Why else would they care if she died of dehydration? Or anything else?

Daisy turned toward the other end of the cabin, toward the poles with their mysterious cargo and the shelves— was there anything *on* those shelves?

She clicked on her penlight when she was only a step or two away. She screamed. Bear paws hung from the pole, row on row, each dangling from a short length of yellow nylon rope.

She dropped the light, then scrabbled in the dirt to find it, forcing herself to stop yelling. There was nothing here to be afraid of. No live bears, only their paws. But why? She made herself approach the shelves, and saw, spread along two of them, a dozen or so dark, pouchlike things, several inches across, desiccated and leathery-looking.

Gallbladders. After her conversation with Gordon Bass, she'd researched it on the Internet. Gram for gram, the bile in these bladders was worth four times more than gold in Hong Kong, Japan and parts of China. As the population became wealthier and more people could afford products made from black bear bile, the demand grew. Even though modern chemistry had synthesized many of the useful compounds in the bile, traditional practitioners resisted the substitute and bears continued to die. The indigenous populations were either gone or almost gone, and pressure had turned to the North American black bear. The animal so revered and respected by the natives of North America was being destroyed for a little digestive organ in its belly....

This had to be the site of the poaching activity in the area, probably the source of the gallbladders that had supposedly been found in the back of Arlo's truck. Ben's cousin *must* have been involved. Was this where he was getting the money to buy Laverne a new horse?

Whatever the truth, these gallbladders were being "harvested" by unscrupulous men who were probably paid a pittance compared to their real worth, so-called hunters who cared nothing for animals or the laws of the land. The Chips and Dales of the world. It would be the brains behind this operation, not the hunters, who'd profit. The arranger. The expediter. A person who hired minions to do the actual work and wouldn't even get blood on his hands.

She took out her camera and snapped some pictures blind, jumping at the shock of the flash's white brilliance. If she ever got out of here, she'd have photos....

She froze. Thunder? No, an engine. Were they coming back to get her already? Or was someone coming to rescue her? Maybe Ben had found the convertible and tracked her down!

She thrust everything in her bag and slung the strap over her head and across her chest so it wouldn't fall. Then she positioned herself near the door, opposite the hinge side; that way, if it was opened, she might have a chance of surprising Chip and Dale. She assumed they were the people approaching. She'd dash out. Then what? Run?

The image of herself running through the bush, stumbling, falling, being chased by men in camouflage gear, possibly even carrying weapons, petrified her. And even if she escaped, where would she run?

The engine grew louder and she recognized the growl of an ATV, the up-and-down roar and whine as it lurched and snarled over uneven ground.

One vehicle? Two? It was impossible to say. And there was another sound, too, a distant rumble, that was definitely thunder.

The vehicle stopped outside. Daisy held her breath, her heart deafening her.

"Okay." She heard a half-familiar voice. Who? "This is it, kid. End of the road."

Footsteps approached, one set heavy, the other light. She frowned. Not Chip and Dale, then.

There was a curse as someone slammed at whatever was holding the door shut, then she heard her name. "Wakey-wakey, Daisy! You've got a visitor."

Visitor? Daisy's mind tried to process that information, but suddenly the door was wrenched open, sunlight nearly blinding her. Instinctively, she threw her arm across her eyes. Before she could make her knees move, run for freedom, there was the sound of a brief scuffle and a body was pushed in and the door slammed shut.

"Daisy?" A thin, wispy voice. Scared. A child's.

Omigod! She threw her arms around the boy. "Junior, oh, Junior! What in the world are you *doing* here?"

"Sir—*sir!* Have you got an appointment?"

"No," Ben called over his shoulder as he strode down the corridor of the Glory RCMP detachment. "I don't."

He pushed open the door to Bass's office. "Daisy's missing," he announced, stopping in front of the gray metal desk.

"Oh?" Bass pushed back his chair and looked up. "Since when?"

"Since yesterday. Nobody's seen her since noon yesterday, and don't give me any of that seventy-two-hour missing persons bullshit because you and I both know she's chasing a story she shouldn't be and *wouldn't* be— if you'd been a little more forthcoming."

Ben held the brown paper bag he was carrying high over Bass's desk and tipped it the contents.

"Shit!" Bass leaped to his feet as the bear paw bounced in front of him. "What the—"

"It's exactly what it looks like." The paw lay in the middle of the document that Bass had been reading.

"Where'd you get this?" Bass's jaw was grim.

"Her car." Ben glanced inside the empty bag, then crumpled it and tossed it in the wire trash basket that stood by the desk. "Her car's parked on the Old Sawmill Road. Overnight. Tiny LaPointe saw the Thunderbird on his way to work this morning."

"You had keys?"

"No, I broke in. It isn't hard," Ben said impatiently. "This was on the floor of the back seat. Little gift from someone who knows what's going on around here, from the look of it."

"Hmm."

"Or maybe just bait." Ben hated to put his worst fears into words like that. He'd wondered if someone had used this paw to trick Daisy into a meeting. The whole town knew how obsessed she'd become with the poaching story and with what had really happened between his cousin and Wayne Petrenko.

"I'd have thought her parents might be the ones to bring this to police attention."

"Her parents aren't here," Ben replied. "They're away on vacation. I don't want to contact them just yet." He raked his hands through his hair and took a step back, walked toward the window overlooking the parking lot, then spun around to face Bass. "Oh, hell. Maybe she's just—you know, gone berry picking or for a hike or something." He could hope, couldn't he?

"Yeah. And Goldilocks just happened to find this—" Bass indicated the bear paw with his ballpoint pen "—on her little stroll through the woods."

"I don't want to worry her folks unnecessarily," Ben said. "Maybe she's okay. I don't see the point of upsetting them until we know for sure she's missing." *Or worse.* Ben couldn't think about that. "You know what I mean, *seriously* missing."

"And where, exactly, do *you* come into this?" Bass continued calmly.

Sonuvabitch! Ben was boiling over with frustration. "Me? I'm the only one who's bothered to listen to her theories about what's going on around here. She thinks bear poaching's behind all of it—and so do I. Look at this paw!" Ben picked it up and dropped it back onto the desk. "I'm not sure I believe all that crap about gallbladders in the back of Arlo's truck, or your story about Arlo and Wayne, a couple of pals, *shooting* each other—"

"Where'd you hear about the gallbladders?" Bass's eyes were narrowed. Cool, calculating, professional.

"Everyone in town's heard it. At least the lowlife element has. I got it from Morris Jack, he heard it from Casper Desjarlais and a bunch of other guys."

Bass's jaw tightened. "I think you're right. I think

Daisy's got herself in some trouble she could've avoided quite easily if she'd listened to my advice. I warned her to stay out of this—''

"Warned her!'' Ben slammed his fist on the desk. "Advice! *Everybody* warned her, including me. But you know what? She didn't listen to us. She paid attention to her instincts as a reporter. And she's a damned good reporter, you know that. I believe she's onto something and that's why she's missing now. You've got to go after her.''

Ben's gaze held the staff sergeant's. It killed him to have to come here like this, beg a *cop* for help.

"Okay. I'll get my officers on it right away. The Old Sawmill Road, you say?''

The phone on his desk rang and Bass picked it up. He listened briefly, then put the receiver down very gently.

He looked at Ben. "Marie just called the switchboard. Junior's missing, too.''

CHAPTER TWENTY-SEVEN

DAISY HUGGED the boy hard. Her nose prickled dangerously, but there was no time to waste bawling. Plus she'd just frighten Jurior. They had to get out of there. *Get out—*

"Hey!" She slammed the door with her knee and the flat of her hand, but of course it was already shut and secured as firmly as it had been before. *"Open up!"*

She heard the roar of an engine and shifting gears as the driver sped away. Daisy felt panic rise until it almost choked her.

"Miss?" The boy's voice was faint.

"What, honey?" She put her hand on his sleeve. She couldn't screw up—she *couldn't!*—not when she had this boy to look out for.

"Why is it so dark in here?"

"There's no light. Don't worry, Junior. Your eyes will get used to it in a few minutes." She thought about turning on her penlight to provide a little light and decided to save the batteries. Besides, this way, she hoped the boy wouldn't see the horror at the other end of the cabin.

"Did you ask for me?" the boy's voice went on. "*He* said you did."

"Who said?" Her mind was spinning. Somehow she had to think of a way the two of them could break out of here.

"I don't like to say his name." Daisy felt the perspiration freeze on her scalp. It was cool in the cabin but she was sweating. *Fear.* "Why not?" Her voice croaked.

"'Cause he's bad," Junior said, so quietly she could barely hear him. "*Really* bad. He made my dad die."

What was the boy saying?

Now that she was accustomed to the darkness, Daisy felt she had a second form of sight available to her, a visceral, physical sense of knowing where she was in space, a feeling that seemed to be enhanced by the darkness.

Like an animal in the night.

All she could think about was trying to escape.

"You know what we've got to do, Junior?" She tried to inject a bright note in her voice. "We've got to get out of here."

"How, miss?"

Good question. "I don't know." Daisy hunkered down on her heels and held the boy's arms. He was a sturdy, well-formed boy, as she recalled, but now he seemed so small and thin. "Somehow we'll do it. You and me, okay? We'll figure it out. And whoever that bad guy is, the one who brought you here today, he's going to get caught." Why not go whole hog? "And those bad guys who brought *me* here are going to get caught and go to jail, too. But, first, Job Number One, we're busting out of this cabin."

"Okay, miss."

"And one other thing, Junior. Call me Daisy, okay?"

"Okay." She heard a faint note of relief in his voice. She could feel him relax a little. She was glad she hadn't said they were partners. They weren't partners. He trusted her to take charge, to do the right thing. She was the adult. He was depending on her, as children deserved to depend on adults.

The nightmare vision that had haunted her for months emerged from the darkness but she beat it back. Yes, she'd been stubborn. She'd believed the public had the right to know about the baby-selling ring, the right to know what was going on in their city. She'd been impatient with what she saw as foot dragging by the police and the civic authorities and had tried to force the issue. There was no way of knowing how things would have turned out if she *hadn't* been stubborn. Maybe both babies would have died....

She couldn't live her life over again. What mattered was here and now. This boy was counting on her. No matter what happened, she wasn't going to let him down.

"Are you scared, honey?"

He nodded. Tears threatened again, but Daisy managed to blink them away. "So am I." She'd cry when she was out of here, back in Ben's arms and one hundred per cent safe. "But we're getting out of here, trust me!"

And those bad guys *were* going to jail.

Daisy led the boy to the bunk. "You sit down for a few minutes and have a rest. I'll see if I can find something to bash the door with. If worst comes to worst, we'll dig our way out."

"How come it's so stinky in here?"

"Garbage. Junk. It's a yucky old cabin, that's why." Daisy hoped her explanation was enough. She made her way carefully over the dirt floor, feeling with her feet for a rock or a chunk of wood, anything she could use on the barred door or a window.

She stubbed her toe. It was only a leg on the wood stove in the center of the cabin, which she hadn't really noticed. She bent down to feel around the floor beneath it.

A rock! Each leg of the stove sat on a flattish decent-size rock and she shoved, trying to dislodge one.

"What should I do, Miss—"

"Daisy."

There was a brief pause. "What should *I* do, Daisy?"

"Here." Daisy had managed to remove a stone the size of a saucer. "You use this and I'll use this one." Ha! The stove, a little wobbly now, had given up another rock. "And we'll smash our way out. How does that sound?"

"Good."

Daisy went to one of the windows first, but she quickly rejected that idea. As she suspected, they were boarded over on the outside, as well as the inside. If she had a crowbar...

The door looked solid, but there might be a chance there. As usual with an outer door, the hinges were on the inside and Daisy attacked the rusted upper one while Junior hammered on the hinge below. She wasn't getting anywhere yet, but if they spent some serious time at this, if they could maybe break off the screw heads holding the hinges, or if they could smash the hinges themselves—

"Ouch! Damn!" Daisy threw down the stone and put her middle finger in her mouth, tasting blood.

"I've got an idea," Junior said, looking up at her. For some reason, it seemed a tiny bit lighter in the cabin now. Maybe she was just more used to it. She heard the crack and rumble of thunder again, sounding a lot closer. "Why don't we try and get out the roof?"

"The roof?" Daisy stared up. Kicking the stones from under two of the stove's legs had unbalanced it, wrenching the stovepipe away and revealing a crescent-shaped sliver of light where the metal pipe pierced the roof several feet above their heads. The stovepipe went straight up between two rafters, through a rickety-looking protective tin plate of some sort. There was no ceiling.

"We could knock down that chimney."

"The stove!" She reached down and hugged the boy. "What a terrific plan! You're very smart, aren't you?"

"I am?" The boy sounded pleased.

Daisy could have kissed him. "Of course you are. If

you hadn't come to help me, who knows how long I might've been stuck here?'' She had to keep this light. She couldn't stop thinking that she had to protect the boy from their grim reality, if possible. He was barely nine. He probably had no idea—as she did—why they'd been hidden in this cabin. And so far, thank heavens, he hadn't noticed the bear parts.

Of course, what did she know about kids? He played video games. Maybe he'd already thought of all kinds of gruesome reasons the ''bad guys'' had brought them here.

But why *Junior?* She could see why someone might want to get rid of her—she'd been asking a lot of pesky questions, as so many people in the community had helpfully pointed out. Not just about Arlo and Wayne, but about poaching. Maybe she'd stumbled too close to the truth and whoever was responsible wanted her out of the way. For good, or at least to give her a scare—

''Hey!'' She'd just realized what had been nibbling at the back of her mind ever since the boy was shoved into the cabin. ''I thought you couldn't talk.''

Junior dropped the stone and dusted his hands on the knees of his pants. ''I was just pretending.''

''Why?'' Daisy blurted before it occurred to her that maybe she shouldn't probe. Junior's silence, self-imposed or not, was probably rooted in some emotional cause beyond her understanding.

Junior sighed. ''I was scared. *He* killed my dad and his friend, and I thought if I didn't talk…'' His voice trailed off. ''I was afraid he'd hurt my mom and my sister or my dog,'' he whispered.

''He?''

''Granny says it isn't good to say bad people's names,'' he continued quietly, looking down at his knees.

''Can you tell me what he did?'' she asked gently. ''You

don't have to say his name. I wouldn't want you to, if you think your Granny wouldn't like it.''

Daisy was torn. On the one hand, she didn't want to waste a moment getting out of their prison, especially with a storm coming and especially now that it looked like she night be able to push the chimney down and break through that tin plate up there with a pole or something. On the other hand, if the bad guy—or guys—wanted to hurt them, why hadn't it happened already? If Junior's kidnapper had driven away not half an hour ago, Daisy felt it was logical, even in her fevered state, that he wasn't going to return in the next fifteen minutes.

Junior seemed ready to talk. He seemed to know something about how his father had died, or he thought he did, anyway. Who knew what went through the mind of a kid? She wouldn't push him, but if he wanted to confide in her, it couldn't hurt to sit here for a few minutes and hear him out.

And it couldn't hurt to turn on the microrecorder in her canvas carry-all either.

Just in case.

BEN LEFT the detachment and got into his truck. He sat there for a minute.

Junior gone!

Why the hell were people going missing all of a sudden? Coincidence? Probably the same old thing, the kid taking off without telling anyone. He'd been doing that a lot since Arlo died, driving Marie crazy. But now, with Daisy missing, too, Ben couldn't help the cold clutch of fear in his gut. *What if the disappearances were related?*

But that made no sense at all. Daisy might well be in trouble because of her persistence in chasing that stupid story, but Junior had no connection to any of it.

No, he'd just taken off again, damn kid, at the worst possible moment.

Poor Marie.

He decided to go to the reserve first. Marie would've checked with Florence before calling the cops. These days, Junior spent as much time at his great-grandmother's as he did at home. Ben wasn't sure what the big attraction was. Probably Queenie's pups. And, to give her credit, Florence was a very undemanding woman. She wouldn't be pestering the boy, trying to get him to talk, trying to "fix" him. She'd just go about her work, as she always did, gardening, repairing things, mending her traps, getting ready for next winter's trapping season.

Florence always had time. Ben remembered that from when he was a kid. She'd spend an hour watching a robin build a nest. To her, that was doing something. She never hurried, never watched a clock. He'd seen an old man's wristwatch on her window sill, over her sink—Grandpa Henry's?—but Ben didn't recall any other kind of time-piece in the cabin. Certainly no alarm clock.

There was nothing to get up for but the sun.

Ben understood why Junior, wounded as he was, would seek out the old woman's company. But Ben also knew that Marie was worried her son wasn't spending enough time with friends his age. He didn't seem to be getting over the shock of Arlo's death.

Ben slowed as he spotted a familiar pickup coming toward him, then braked when the vehicle stopped. He rolled down his window.

"Hey, Ben." It was Casper Desjarlais, with two of his "gang" in the cab with him. "Any sign of Daisy yet?"

Ben was surprised. Evidence yet again that there were no secrets in small towns. "No. I talked to Bass and he's putting some men on it."

"It's been, what, a day since anyone's seen her?" Casper shook his head. "I've asked around some myself. Nobody seems to know where she could be."

"Don't worry. The cops'll find her." Ben put his pickup back into gear and eased up on the clutch. He was no friend of the cops, but he'd never thought they couldn't do their job. Nor did he want to give Casper the impression that he was panicked about Daisy, which he was. "Say, you or any of your boys see Junior around?"

"Hell, he missing too?" Casper sounded incredulous. He glanced at the "warrior" sitting next to him. His passenger shrugged. The light wasn't too good, but Ben was pretty sure he recognized Alan Poundmaker.

"Probably just went over to visit his friend Stevie," Ben said. "I'm taking a run out to check."

"The little dickens," Casper said with a grin. "Runnin' off again, eh? Marie's gonna have to put a line on the little bugger, tie him down."

Ben saw another pickup coming from the reserve, behind Casper's, so he let in the clutch and continued on. Since Daisy had surprised him in the shower—was it really less than a week ago?—he'd felt a little guilty about neglecting Marie and the kids. Daisy had turned his life inside out and upside down, and there was no going back. He wanted to clear up this damnfool business with Junior and do what every nerve and sinew in his body was begging him to: look for Daisy.

The reserve wasn't far from his ranch if you knew the shortcut that went over the spine of the hill. Junior could have walked there in forty minutes, if he'd been so inclined. The same path branched off in a slightly different direction toward Florence's end of the valley. Ben didn't know if the paths were a series of game trails or old aboriginal hunting trails but, as kids, he and Arlo had walked through the bush to their grandmother's many times.

Just yesterday, Ben had offered to take Junior to see his

best friend, Stevie Walks With A Stick, at Pekisko, and for a few minutes he thought the boy had actually considered it. In the end, Junior'd gone home and when Ben asked Marie, she said he was in his room playing video games. Still, Ben didn't think he'd imagined the spark of interest. Maybe Junior had walked to Stevie's on his own.

Big dark clouds were collecting to the west. Looked like Harold had been right; rain was coming. Good thing, too, since the bush was tinder dry. He was luckier than most. His river flats hay crops always wicked moisture from below, and this year he'd had a bumper first cut.

Find Daisy. It was hell, being torn two ways like this— three ways, if you counted Harold needing him. He kept telling himself to settle down, be rational, the cops would find her. They had manpower, equipment, they had a helicopter they could call in if necessary. He kept telling himself she'd just wandered off, gotten turned around somewhere....

That was what he desperately wanted to believe.

Ben pulled up at the Walks With A Stick residence, a comfortable seventies-style rancher with evidence of children around—swing set, home-made sandbox with grass growing in the corners, a couple of dogs lazing in the shade, bicycles, a basketball hoop in the driveway. Stevie was shooting hoops with another boy when Ben drove up.

"Hey," he said, getting out of the truck.

"Hey, Ben!" Stevie fired the ball his way and Ben caught it and tossed it at the basket. Missed. The boys laughed.

Ben crouched down and came in on a layup the older boy was attempting and got the ball from him. He dropped it in the net. "Not bad for an old guy, huh?" He grinned. "Listen, you guys see Junior?"

"Junior?" Stevie frowned. "I haven't seen him since school got out. Have you, Leonard?"

The other boy shook his head and Ben's heart sank. "You mean he isn't here? I thought he might've come over on the back trail."

"Is he talkin' yet?" Leonard's expression was curious.

Ben shook his head. "Not yet, but the doc says he'll be feeling better soon. He's going through a tough time. I guess you know that."

"Yeah. I saw him the day his dad died," Leonard said. "Whew! That was a real bad day." He shook his head.

"You *saw* him? Where?" Ben's recollection of events that day was sketchy. Marie had taken out the school bus in the morning and she hadn't been notified of Arlo's death until she got home, around noon. Marie drove a different route than the one her kids were on and, besides, Junior had spent the night before at Stevie's house....

"Walking down the road there." The boy pointed to the north. "Me 'n' my dad had to go out and get our pinto that kept breaking out of the fence. Dad said I had to help 'cause it was my fault he got out. We were coming back and it was pourin' rain and I saw Junior standing by the side of the road."

"Waiting for the school bus?" Ben was thoroughly confused.

"He never got on no school bus!" Stevie said. "He was supposed to, but I told my mom he walked home instead 'cause he felt homesick but really he was—" Suddenly the boy colored. His eyes shot to Ben, and then to his friend.

"What, Stevie?" Ben asked urgently. "You can tell me. It could be important. After what happened to Junior's dad, you can be sure his mom's plenty worried about where he is."

"It isn't that. Junior said it was a secret. I wasn't supposed to tell nobody and I didn't, and then after—after it happened—" He broke off and swallowed. Ben could see he was about to burst into tears. "Junior didn't go home 'cause he felt homesick, that was just a story we made up so nobody'd try and stop him. He met up with his dad. They were supposed to go fishing and not tell anyone. It was a birthday surprise from his dad 'cause Junior's mom would've been real mad if he missed school for that."

It was exactly the sort of thing Arlo would've done. Ben's ears felt fuzzy. He couldn't take in what he was hearing.

"And he had my cap, too!" Stevie said. "My new Stampeders cap, and now his dad got killed and he never brought it back."

"Calgary *Flames?*" Ben felt horror tugging at his gut.

"No. Junior had a Flames cap already. He wanted to wear my Stampeders cap."

Ben wheeled and headed for his truck. "Thanks, guys," he said through the open window. He reached for the ignition, trying his best to keep his voice level. Ordinary. "If he comes over, you call his house and tell Marie, okay?"

"Sure, Ben."

He left the boys shooting hoops and arguing amicably, just as he'd found them.

Flames or Stampeders?

He fumbled for his cell in the glove compartment. Either way, he had to talk to Bass.

CHAPTER TWENTY-EIGHT

FLORENCE WAS FEEDING the hens when Ben arrived. She set the coffee can of grain on a fencepost and walked toward him.

"Quiet!" she said when the dogs barked. At five weeks, Queenie's litter was running all over the yard. They yipped and ran straight for mama, though, when Dodger jumped out of the truck and started sniffing their back ends, frightening them.

Her grandson looked rougher than he had at his cousin's funeral a month and a half ago. He needed a shave and a haircut. It was because of that woman, Daisy. Marie said she'd gone missing the day before and now little Junior had run off....

"Any word on the boy, son?" she asked as she approached the pickup. Ben waited for her, slumped against the front fender. Tongues of lightning flashed to the southwest, followed by the deep rumble of thunder.

"Nothing, Nan. I thought he might be at the reserve, at Stevie's." He sighed and ran his hands through his hair. Looked like he hadn't slept for a week. Might've been going without sleep even *before* the newspaper lady went missing, if what she'd heard from Marie was true and it probably was. Marie might not be her favorite relation but she wasn't an everyday liar.

Good for him. Ben deserved some happiness.

"Storm coming," she said, not sure yet why he'd come.

He'd arrived in a cloud of dust and now he was just standing there staring into space.

"It'll be over soon," he said, not really paying attention to her. He was working something out in his mind. "Little thunder and lightning, and that'll be it."

"I don't think so." She glanced at her hens. Long ago, she'd noticed that the hens knew about rain. In a shower, they stayed out in the yard, pecking and scratching, getting their feathers wet. When the rain was going to last, they went into the henhouse before it started and didn't come out until it was over.

You couldn't fool hens.

"Nan, your trapline runs back of the Old Sawmill Road, doesn't it?"

She considered, going through the geography in her mind. Maps didn't mean much to her; landmarks did. "I suppose it does. It takes a bend north just at the fork in Mosquito Creek and then heads west along the flats. The old mill site's not far from the flats. There's nothing there now. Why?"

"Besides the mill site, do you know of any buildings in the area? Maybe a cabin of some kind? Any shacks left by the oil companies? Loggers' skid shacks?"

"Nothing. Hasn't been for years, not since Old Man Standish had a trapline, but that'd be over forty years ago."

"You think he built a cabin?" Ben's eyes were sharp on hers.

"He built a good-size cabin there once, yes. Was going to move Mildred and the kids in, but she put her foot down. It'd be too far off the road, she said, when the kids got old enough to go to school."

Ben went to his truck and rifled around. He came out with a torn envelope and started drawing something on the back. "You think you could give me an idea where it is,

Nan? Say, here's the road to Castello Mountain and here's where the Old Sawmill Road crosses it.'' He showed her the scrap of paper, which meant nothing to her. ''Now, here—'' he drew a wiggly line ''—this is where your trapline runs. Would the cabin be in here somewhere?''

He looked so hopeful, poor boy. Florence concentrated. She forced herself to remember walking through the woods, along the river, up over the hill he was talking about. There was a big windfall on that hill, a pine turned over, and she'd seen a lynx crouching on it one winter and wondered if it had a den nearby. Then she tried to think of standing on the hill by the windfall and turning around toward the old sawmill, which was only a heap of rotten sawdust now, maybe some angle iron, a grinder's wheel or two, and looking out over the country. She thought of where the Standish place was from there. Funny, she saw it in winter, with snow on the ground, the way she'd always seen it.

''Here,'' she said, putting her finger on the envelope.

Ben stared at the spot she'd touched. He drew an X on the paper. ''Could I drive there?''

Florence shook her head. ''Too rough. Mile and a half at least, maybe more. There are a few paths through here.'' She moved her finger across the paper he held out. ''Game trails. A horse could make it or a Ski-Doo in the winter.''

''Thanks, Nan.'' He gave her a weary smile and stuffed the envelope in his shirt pocket. ''I'm going to look for Junior up there. I don't know what else to do. The cops are searching for Daisy. I've got a bad feeling about this. I keep thinking if we find Daisy, we might find Junior, too.''

She gave him a wondering look. ''You think he might be way up there? Junior didn't come here today, son,'' she said sadly, shaking her head again. ''Marie insisted he did, but he didn't. No one came here today except her, looking for the boy. And you.''

"*Who* said Junior came here?" Ben frowned.

"Casper told Marie he dropped the boy off at the lane and Junior walked in.''

"I saw Casper coming from the reserve and he never—'' Ben stared at her. Then he swore in a way that she didn't really approve of; she'd never allowed her men to swear. But she wasn't going to say anything.

He whistled for Dodger and the two of them drove away.

CLOUDS PILED UP and lightning and thunder streaked across the sky while they were widening the gap between the rafters the stovepipe had filled. Daisy had swallowed her nausea and removed one of the long poles set into boards that were nailed to the walls, sliding the grisly cargo off the end of the pole into a dark heap in a corner. She was grateful Junior didn't ask what she was doing.

Then, with the boy supporting her for balance, she'd poked and prodded at the tin plate until it bent and folded. One whole side came free, and a board broke away. The roof was rotten.

"Okay, Junior. I think we've got it." The electrical storm frightened her, but not as much as the thought of those men coming back. If they did come back, there'd be no warning. She'd never hear an engine over the thunder now. It was only late afternoon, but clouds seemed to blot out the sky. Flashes of lightning intermittently lit up the interior of the cabin, and the wind sucked and blew through the hole in the roof.

"I'll hold you, and you try to get up there. Think you can do it?" Daisy had jammed the rocks back under the stove legs to stabilize it and intended to stand on the stove, using the pole for balance. The stove was made from an empty steel oil drum and seemed sturdy. She hoped she'd be able to lift Junior high enough so he could get his hands on the edges of the roof planks and then she'd heave from below. She prayed the roof would hold him.

Daisy hoped that once he was on the roof, he'd see a way to get himself down, then open the door for her.

"I think I can." The boy sounded more confident than she felt.

"If we don't get the job done right away, we'll just keep trying until we do, okay?"

"Okay."

Daisy clambered onto the stove and reached down to help Junior up. The top of the stove was about three feet off the floor. Daisy was five feet five inches. She weighed 110 pounds. Well, okay, 114 pounds. From the feel of it, she thought, pulling Junior up, he weighed about as much as she did.

Impossible. But she definitely wasn't the strongest person in the world; she knew that. Why didn't she spend time at the gym? Work out the way Emily did?

"Okay. Now, I'll grab you around the middle." Even as she said the words, Daisy knew there was no way Junior was going to be anywhere near the roof. She heaved him up, just to give it a try, then set him down again.

"Damn." They stood together on the stovetop, which was about eighteen inches wide and three and a half feet long. "Oh!" Daisy jumped down and got her canvas bag. "I nearly forgot. Here." She handed him two granola bars and a package of gum, which was all the food she had. There was sugar in the gum. Sugar was energy, in case he needed it. "Put these in your pocket. Remember, if you can't get the door open, you're to leave me here and go for help. Promise?"

"Promise."

They'd agreed that Junior would follow the ATV trail

out to the road and walk for help. "Don't worry about water. I'm sure there'll be plenty around with this storm."

As though in response to her words, a huge whooshing sound filled the cabin, accompanied by an earsplitting crack. The cabin lit up like a fluorescent tube. All around them the atmosphere hissed and zinged, and Daisy felt her hair stand on end. She smelled burned air—was there such a thing? The thunder right above them deafened her. She'd been scared before but now she was terrified.

"Here, Junior," she yelled. She climbed back onto the stove and bent over, bracing her arms against her knees. "You get up on my back—that's it!" The boy was whimpering, but he was following her orders. "Now stand up slowly, hang on to my shoulders until you get your balance, and see if you can grab the edge of the hole. Take your time!"

She didn't *really* mean take your time, she just wanted to encourage him. Daisy prayed her knees would hold out. He was heavy, but fear had given her extra strength.

"I think I can reach it!" She felt his weight on her back ease, then one foot lift up, then the other. She whirled around and began to push, getting her shoulder under his feet, helping take his weight while he hoisted himself onto the roof. "I'm okay!" he yelled back.

Then he was gone. He was a wiry little guy but strong. *Oh, thank heaven!* Daisy felt the tears run down her cheeks—or was it rain? She didn't care. At least Junior was out. And safe, she hoped. That child had been through hell. Even if the men came back right now, he could hide in the bush, as he'd done before. They'd never find him.

She heard him walking around on the roof, going one way, then the other. He shouted something she couldn't make out and after that she couldn't hear his footsteps anymore. He must've managed to reach the ground.

She could still hear hissing and crackling. In her numbed

state it took her several minutes to realize that what she was seeing through the jagged hole in the cabin roof wasn't lightning—it was fire. The lightning strike that had nearly deafened and blinded them had hit a tree nearby. In this dry country, no rain for over a month, the bush would be like tinder and that tree wasn't far from the cabin....

She couldn't think about that. She got down from the stove, her knees shaky and her arms weak, and leaned against the wall.

Junior had made it down from the roof. He was nine years old. Would he be able to open the door to let her out?

BEN RAN AND RAN, his lungs burning. The storm had rolled in quickly and lightning flashed all around. There'd be work for forest fire crews out of this, he thought, grabbing for his next breath. Dodger was all business, racing beside him.

The trail forked. Which way. Which *way?* Dodger ran a few steps down the path that seemed most traveled and looked back at him.

It was a sign.

Ben pounded down that trail. He must've run a mile and a half already, maybe two.

A huge streak of flame split the sky and Ben stumbled and fell, got up again. That one was close. Not more than a few hundred yards away.

He didn't know why he was so sure Daisy was in this area but he was. Her car had been left just off the highway, on the narrow little-traveled sawmill road, and if she'd been kidnapped, she could've been taken anywhere in a vehicle. But the feeling that she was nearby persisted....

What was that? A small clearing off to the right contained what looked like a shed.

Ben veered off the trail and came to a stop, hands on his knees, panting. No, it was a work yard of some kind. An open shed with an older all-terrain vehicle in it, room for two, one missing. Some wooden boxes stacked up. A gas can. An old campfire, used quite a lot over a period of time, from the look of it. Pile of empty tin cans, beans, corned beef, pineapple. Empty liquor bottles, mostly rye. Partyers? Kids?

Ben ran to the ATV. No key. He reached under the handlebars and ripped out the ignition wires, fumbling as he worked, his fingers thick, his chest hurting.

Thank God he'd learned a few tricks as a juvenile delinquent. The ATV started with a roar—hey, he still had the old magic—and Ben clapped his hands for Dodger to jump into the heavy metal cargo box welded to the front of the machine. He followed the trail that led from the clearing, since he didn't know what else to do.

There was smoke in the air. Little fires would be springing up all over the bush thanks to this lightning. With any luck, Florence was right and the rain would last, extinguishing most of them before they got out of hand.

The wind carried rain already, lashing his face, although the storm had not broken fully. The other-worldly scent of ozone filled his mouth—

Shit!

Ben let up on the gas. Another ATV was roaring toward him on the trail, full speed. Who was that? One of the Mounties? Ben stopped and jumped off the machine. He hoped Bass's men were around; he'd seen a couple of cop cars but no manpower when he'd left his truck at the end of the old logging road and started running.

Casper Desjarlais.

Casper looked scared. His face was greasy with sweat and his hands were dirty. He had on work pants, an old sweat shirt and hiking boots.

"Ben!"

"You sonuvabitch! *Where's Daisy?*"

"What you talking about?" Casper's face was pale. He glanced automatically over his shoulder and Ben's gaze followed his. There was nothing but trees, swaying in the wind. "I'm looking for her, just like you. I thought I'd take a ride up here, see if I could find her—"

"You lying bastard!" Ben lunged for his boyhood friend and knocked him off the machine. An empty gas can fell off the back of Casper's ATV.

"Leave me alone, Ben! I swear, I'm doing the best I can to find her, just like everybody else. And the boy!" he shouted. "I'm looking for Arlo's boy."

"You goddamn liar! You told Marie he was at Florence's. You've done something with him. With both of them!"

This time, Ben looked up the trail and saw smoke rising. *Black* smoke suddenly billowing above the trees. Hydrocarbon. Wood smoke was white or gray.

He jumped back on the ATV. Bass would have to handle Casper; Ben had no time.

He roared around the bend in the trail and then another, and his heart stopped. To the east, downwind, wisps of white smoke curled up as the grass and low bushes caught. A big poplar, nearly burned already, was the source of the ground fire, blown up by the wind.

But the black smoke...

A cabin was on fire. A derelict log cabin, which burned evenly, unnaturally, from the ground up on all four sides.

"*No!*" Ben hit the throttle and surged toward the cabin. *Daisy was in there. He had to get Daisy out—*

Where was the door? Ben raced around to the south side of the building. There was a wooden door, barred with a piece of two-by-four. The windows were sealed, boarded up. He ripped at the two-by-four, the heat of the fire searing his skin.

"*Daisy!*" Was that his voice? He sounded like a man demented. He *was* demented; Daisy was in here, maybe Junior, too. His life was over if they died in here. He had to get them out. There was no other way, no one to help him....

He flung the two-by-four away and pulled at the rope latch. The door opened and Ben darted inside. The dark cabin vibrated with a ghastly red glow from the roof, which was fully ablaze, with pieces of burning rafter and cladding falling inside. "Daisy!"

There was no answer. He stumbled into the corner, gagged as he tripped and fell down, right beside a pile of stinking fur. He could see claws glowing in the light from the fire. *More bear paws.*

This was the poachers' lair, all right—but where were Daisy and Junior?

Dodger stood at the door, barking frantically. Pay attention to the dog. Get out of here. *Now!*

Ben staggered to the bunk on the other side of the cabin and felt around. No Daisy; no Junior. He lunged for the door and a beam fell, smashing him on the side of his chest and knocking him down. He got up and grabbed the door jamb and pulled himself through, just as most of the roof collapsed into the cabin in a fiery heap.

He was safe. He was alive.

But where was the woman he loved?

CHAPTER TWENTY-NINE

BEN LAY SPRAWLED facedown on the wet grass, trying to catch his breath. His side hurt but the rain, which had started to pelt down, felt good.

How long he lay there feeling the heat of the cabin burning behind him, he didn't know. How much of the wet on his face was sweat or rain or tears, he didn't know.

Dodger licked his hand and he started. He'd forgotten about the dog. The storm had moved on. Thunder pounded farther to the east now.

He forced himself up onto his elbows, favoring his right side. He must have cracked a rib or two. It hurt to breathe.

"What is it, fella?" Dodger was whining and barking in short sharp yips as he did when he wanted Ben to get up from watching a hockey game on TV and follow him to the cupboard where the dog cookies were kept.

Ben got to his knees and began to cough. It was agony. He hung his head for a minute, trying to clear his brain, then stood up. The cabin was fully ablaze. He backed up a few steps and watched as one end of the dwelling fell outward, sending sparks flying, setting the long grass on fire.

He should get out of here. The fire was going to surround him if he wasn't careful.

Dodger raced around him a couple of times. Each time he circled Ben, he darted off toward the east, where the grass smoldered and the big lightning-struck poplar burned.

"That's not the way, pal," Ben muttered. He started to skirt the cabin, heading to where he'd left the ATV, but something about the way Dodger was acting bothered him. Ben whistled, but Dodger just whined and ran in a little circle and looked at him again, head to one side.

He wanted Ben to follow him.

Maybe the cabin had been empty all along. Maybe Daisy and Junior had never been there. Maybe they'd been taken someplace else.

But then why would Casper have hurried here to pour gasoline around the place and set it on fire? As soon as Ben had seen that oily black smoke, he'd guessed what Casper had done.

Maybe to destroy some kind of evidence now that he knew the bush was alive with cops combing the woods, looking for Daisy? Evidence of poaching?

That made sense.

But the tinder-dry forest was already on fire—why would he risk coming up here himself?

Ben shook his head groggily. Okay. That *didn't* make sense.

He couldn't think straight. He decided to follow Dodger.

The dog led him over windfalls and through some muskeg, right through a section filled with wisps of smoke. In several places, in the distance, he saw trees on fire, but the rain was getting heavier by the minute.

Ben was soaked. He clambered down a steep rocky slope, hoping he'd be able to retrace his steps when he got to the end of Dodger's wild-goose chase. He tripped, rolled a few feet, nearly to the bottom of the incline, then lay on his back, panting. Listening.

"Dodger!"

He heard a faint cry mixed with Dodger's yelps and he leaped to his feet and nearly fell again.

Daisy! Junior!

He staggered down the rest of the hill, which ended in a low, boggy area and followed the sound of Dodger's barking to a place where the wet ground gave way to a narrow, deep stream.

"Ben!" It was Junior!

"Where are you, boy?"

"Over here! By the willows!"

Ben lunged along the bank, then pushed aside a clump of willows and gazed at a sight he'd never expected to see. There was Arlo's son, sitting on the bank with Dodger in his lap, and there was the woman he loved with all his heart, looking like hell, with her face dirty and her hair burned, her arm in a sling made out of a shoelace, her pants torn. She was wearing only one shoe; the other foot was bare. Bright-orange polish on her toes.

The canvas bag, dirty and wet, was plopped beside her on the bank.

"Ben!" She reached up to him with her good right arm and he scooped her up, ignoring the fierce pain in his side, and covered her face with kisses.

"Daisy! Oh, my darling," he muttered, his throat tight. "I never thought I'd see you again." He turned to the boy. "You okay, Junior?"

"I'm okay, Ben." Junior stood in front of him, his face alight with joy and pride through the grime and the soot. He seemed an inch taller and, miracle of miracles, he was talking again. "I saved her, Ben! I got Daisy out. I remembered everything my dad said to do when you're in trouble in the bush. Even put a sling on 'cause her arm got hurt. We lost her shoe and we drank creek water and I tore my shirt!"

Ben looked down. Daisy was trying to say something. "Don't forget my bag," she whispered hoarsely. "I've got pictures—"

Then she fainted in his arms.

BEN PULLED UP in front of the Sutherland residence. He started to take a deep breath, then winced. He couldn't sneeze, he couldn't cough, he couldn't even laugh with his ribs taped, but the doctors said the bandages could come off in two weeks and they'd told him at the hospital that it could've been worse. He was lucky.

Yeah. He was a lucky man, all right. And he'd know soon if he was going to be a whole lot luckier.

He hadn't seen Daisy since it happened, three days ago. Just that glimpse of her and Junior being loaded into the ambulance. She'd protested weakly, but Junior, hardly recognizable because he was so filthy—although fortunately uninjured—had asked if he could switch on the siren.

Halfway back to where he'd left the truck, he'd come across some of Bass's men as he carried Daisy half-conscious in his arms, Junior hanging on in the seat behind him on the ATV. They'd had to take it slow, Ben cursing every bump, praying that the only thing wrong with her was exhaustion and shock from the injury to her arm. A burn, he thought.

Bass had taken Casper away in handcuffs. Ben would never forget the look on the bastard's face. He'd betrayed them all. Him, Arlo, Wayne, Marie—everyone, all for the sake of a little cash. Maybe not a little; he'd been paid plenty for the gallbladders by a Vancouver intermediary, who'd been arrested by Vancouver police. But as Bass pointed out, the fool didn't even know that bear paws, a contraband Far East delicacy that rich patrons paid over a thousand dollars a plate for in Taiwan or Seoul or Hong Kong, had to be fresh or frozen. There was no market, legal or illegal, for the dried, rotting bits of gristle, claw and fur that he had stored in that cabin.

Ben shuddered. That was a nightmare he'd never forget: the cabin ablaze and his belief that Daisy and Junior were inside.

He left Dodger in the truck, grabbed the Henderson's Hardware bag and rang the doorbell. Marian Sutherland answered almost immediately. She smiled and held the door wide, but Ben hadn't missed that split second's hesitation and surprise.

"Welcome! Daisy will be *so* pleased to see you," she chirped, escorting him into the cool, dim foyer. Sunshine poured in the long windows in the living room, off to the right and at the end of the hall, and the place smelled of flowers and beeswax. He pondered whether to mention the broken clasp on the east basement window but decided maybe another time.

Ben followed her stiff back up the stairs. He'd have his work cut out with this woman. But he wasn't worried about meeting Marian Sutherland's expectations, formidable or otherwise. Her daughter was another story. The rescue was over; reality had returned. She'd had time to think about things and so had he.

Daisy was in bed, propped up against a half-dozen white linen pillows, an overturned paperback book on the blanket by her right hand. Her hair was short, fluffed out around her face. Her eyes were bright.

"Ben!"

She was happy to see him.

He looked around and sat down in the delicate chair positioned by her bedside. Flowers and cards filled the room. It reminded him of something. A funeral? No, maybe a birth...

Oddly, he felt awkward, now that he was actually here. "How are you, Daisy?"

"Oh, Ben, I'm so—" Her eyes filled with tears. She glanced over his shoulder. "How are *you?* Uh, Dad told me you'd cracked a couple of ribs. Are you okay?"

He nodded. "I'm fine." He cleared his throat. "Your hair—" He couldn't go on for a split second, then got his emotions under control. *She could have been burned to death. His life would have been finished, too.* "It's beautiful."

A tear spilled over and she put her good hand on her crown, covered in short golden curls. "Oh, it's not. It's not, Ben. It's *horrible.*"

Ben cleared his throat again. Mrs. Sutherland was still in the room, humming a little, adjusting a blind, touching a flower arrangement, running her finger along a tabletop as though checking for dust. The Sutherlands' had returned from their trip to Saskatchewan as soon as they'd heard about Daisy's ordeal.

Daisy cleared her throat, too. Very audibly. And stared directly at her mother for several seconds.

"Oh! I'll be right downstairs if you need me, dear," Marian Sutherland murmured. "Just call if you want anything, anything at all."

She left the room, leaving the door ajar, and Daisy grabbed at Ben's hand. "All I want is *you,*" she said fervently. "All I could think about the whole time I was locked up in there was that I had to get out so I could get back to *you.*"

Ben leaned forward. Her mouth was soft and sweet, exactly as he remembered. *Everything was all right.* He kissed her, pressing her back into the pillows, until he realized her face was wet with tears.

"You okay, honey?" He wiped awkwardly at the curve of her cheek with the side of his hand. "Really?"

"I'm fine," she said, not looking fine at all. "It's just the emotion—it overwhelms me sometimes. I'm weepy. I keep thinking about poor Junior. That boy's been through hell, Ben."

"Marie says he won't stop talking," Ben interrupted dryly. "Kids recover fast."

"Oh, I know he's okay, but—" She reached for a tissue

on the table beside her and blew her nose. "Honestly! I don't really need to be in bed at all. The doctor said I should take it easy and Mother won't let me out. I'm so glad you're here." She squeezed his hand. "Did Gordon tell you what happened? That tape in my bag—it's all on there. And I got pictures—"

"You would."

"That terrible, terrible man is going to jail forever." She blew her nose again.

"Don't think about that, Daisy." Ben wiped a fresh tear from her cheek. "It's over now. Time to think about the future."

She took a deep breath. "Alice Petrenko came over yesterday. She told me Wayne had been involved in a real mess back East, and he'd been sent here for punishment. Just as Dad suspected. He'd dipped into some of the evidence he was supposed to collect from his undercover drug work and ended up in detox—"

"Shh, honey." Ben framed her face with his hands. "Don't talk about it. Please. There's plenty of time to go over the details later."

But she was out of the gate, and Ben decided he might as well let her run....

"The cops apparently tried to keep it quiet, Ben. He was an embarrassment—that's why he was sent out here. Then he got mixed up with Casper and tried to go undercover on his own—"

Ben finally kissed her, just to shut her up. Well, he might have had another reason....

She smiled when he sat back, holding her hands in both of his. "Okay. We can talk about it later. I'm just so—so happy you finally came to see me. What took you so long, Ben?" Her voice cracked a little.

"I needed to sort a few things out," he said gruffly.

"Like what?"

"Like find out if I was ready to take a big step in my life."

"Marry...Marie?" Was she really only kidding? Her eyes had a tiny hurt look, as though she'd actually thought, even for a moment, that she wasn't the only woman in his life, that he might not come to see her as soon as he could.

"That's not part of the plan anymore."

"Oh?"

He stared into her eyes. He'd always thought she had the bluest eyes he'd ever seen. "I'm not sure that it was ever much of a plan. The truth is, I've only met one woman I want to spend my life with."

"And?"

"That's you, Daisy."

She sat straight up, smiling. "Are you asking me to marry you?" She was utterly, perfectly beautiful to him, with her short-cropped hair and her bandaged left arm. Her direct gaze. Her impish smile.

"I guess I am." He tried to smile, too, but it was hard when his heart was so full....

She reached up and pulled him close, her right hand on the back of his neck. "Is that cowboy talk for 'I love you?'" she demanded, her face inches from his.

"Yeah, that's what I'm trying to tell you. I love you, Daisy." His voice grew firm as he found the words. "I love you and I want to spend the rest of my life with you, no matter what. I don't have much to offer, just a few pie-in-the-sky bucking horse prospects and some damn fine river flat hay country but if you'll have me, I'd be honored. You're all I want."

"You're all I want, too, Ben. Oh, yes, yes, *yes!*" Daisy pulled him even closer and planted her lips on his. He tried to remember not to hurt her bandaged arm. She had no such scruples and he was groaning when she let him go.

"Oh!" She drew back. "Your ribs. I'm so sorry!"

He grinned. "Don't be." His head was reeling. How could anything hurt when he was so happy? He'd never dreamed this would ever happen to him—he'd fall head over heels in love with the most unsuitable woman he could've imagined. Crazy and impetuous, yes, but also loyal and determined. Honest. Bold. Brave. Passionate. About him, about justice, about making things right in the world.

Damn, he needed to kiss her properly. He got up to close the door and noticed a huge bouquet of yellow and white roses on the dresser, in front of a gilt mirror, with a weird-looking bare wooden branch in the middle of the blooms. "Nice flowers," he said. "What's the stick for?" Much as he disliked cut flowers, he now wished he'd brought some. It was a romantic gesture, after all. Not one that had ever crossed his mind before.

"Supposed to be an olive branch, I think. They're from Gordon," she said softly. Slyly. "Did you bring me something? I see you have a bag with you."

"Yeah." He reached into the Henderson's Hardware bag and pulled out a brand-new paint roller, still in its cellophane wrapper. He left the second roller in the bag. "Maybe I should've brought flowers—"

"What's *this*?" she squealed, obviously delighted.

"Just what it looks like. I thought maybe when your arm gets better, we could open up a gallon of that Coral Tassel paint I bought at Henderson's this morning and get started."

"Oh, Ben!" She buried her face in his neck. That was the color she'd wanted to paint the spare room where he kept his pool table. The pool table they'd already christened—although the balls and cues hadn't left the rack.

He wrapped his arms around her and held her tight, ignoring his protesting ribs.

Coral Tassel. Silky Wheat. Genoa Aubergine. He didn't care. She could paint his house any damn color she wanted—just as long as she agreed to share it with him.

CHAPTER THIRTY

"YOU MEAN Arlo's son was there—actually *saw* the whole thing?" Emily gave Daisy a horrified look.

The two of them stood by the fence that separated the rodeo ring from the spectators. In the ring, constructed by volunteers from temporary fences, children aged five to seven or eight were riding sheep bareback, while the spectators cheered them from seats in the ball park bleachers.

"Yes," Daisy said, frowning, "It's pretty awful to think about, isn't it? Although I must say Junior seems to have come out of it fairly well."

"Is that him over there?" Emily pointed to the opposite side of the ring, where a group of young boys clustered around the entrances to the various animal pens, steers that would be ridden by the older boys and the sheep that were favorites of the younger children. The clown, a role played by one of Laverne's friends, rode a burro decked out with a sun hat and scarf, although the goggles the children had originally inflicted upon the beast had fallen off somewhere.

"Yes. Apparently Arlo had secretly arranged to take Junior fishing that day. Junior said his father told him he was meeting Casper for a few minutes before they went fishing and then, when they got to the meeting place, they saw Wayne and the police cruiser. No sign of Casper. Arlo got out of his pickup to talk to Wayne, and there was a shot and Wayne went down. Poor Junior!" Daisy shook her head. "He's a brave boy. He told me all this while we

were stuck in that cabin and then he repeated most of it
to Gordon when we were in the hospital.''

"Speaking of which, how's the arm?''

Daisy looked at her left arm. The bandage had come off
but she knew she'd have a scar when it healed fully. It
seemed the whole forest was in flames when they'd managed to get out of the cabin and were running for the creek.
A burning branch had fallen from somewhere and landed
on Junior. He'd been knocked down but luckily not
burned. Somehow, Daisy had managed to drag the branch
off him, burning her hair and arm in the process, and
they'd continued on to the creek, which Junior told her
was the safest place to be in a forest fire. Fortunately, Ben
and Dodger had found them not long after, and the rain
over the next two days had put out most of the small fires
the lightning had ignited.

"It's fine. Hardly hurts.'' She waggled her hand in the
sunlight and Emily grinned.

"I suppose that diamond takes away some of the pain.''

Daisy threw her arm around her friend's neck and
squeezed hard. "Hey, that's got nothing to do with it!''

"Okay. So what happened then?''

Daisy felt sick whenever she thought of the events of
that morning. "Wayne was shot and Arlo started to run
toward him and suddenly Arlo was down. Junior was terrified. He started to crawl over the driver's seat to get out
and help his dad, but Arlo managed to grab on to the side
of the truck and told Junior to hit the ditch and run as fast
as he could into the bush. Before Junior could obey, there
was another shot and Arlo fell again. Junior squeezed under the dash of the pickup. He was scared to death. He
saw Casper go past the open door of their vehicle to the
police cruiser. He saw Casper come back and bend down
and stick something in his dad's hand. Then he went to
the back of their truck and opened the canopy—''

"Just a minute. What did he put in Arlo's hand?"

"A gun. A police revolver."

"A *police* gun?"

"Yes. A 9 mm Beretta that'd been stolen two months earlier in a break-and-enter on a cop's house in Cardston. The cop was in the hospital and his gun was in his house and it was stolen." Daisy shrugged. "I guess these things happen. Anyway, Casper used the stolen gun, apparently thinking that if the bullets were clearly from an RCMP gun, there wouldn't be any ballistics tests to find out whether they'd come from that exact gun. And, in fact, the natural assumption was that the two of them shot each other."

"And Arlo would get blamed for the B and E, too."

"Yes."

Emily digested the information for a few minutes, staring into the ring. The crowd had burst into laughter because one of the "wild" sheep had trotted around a bit then started grazing with a four- or five-year-old on its back. "So Junior managed to get away," she mused. "Lucky kid. I don't think that man would've stopped at anything."

Daisy shuddered. "I think you're right. It's been pretty hard on Ben, knowing that one of his old gang, someone he'd protected and believed was a friend, murdered his cousin and Wayne in cold blood."

"And would have murdered the two of you!"

"I'm not totally convinced of that," Daisy said. She'd thought many times about the pail of fresh water in the cabin. "I'm not so sure he wasn't just trying to give me a good scare. Maybe keep me in that cabin for a few days, then let me go. Shut me up. Scare me off my investigation. After all, I didn't know who those Chip and Dale characters were and there's no way I'd connect them to Casper."

"But Junior knew who he was."

"Yes. But I think Casper figured the boy was never going to talk again, certainly never going to turn him in. He'd threatened Junior several times when he got him alone, told him he'd hurt his mother or sister. I don't believe Casper had really thought the whole kidnapping thing through. Grabbing Junior was an impulse. That's how he did things."

"Well, he's going to spend the rest of his life where he belongs—in jail! Where does Junior's dad fit in?"

"Nobody really knows for sure. Arlo didn't think things through very well, either, from all reports. Morris Jack told Ben that Arlo'd been couriering parcels here and there—to the airport, places like that, thinking it was all legit. But he'd begun to figure out what Casper was doing. According to Morris, Arlo got cold feet and was meeting Casper to tell him he was quitting. I suspect Casper learned that Wayne had turned on him, too, and wanted to get rid of them both, make it look like Arlo did it."

"Well, Casper didn't know you and Junior weren't in the cabin when he set it on fire."

"That was probably to destroy the poaching evidence—"

"Are you *defending* him?" Emily looked astonished.

"Never! He's a creep and a slimeball and a murderer. I'm just trying to be fair, that's all."

"Creep, slimeball—not criminal offenses," Emily said, smiling. "Murder, poaching and kidnapping—criminal offenses."

"Well, that's true." Daisy reflected. "And those idiots who called themselves Chip and Dale, they've been arrested, too. They were two of the bear poachers and Gordon thinks they were behind the B and E at the cop's house."

"All's well that ends well," Emily said philosophically.

She smiled and patted Daisy's hand. "You're safe, Daisy. That's all that matters. You and Junior are okay, and now you're going to get married and I'm going to be the only old maid in our graduating class."

"Not for long, I'm sure," Daisy said, with a sly glance across the ring, where some of the men, including Ben, his friend Adam Garrick and Jesse Winslow, were in charge of the so-called roughstock.

"We'll see," Emily said enigmatically. "You know I like to play hard to get. Hey, the barrel racing's up next, I think."

Daisy looked toward the stands, in time to see Marie Goodstriker moving into the bleachers, accompanied by Ed Sawchuk, who was carrying a tray of drinks. She elbowed her friend. "There's Marie and one of her suitors. You know, Ben told me he had his eye on her at one time."

"No!"

"According to him, half of Tamarack was in love with Marie before she married Arlo." *And after,* Daisy added to herself. She contemplated telling her friend the whole story, but decided some secrets were better kept. Much as she loved her, she knew Emily wasn't always the most discreet. Ben had told Daisy he'd long suspected—and his grandmother had been certain—that Laverne was Wayne's daughter, not Arlo's. Arlo had been away at bull-riding school that summer, and Wayne had spent a lot of time with Marie. Then Wayne abruptly left for the RCMP training school in Regina that fall, and Marie suddenly agreed to marry Arlo. Six months later, Laverne was born.

Ben had never known if Arlo had put two and two together but, knowing his cousin, he wasn't sure it would've mattered. As Lonny had said, Arlo was a dreamer, someone who'd never quite grown up, a loser with a heart of gold. He'd adored his daughter *and* his son. Nor did Ben know if Wayne was aware of the circumstances. With his record for sowing wild oats, it wouldn't have been the first "accident."

"What about Wayne?" Emily asked, as though reading Daisy's thoughts. "He doesn't sound like the wonderful guy the town seems to think he is."

"Wayne played both sides at the start, and then he apparently got the idea that instead of going along with Casper, taking a share of the profits, as he'd been doing, he'd bust the operation and—according to Lonny—restore his name and reputation with the force. He was a maverick cop. Even Gordon as much as told me Wayne couldn't be trusted. He was good at undercover, but then he'd get caught up in the games he was playing and end up involved in the criminal life. It had happened a couple of times in his career, and that's why he was posted back to Glory. Gordon Bass was supposed to keep an eye on him."

"Are you going to be writing up any more of this for the newspaper?" Emily's voice was curious.

Daisy sighed. "Yes and no. It's a huge story but I have to agree with Mother and my dad that you don't always need to tell the whole story to tell the truth. Oliver says to trust my instincts. Dad's standing behind me. He says I should print whatever I think is fit to print. But I'm not sure. Nobody really needs to know that Wayne wasn't always such a great guy. Why tarnish his reputation now? He's dead and I can't forget that he did a lot of good as a cop, too. He wasn't all bad. His parents know the truth, and to the town, he's a hero.

"As for Arlo, I think his reputation is restored now that this has all come out, now that Casper's been charged with both murders. Plus kidnapping. Plus poaching—he planted the box of gallbladders in the back of Arlo's truck, you know, to set up the story that Arlo was poaching."

"You're kidding!"

Daisy shook her head. "Not kidding. Plus there's the

money laundering through his so-called flea market business.'' Daisy laughed. ''Not to mention arson for setting the cabin on fire. You know Gordon—he's nothing if not thorough. As I think you said, all's well—''

''—that ends well.''

Daisy watched Ben and Jesse lope across the field toward them, Ben on a buckskin, Jesse on a black. She still kept pinching herself, unable to believe she was really marrying this man in October. That he loved her and she loved him and somehow, crazy world that it was, they'd found each other. The Sutherlands had been surprised at the news but then warmly supportive. Daisy wondered if they were just relieved she was getting married—to anybody!

Jesse swung off his horse to stand next to Emily and Ben stood behind Daisy. She leaned against him and he put his arms around her as they watched the barrel racing, boys and girls, get underway. The first contestant was a twelve-year-old from Granum. The crowd cheered mightily as she ran the barrels in just over forty seconds. Next, a boy from Pincher Creek did a few seconds better.

Then it was Laverne's turn.

Daisy found herself screaming and cheering and jumping up and down as Brownie rounded the barrels, Laverne's time five or six seconds better than either of the other contestants. There were four more to ride.

''Oh, I hope she wins!'' Daisy said, nudging Ben.

He was his usual taciturn self, but Daisy knew he was proud. ''Did I tell you I stopped in at the bank in Glory yesterday and checked out Arlo's account?''

''No!'' She searched his expression for a hint of what his news was, good or bad.

''He had $512.73 in it. No surprises there. Arlo never was much for saving money.'' Ben smiled.

Daisy thought he looked awfully smug about something. "That's all?"

"Turns out he had a safety deposit box, too, so I checked it out."

"And?"

"He had over eight thousand dollars in cash—"

"No!" Daisy tried to keep her voice low; she didn't want to invite Emily's curiosity.

"Yes. I went over to the detachment and mentioned it to Bass and he asked me how the weather was over in our part of the country."

"Ben! He doesn't want to know about it?" Maybe Bass could surprise her after all....

"He just asked about the weather," Ben said with a shrug. "I told him it was fine."

That meant Laverne would get the new pony she wanted. And Marie would have a little nest egg, too.

Laverne's time held, and she was announced as the winner of the First Annual Tamarack Small-Fry Rodeo barrel race event. As the contestants did a gallop-past, Laverne waved to the four of them. Brownie tossed his head like a horse half his age. She'd swear the old cow pony knew he'd won.

"Daisy!" Junior and a couple of his friends came streaking across the field to join them at the fence. "She won! My sister won!"

"You must be Junior Goodstriker," Emily said, sticking out her hand.

"That's what people call me, but my *real* name is Arlo." The boy raised his hand to grip Emily's. "Just like my dad's."

His eyes were shining and so, Daisy was sure, were hers.

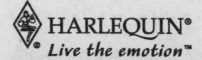

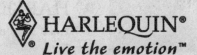

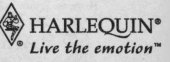

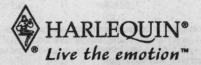

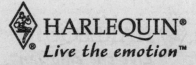

Forrester Square

LEGACIES . LIES . LOVE .

*The Kinards, the Richardses and the Webbers were
Seattle's Kennedys, living in elegant Forrester Square—
until one fateful night tore these families apart.*

*Now, twenty years later, memories and secrets are about
to be revealed…unless one person has their way!*

Coming in October 2003…

THE LAST THING SHE NEEDED

by Top Harlequin Temptation® author
Kate Hoffmann

When Dani O'Malley's childhood friend died, she suddenly found
herself guardian to three scared, unruly kids—and terribly
overwhelmed! If it weren't for Brad Cullen, she'd be lost. The sexy
cowboy had a way with the kids…and with her!

Forrester Square…Legacies. Lies. Love.

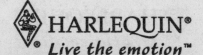